It was while I was at school that I kind of fell in love with writing not that I knew it, kids would play games and I would go into a quiet corner and let my mind wander with dragons, pirates even cowboys and Indians.

Funnily enough, it was never about the people in my mind stories that I concentrated on, but their backgrounds, dragons would be setting fire to everything, pirates would be looking for islands to bury their treasures, and cowboys would be making friends with Indians.

I realised that I would rather write than go out with friends, I started to look through what I had been writing and started to add lines to make the stories more interesting.

B. Wilkie

APHRODITE'S KISS

AUSTIN MACAULEY PUBLISHERS™
LONDON * CAMBRIDGE * NEW YORK * SHARJAH

Copyright © B. Wilkie 2023

The right of B. Wilkie to be identified as author of this work has been asserted by the author in accordance with sections 77 and 78 of the Copyright, Designs and Patents Act 1988.

All rights reserved. No part of this publication may be reproduced, stored in a retrieval system or transmitted in any form or by any means, electronic, mechanical, photocopying, recording or otherwise, without the prior permission of the publishers.

Any person who commits any unauthorised act in relation to this publication may be liable to criminal prosecution and civil claims for damages.

This is a work of fiction. Names, characters, businesses, places, events, locales and incidents are either the products of the author's imagination or used in a fictitious manner. Any resemblance to actual persons, living or dead, or actual events is purely coincidental.

A CIP catalogue record for this title is available from the British Library.

ISBN 9781398458673 (Paperback)
ISBN 9781398458680 (ePub e-book)

www.austinmacauley.com

First Published 2023
Austin Macauley Publishers Ltd
1 Canada Square
Canary Wharf
London
E14 5AA

Chapter One

The bus must have hit a hole in the road, Catherine thought as she tried to find her place in the book again; something in the back of her mind was niggling at her as she skipped through lines that she had already read.

The roads up to the Hill are the best roads in the country and there would definitely be no holes in them. She looked out of the bus window. As it was getting near the end of the fall and winter was only three days away, it was beginning to get dark. What she saw as she peered into the dim light was, tenement buildings.

This is not the way home, she thought as she looked at the broken windows, some with drapes being blown around after being sucked out of the glassless windows like some long-forgotten flags that had worn away at the ends with all of the flapping. The bus came to a stop and a boy and girl got off, the bus moved off again and drove past the two who had just got off. Catherine turned her head as if watching to see where they were going, then she saw the police patrol car parked across the street.

"Stop here please," she asked the bus driver; the bus stopped and the doors opened. Catherine grabbed her school bag and ran to the door, she got off the bus and waited on the sidewalk until the bus had pulled away, when it did, she saw that the patrol car had also pulled away. She looked up and down the street, it was nowhere to be seen, she looked at her watch.

"Five past four, God, Mam will be worried sick and phoning Dad now," Catherine said to herself as she pulled her coat collar up, put both arms through her school bag straps, zipped up her coat and started to walk. She didn't know if she was going in the right direction or not, she just wanted to get away from this place.

Everywhere she looked, there was garbage piled high as if it was a garbage site, there were cars with no wheels on, their seats ripped out laying on the road, one seat was hanging off a street light, which wasn't working, boxes of garbage were scattered all over and the smell was horrendous. She saw a drunken man trying to keep himself upright as he relieved himself and it looked like he didn't care who saw him, she turned away from the man and looked down the street, most of the street lights were off and there were big stretches of darkness. Catherine never knew this part of the city existed; she looked at her watch again.

Four thirty, when am I going to get away from here.

She noticed a couple of kids who looked just a little older than her following her on the other side of the street, she casually turned around and looked behind her, along the side of the street that she was on.

Three of them on this side. She started to walk faster; panic was building up inside of her.

Her father had paid for private lessons in ju-jitsu and karate when she was ten years old, she has been practicing it for five years now and it looked to Catherine that she would have to use it for real pretty soon. Although she had trained to fight up to two people, she knew she had no chance against five, she decided to walk a little faster, hoping that she could lose them.

She turned a corner and saw an opening, she ran for it, praying she got there before they saw where she went, as her eyes got used to the darkness, she saw that it was an alley which curved. She ran down it. As she went around the curve, she saw the big high wall at the bottom. There was no way that she could climb the wall. She looked around the alley for another way out or somewhere to hide; it was really dark in the alley now and she just managed to see and get to a doorway before she heard voices coming from the end that she had just ran down from.

As she tried to regulate her breathing so they could not hear her panting she looked at the skyline above the wall, up to the top of the wall it was an evil, frightening blackness, yet above the wall it was a beautiful darkish blue, almost purple in colour.

"She had to come in here, Flick." She heard someone say.

"All right, spread out, I don't want her getting past us."

Catherine heard them picking up boxes and throwing them around. She heard them kicking stuff and now and again, she would hear a shout of pain when one of them had kicked something that was to hard or big to be kicked. If she had been watching this in the cinema, she would more than likely be laughing but this wasn't the cinema and she felt nothing like laughing; she jumped when she heard.

"Flick, she's here."

She heard them scramble closer to where she was, and a voice, which must have been 'Flick's' say.

"Okay, babe, let's have you out of there so we can see what you look like."

Catherine wanted to scream but she knew it would never be heard and it would only give them the opportunity they needed to jump on her. At least if she kept quiet, they would keep their distance for a while. Catherine stepped out of the doorway, trying not to look frightened.

"If anyone of you lay a hand on me, I'll break it," she said making sure she never stepped to close to any of them.

"We're not going to hurt you, that's if you do what we say." One of them sneered.

"A nice well-dressed babe like you must have some money on her, so if you just hand it over, we'll have some fun with you then we'll let you go your way but if you try to put up a fight, then you will get hurt," the thug said the last five words slowly.

Catherine's eyes were getting used to the dark and she could see the faces of the thugs. Two of them had woolly hats on and two had baseball hats on backwards. The one she thought was 'Flick' didn't have a hat on. He had long hair that reminded Catherine of rat's tails. Their clothes looked as if they had never seen wash or clothes press before.

"All right, I'll give you what money I have but that's all you're getting," she said she knew what they were going to do to her, so she decided to play for time and see if she could figure a way out of this mess or make a run for it. Her back was against the wall beside the doorway. They were in a half circle about five feet away from her. She could still see the big wall at the bottom of the alley. Her heart almost stopped as something caught her eye down the alley. She was sure someone had just climbed over the wall. Catherine had to do something quick or one of the thugs might see whoever it is. She moved slowly back into the doorway, the two who were at her right moved down a little, when she was right back into the doorway. Catherine knew that they all had their backs to the wall at the bottom and that they couldn't see anything behind them. Catherine handed her money to 'Flick' then said.

"Let me take my clothes off, so you don't rip them and I promise not to scream." She felt terrible saying it but it was all she could do to waste time.

"That's okay with us," the leader of the thugs said.

Catherine took the bag off her shoulders; she opened her coat then took it off and let it drop to the ground. Catherine could feel their eyes on her breasts, she could also see them drooling at the thoughts they were having of what they were going to do to her when she finished taking her clothes off.

The thought sent a shiver down her spine and her hands started shaking, her fingers went to the top button of her shirt.

Please, whoever you are, please be quick before anything else has to come off, Catherine thought. She couldn't look down the alley in case one of the thugs saw her and turned around to see what she was looking at.

She started to loosen her shirt, slowly working her way down the buttons, when she finished unbuttoning it she pulled it out of her skirt. The thugs could see her white Bra. She pulled the shirt off her left shoulder…

****

Richard always went onto the roof of the tenements in the fall and winter as it was the best time to watch the stars. He would spend hours laying on an old mattress and just gaze up at them. For some unknown reason, he had walked around the roof and looked down at the streets, he saw the five gang members acting funny. He watched as two of them crossed the street. He knew they would be up to no good. he'd had a few run ins with them since he and his mother had moved to these tenements. They had asked him to join their gang, he refused, so they would pick fights with him every time they meet him but they know there has to be three or more of them, because two tried to fight him once and he slaughtered them.

He ran down the stairs two at a time and dashed to the main entrance. He saw the three who had crossed the street go into an alley. Richard ran through the building and out of the back into the sprawling darkness that no one ever went to at night. Richard knew there were five alleys altogether. Now he wished he had taken notice which alley they had went down instead of just running out here. He ran to the wall of the first one and climbed up, making sure that if they were in there, he would not be seen. He pricked his ears up but couldn't hear anything. He lowered himself back down and ran to the next wall. This wall was a little bit bigger than the first. He went back a little then ran at the wall and jumped, his hands grabbing at the edge of the top, he pulled himself up, his ears searching for the faintest of sounds. He heard a girl's voice saying something about money. Richard slid over the top, keeping his body as close to the wall as possible. He said a silent prayer that there was no garbage on the ground where he was going to land when he lowered down. He landed on the ground silently; he stood where he landed until his eyes got used to the darkness. Richard picked up a piece of wood and started to walk towards the gang, making sure that he didn't kick or bump into anything as he tried to stay in the darkest parts of the alley.

He was about six feet away from two of the gang when he swung the wood at them. The girl was just starting to take her shirt off when she heard the 'whoosh' of the wood just before she heard the bang as it hit the two that were nearer the bottom of the alley. The first one took the full force of the hit; the second one got just as big a shock as the first but was prevented from getting hit by the first. Richard was bringing the wood back for another swing but he knew he never had time so he kicked at the second one, he felt his foot hit the kneecap of the second one and he joined the first one on the ground screaming in pain. Richard knew five was too many to fight; he knew he had to get at least three of them before they realised what was happening. Just as the third one turned, Richard hit him square in the face with his fist and he dropped like a brick. He could see the other two bending over. He thought they were going to pick the wood up that he dropped.

****

Catherine hadn't seen how close her saviour was and she was about to say another prayer when the wood struck one of them or was it two. She wasn't sure as it happened so suddenly. She got just as much a shock as they did. It was when the second one went down that she sprang into action. She kicked with all the force she could and got the forth one between the legs. She knew he was out of it as he went onto the ground clutching at his crutch and screaming in pain. The fifth one grabbed at his crutch out of instinct. He knew it was the wrong move to make the moment he felt her fingernails digging into the skin on his face and started pulling at it. Catherine could feel his blood running down her hands and arms, the thug grabbed her hands, it was just what she wanted him to do.

Catherine already had her leg in the required position for one of the most devastating kicks anyone could give a person in the crutch. When it connected, he lifted off the ground and landed three feet away with a dull thud.

A hand grabbed her shoulder, she turned around; her hand was already in the shape of a fist and heading straight for whoever grabbed her. Richard saw it coming and ducked under it just in time as it flew over his shoulder.

"It's okay," Richard said. "It's okay," he repeated, when he was sure she knew that he wasn't one of them he said.

"I think we had better get out of here in case more of their friends come."

Catherine started to button up her blouse but she was shaking too much.

"I don't think we have time to do that."

Catherine nodded her head and she could feel herself crying, though she kept it from him. She didn't know if she was crying with the excitement or the fact that she was about to be mugged or worse, and had got out of it. She picked up her coat and put it on and pulled her bag onto her shoulders. She felt him pulling her down to the bottom of the alley.

"We'll have to go this way," her rescuer said as he pulled a box over to the wall and climbed onto it. He took hold of her hand and pulled her onto the box as well, then he cupped his hands and spoke.

"Put your foot in my hands and I'll lift you up."

Catherine did as she was told. She put her foot into his hands and felt herself going up. She grabbed the top of the wall and pulled herself the rest of the way up, she sat on the top and waited for him to climb up. When he did, he lowered her down the other side and she waited again for him. He jumped down. He took her hand.

"Come on, we'll have to get as far from here as we can," he spoke.

They ran. Catherine didn't know where or for how long they ran, they just did. Catherine could see the change in the area that they were running through, for one thing that horrible smell was gone and more and more streetlights were working. She felt him ease his hold of her hand as they started to slow down until he let go of it altogether. By the time they had stopped, they were under a street light. He had never looked at her and she had not had time to look at him. When he turned to face her, her mouth dropped open.

He is gorgeous, Catherine thought as she looked at his soft boyish face with his hair hanging down onto his shoulders but it was much cleaner and tidier than the hair the thugs had and he was taller than she was. She wished she could see his eyes but it was too dark. She started to fasten her blouse again.

"I think we'll have a sit down over there," he said, pointing to a few wooden benches.

"If you tell me where you live, I'll know which way to go to get you home."

Catherine was still trying to fasten her buttons; she could see that he didn't want to be seen watching her in case she thought he was leering. Without looking up, she said.

"I live on the Hill." She never saw the sneer on his face.

"Yeah, sure you do and you just happened to be passing by here like you do every day," he said sarcastically.

"What?" Catherine answered as she lifted her head up, still unaware of his sneering.

"Look, there is no way someone from Snob Hill would be walking around here, or was it some kind of silly little girl prank with some of your friends."

Catherine stood up, shocked at his attitude.

"How dare you even suggest that I'm some kind of spoilt kid, if you don't believe me that's your problem. You have to deal with that, I don't. Just point me in the right direction and I'll make my own way home." Her voice was getting more and more quivery as if she was going to start to cry. Richard stood up.

"Look, I'm, I'm sorry okay. I didn't mean to say you were, were…Look, come on we have a long way to go." Richard was sorry as soon as he said it. Catherine started to shake, then she started to cry. She didn't want to cry it just burst out of her. Richard put his arms around her. They stood there for five minutes, Catherine crying and Richard trying to make her feel better and to get her to stop crying. Then in a much softer voice, he said to her.

"We will have to make a start if I'm to get you to the Hill."

Catherine took a deep breath, picked up her bag, then said.

"I'm okay now and thank you very much for what you have done for me, I'm sorry for losing my temper." She looked at the ground, guilt, mixed with her shyness coming over her.

"That's all right; we'll put it down to the excitement, eh?"

Catherine could feel her temper rising again until she looked up at him and saw the smile on his face, then the both of them burst out laughing.

"That's better; you look beautiful when you smile. My name is Richard."

"Mine's Catherine, thank you again, Richard, for what you did for me."

"Now don't lose your temper again okay but do you really live on the Hill?"

Catherine looked at him and knew he was not trying to be funny or sarcastic.

"Yes, why?"

"What were you doing in that part of the city?"

"I got on the wrong school bus," she answered him.

"People from the Hill don't get the bus from school." He was about to sneer again but stopped himself.

"Some of us do," she replied. She could feel her heart pounding inside of her but she didn't know why.

"We'll start walking now, okay." He walked in front of her until she caught up to him. She wanted him to take her hand, she was thinking of putting her hand into his, then she knew why her heart had started pounding.

"It's going to be a while until you get home; the Hill is on the other side of the city."

Catherine kept taking looks at him without him noticing.

I couldn't care if it takes us forever as long as I'm with you. Please take my hand again, she thought. After an hour of walking, Richard led her to some seats.

"We'll sit down for a few minutes." They both sat down.

"Do you live in the tenements?" Catherine asked him.

"Yeah, I know there not as pretty as the Hill but it's where I have lived all my life and there not as bad as people say they are," he answered her, then he asked.

"So how come you got on the wrong bus?"

"My friend Cora had to stay back to learn how to do the make-up thing that she is into, so I opened my book and started reading. A bus stopped and I got on and sat down. I never once looked up or at anyone else until the bus hit a hole in the road. Then it was too late so I waited until I saw a police car. I jumped off the bus but the car had gone. Then they started following me and I panicked and ran down that alley."

Richard stood up again and held out his hand.

"Come on, we'll have to move again," he said.

Catherine took hold of his hand and felt herself being pulled up off the seat, she said a silent prayer for him to keep a hold of her hand but as soon as she was standing up, he let go of it.

"Do you think we should go through the park or around it?" Richard asked her.

The Park is generally known to be the border between the old part of the city and the new or as the people say, 'the haves and the have nots'. Whereas the tenements are known as the worst. Cloister Hill, also known as Snob Hill is regarded as the best. Cloister Hill is not a Hill as such; it is more of a Mountain, which has houses with no less than ten bedrooms or so Richard's mother told him a few years ago.

"I think we should go through it," Catherine answered him.

"Well, I can take you to it but you will have to lead the way once we are in there," Richard told her.

"Why is that? Surely you know the way to the Hill once you are in the park?" Catherine said.

Richard smiled, then after a few seconds he said.

"I can take you to the park from anywhere in the city but as I have never actually been in it myself, I…" He shrugged his shoulders. Catherine stopped walking and stared at him in disbelief.

Richard looked at the ground almost in embarrassment and he never saw the grin coming to Catherine's face as a plan was forming in her mind.

"It is the most incredible place in the city." She could see that Richard was telling her the truth. Richard looked up at her, it was the first time that the light had been just right and it shone on her face, showing Richard just how beautiful she was.

She is beautiful. The thought shot through his head before he could stop it. Her hair was almost waist length now that she had shook it out of its bun and it was jet black, her face looked soft and kind and her smile looked as if it was there permanent.

"What are you looking at?" Catherine said.

Richard pulled his eyes away from her face and looked down instinctively.

Catherine pulled her coat closed.

"Now what are you looking at?" she said again.

Richard's mouth was wide open. He took hold of her coat and opened it. Catherine just stood there unable to move.

"You're covered in blood," Richard said.

Catherine was almost too frightened to look down.

"I'm sorry I never asked you if you were hurt. I think we should get you to a hospital," he spoke.

"I'm not hurt; it is blood of one of the fools who attacked me. It must have got on my shirt when I was trying to fasten it."

"Well make sure you warn your parents before you take your coat off or they will die of fright." Catherine could feel the concern in his voice.

They started to walk again. They were talking a lot more now as the tension of the last couple of hours eased. Every time Catherine brushed against him or felt his arm as he made her laugh, she got nice warm feelings shooting through her body.

They came to the small wall that surrounds the park, it was only a foot high. Richard took Catherine's hand and helped her over it.

It's now or never girl, she thought, now was the time to put the plan that had been forming in her head into practice.

As Richard tried to let go of her hand, she grabbed it tighter.

"It's dark in here, Richard, and we might get separated so it's best if we keep together." She felt him ease his hand and let her keep hold of it. He never saw the look of pleasure that she had on her face.

Catherine knew it would not be long before they were at the Hill, so she took him around the longest way, along all of the different paths, making sure she never went down the same one twice. After an hour, they came to the other side. They climbed over the wall and walked up the Hill. There were no sidewalks, just a small road with hedgerows on both sides. They reached the top and started to walk down the other side. Richard saw the flashing lights of the patrol cars.

"That must be your house, Catherine, so if you don't mind, I'll leave you here; you should be okay now."

Catherine's grip on his hand tightened.

"What?" She was taken by surprise by his words.

"You can't, you must come home with me, my mother and father will want to thank you. The police will give you a ride home, Richard, please come with me." Catherine was thinking of everything to get him to stay but she knew it was no good when he pulled his hand out of hers.

"Catherine, I can't go down there with you, the police will arrest me. My mother will be worried sick, so I'll leave now and save everyone a lot of trouble," Richard said as he started to walk away. Catherine ran after him, she grabbed his arm and turned him around.

"Please Richard, the police will not arrest you, I'll make sure of that," she pleaded with him.

"Catherine, when the police see all the blood on you, you will not be able to stop them from arresting me. I have to leave you here, Catherine. I have to, okay?"

Catherine saw the determination in his eyes and knew that he was not going to go home with her.

"All right, Richard, but I want to see you again, please, please say you will see me again."

Richard couldn't believe what he was hearing. Catherine was without doubt the most beautiful girl he had ever seen and she wanted to see him again.

"Okay. I'll see you in the park on Sunday at one, if you really mean it."

****

Chapter Two

When Catherine walked down her driveway that night five years ago, for all the trouble she had been through she had a spring in her step that had never been there before. A police officer saw her and took her into the house, her parents were so relieved to see her; her mother started to cry.

"Mom, Dad, I'm okay," she kept saying.

"Now please don't get a shock. Richard said that I have to warn you before I take my coat off. The blood you'll see is not mine." Then she opened her coat and took it off. Her mother's hands went straight to her mouth to stop a scream coming out and her father put his arms around his daughter, squeezing her gently.

"I did say it wasn't mine, Richard was right, he told me I had to warn you."

The police doctor came into the house to check her over and they took her shirt and the rest of her clothes away to see if they could get any clues off them to help capture the gang. She had stayed up all night explaining to the police and her parents of her whereabouts; she told them everything including Richard's part in it all.

She did panic a little when the police officer asked her for Richard's second name and where he lived. She couldn't answer him because she had forgotten to get his name and address but she soon realised that it didn't matter because she was meeting him on Sunday. She never told the police, she was afraid they would be there and frighten him away again. When the police had finished questioning her and they had left, her parents had told her that she need not bother going to school because she'd had no sleep. It was as her father brought them all cups of coffee in from the kitchen that she told them, "Mom, Dad, Richard is going to be at the park on Sunday. I didn't want to tell the police because they might have turned up and if Richard had seen them, he wouldn't show." She was waiting for her father to explode at her deceit but all he did was look at her mother.

Alvin and Beverly, her parents, had paid for private investigators when the police had failed to find the gang. Catherine's parents were one of the wealthiest in America and they left no stone unturned looking for them but it seemed that they had all, vanished off the face of the earth.

****

Catherine and her best friend Cora were sitting in the storm shelter at the bottom of the garden.

"Have I told you it is five years today that I met Richard, Cora?"

Cora was sitting on the bench with her hands over her ears and her eyes tight shut. After a minute, she opened one eye and saw that Catherine was smiling at her and had stopped talking.

"Catherine, I promise you if you go on about him one more time, I'll kill you."

"But Cora, if you had just seen him, he was…" Catherine continued as if Cora had said nothing.

Cora let out such a scream it hurt their ears for a few minutes. Cora grabbed Catherine and the two of them were pretending to fight each other; they ended up rolling on the bench laughing.

After a while, Catherine said to her friend.

"Cora, I'm serious now. Why do you think he never turned up at the park on the Sunday? He seemed so pleased that I wanted to see him again, even when I kissed him on the cheek, he never pulled away. Should I have kissed him on the lips? Do you think he said he would meet me just to get away from me?"

Cora could see the sadness in her friend's face and she wished she could see this Richard, she would give him a piece of her mind; just the thought of him hurting Catherine the way he has brings her blood to the boil. Cora put her arm around her friend.

"Listen, Catherine." Cora was just about to tell her what she thought of him, when she remembered the last time she had, and how Catherine went into a quiet mood for hours with her.

"Listen Catherine, there must have been a reason why he never turned up or maybe he did but at a different part of the park; you did say that he had never been there before, so maybe he was at one end and we were at the other?"

Cora had been shocked at Catherine's behaviour when he had not turned up at the park; they had waited until six-o-clock still hoping for him to walk up to them. Catherine cried so much. Cora knew when Catherine had started talking about him all the time and that she was as happy as she had ever saw her friend but she didn't know how much he had affected her. When Cora said it was time to go, Catherine started shaking, she said, "Cora, where is he, oh where is he?" Cora put her arms around Catherine and had hugged her so much.

Cora hated this Richard for doing this to her friend.

****

It was almost two-o-clock in the morning when Richard had got home. He tried to slip into the house without waking his mother up but as she had fell asleep on the sofa, she woke up as soon as she heard the door open and close. She looked at the clock.

"Richard, where have you been until this time of night, please tell me you have not been in trouble."

Richard smiled at her.

"No, Mom, I fell asleep on the roof. I'll make us a cup of coffee. Anyway, what are you doing sleeping on the sofa?" he said from the kitchen.

"Because I want to tell you about the two bits of good news I have," she spoke.

Richard came back into the room carrying two cups of coffee. He could see that his mother was trying to hold her excitement in until he was here.

"Well, come on then, tell me." He smiled at her, he loved her when she was like this; she was just like a little girl who had been given some candy.

Everyone who sees Richard and his mother together think that they are brother and sister, when in fact they aren't even related. Sharon had been living anywhere she could in some old tenements at the other end of the city, she had made a nice little room for herself and she was quite cosy in it, in an empty part of the building. When one day Richard walked in and lay down beside her and fell asleep. She was about ten years old and Richard was about five or six. She had tried to find out where he came from but all her inquiries came to nothing, so she decided to look after him. His smile was a big help, because everyone who meets them and he smiles at them, he melts the hearts of the women.

Sharon had to pretend that he was her younger brother to get him into school and she had to tell him not to call her mother when they were in school. After school, she would take him to the store where she packed shelves, then she would take him to the late-night coffee store where a friendly cook would make them something to eat for cleaning the tables, then it would be back to the tenements to sleep.

"You know that the tutor at my typing class put my name down for a position at the De Charger factory."

Richard could see his mother getting more and more excited.

"Yes," he said.

"Well, I got the job." Her smile was a mile wide. He put his cup down and gave her a big hug and whispered in her ear.

"Oh, Mom, I knew you would get it."

She pushed gently away from him.

"And, and, and we have also been given a house in the new project the county is building across the river." She felt him squeeze her harder.

"Mom, this is great, a new house, a job, now we have a new life away from here." He squeezed her again and again and again.

"We start moving on Saturday and should have everything sorted by the Monday when I start at the De Charger factory." She saw the frown appear on Richard's face, it only lasted for a split second but it was there.

"Richard, what's wrong?" she asked him.

******

Catherine and Cora were now at the State University studying Drama. Cora was more interested in the make-up and costumes and she loved the hustle and bustle of back stage, whereas Catherine loved to be on the stage performing.

At this time of year, the State University and it's Annex, in the downtown part of the city, join their drama groups together and put on a show for charity. This year, it was being performed at the Annex.

"I've never been to that part of the city," Cora said.

"And I've never been back," Catherine replied, shivering, and then a smile came to her face.

"What are you smiling for? I know I wouldn't be smiling thinking of it," Cora asked puzzled.

"Do you think that we might, just might mind you, bump into Richard?"

At that point, Cora went straight for Catherine's throat. Catherine ran as fast as she could up the path leading to the house, Cora in hot pursuit screaming after her.

The following morning saw Cora sitting on the steps to her house waiting for Catherine. Cora lived in a well to do area, not as exclusive as Cloister Hill and as it was on the way to the Annex Catherine had suggested that she pick Cora up instead of Cora coming all the way to the Hill to pick her up, then to drive all the way back. As it was the first day at the Annex, they had decided to get there early in case of wrong turns or traffic jams. Catherine's father had told them how to get to the Annex and they drove to his instructions, as they came off the freeway at the turning. He had said the Annex was right in front of them. There were plenty of spaces to park their car. They got out and asked a student who was passing if he could tell them the way to the Drama building. It had taken them exactly forty-five minutes to get here and as they had allowed an hour and a half, they had half an hour to kill before they started their class.

"Let's go for a walk, so we know the place just in case we can't park here every day?" Cora said.

"Okay." Catherine agreed, nodding.

The buildings weren't as old as the universities and they were not as big but they were very colourful. They were covered in what people call 'street art', some had many paintings on them and some had only one that covered the whole of the building. The pathways around the buildings were all clean and where grass grew, it was neatly cut with small white painted chains around them, as usual it was Cora who saw him first.

"Oh my God, Catherine looks at him standing there. If ever there was an A.D.O.N.I.S., he is it."

He was standing under a tree reading a book, his army fatigues coat was hanging on one shoulder, he had a white T-shirt on that didn't hide any of his muscular frame. Cora started to walk towards him.

"He just has to be an instructor of L.O.V.E. techniques," Cora said as she left Catherine.

"Where are you going?" Catherine tried to grab hold of Cora's arm but missed.

"I'm going to have a chat with Mr Love Machine, honey," Cora said over her shoulder.

"I don't think Tom will be too happy about this, Cora," Catherine said.

Cora stopped just as she was about to step over the small chain fence.

"I'm not going to do anything out here, Catherine, I just want to hear his voice so that at nights when I'm cold and lonely, I can fantasise about him keeping me warm."

Catherine saw the smile she gave her as Cora stepped over the chains, Catherine following her but catching her foot and falling. Cora turned around when she heard her friend cry out.

"I think I have twisted my ankle, Cora," Catherine said, rubbing it gently.

Cora walked back to Catherine and helped her get up off the ground.

"Are you sure you can walk, Catherine? If not, just stay here and I'll go and get a medic."

"No, Cora, I'll be fine, let's just go and find the medical centre," Catherine said trying not to show Cora how much pain she was in.

Cora shouted over to the Love Machine that it was okay and where was the Medical Centre when she saw that he had put his book down and was starting to walk towards them. He stopped walking and pointed to the building next to where they were. Cora was mumbling under her breath so that only Catherine could hear her.

"It's all right I don't need your help just now but some other time, definitely."

Catherine was trying not to laugh at her friend but the faces Cora was pulling were unbelievable, then Cora started to laugh. Cora let out such a big sigh when she saw the Love Machine walking away from them. She looked at Catherine with her 'I'm going to kill you, girl' look.

"Catherine, if you did this deliberately..." She pulled her up with one big pull.

"If you did this deliberately so that I wouldn't be able to talk to the Love Machine, our friendship will be at an end." Then the smile Cora gave her went from ear to ear.

"Cora, I never did this deliberately," Catherine said, wincing at the pain in her foot. The two of them started hobbling to the medical centre, Catherine with her arm over Cora's shoulder and Cora trying to take the weight off Catherine's foot.

The Medic put a big heavy bandage around her ankle and told her to take it easy for a couple of days. The following day, Catherine stayed at home and on the Wednesday, she went back, Cora picking her up.

"I went back to the tree yesterday but he wasn't there, pity really, I think I could have liked him," Cora said with a straight face.

"And what about Tom, you know, Tom your boyfriend, Tom the boyfriend you've had for two years."

"Catherine, I said I only wanted to talk to him." A mischievous grin coming to her face.

****

Richard starts his classes early on Mondays but the rest of the week, he starts two hours later. He'd seen the two girls walking over to him and when one of them fell, he wanted to help but the other one said it was all right, so he went to his class. He was doing really well at university just like he had done at school. He was one of only three students to get a free ticket to come here. It had not been easy to get here. He had to work hard at it and so had his mother. She worked all the hours she could so that he could get his books. He had a small job teaching young children the basics of computers although he never classed it as a job because he loved to teach children and as always, he was amazed at the speed they pick things up.

His mother was so proud of him that she would have worked day and night to get him his books. When they had moved from the tenements, it was as if a great black cloud had moved away from their heads. She had been so worried about all the bad things that were going on in there and she didn't want Richard getting mixed up with it. All her doubts vanished when she heard that he had won a ticket to university, not just to go to the local one, he was getting letters from universities all over the country. She never once tried to influence him in his choice of university. When Richard had asked her which one should he go to, she had said, "Richard, I have never been to university, so it would be wrong for me to tell you which one to go to."

She had to hide a tear when he had picked the local one and he wouldn't be going away.

Richard would finish his classes at four, by the time he got home and cleaned the house then changed his clothes, make his mother's meal so that all she had to do was come in, take her coat off, wash and eat, then they would do whatever they had to do. He would jump on a bus and go to one of the schools, teach the children for two hours then get home for about nine thirty, do some revision, then it would be time for bed.

That would be Monday until Thursday. Friday, Saturday and Sunday, he would sometimes do a few hours at a school for afterhours learning, mainly computer work but sometimes if there was another volunteer off, they would ask Richard if he would fill in for them, he always said yes.

It was Friday morning and he only had one class which started at ten thirty. He was sitting in a study room reading his books until it was time for the class to start. There were other students in the room, some were talking to their friends, some were reading books or magazines. It was all quiet talking and Richard noticed as soon as the hushed talking ended, he watched as two known bullies entered the room and went over to a young student who was just reading. He saw them pick the young student up out of his seat and push him away, then they scattered his books all over the floor. The young student went to hit one of the bullies but his friend stopped him. Everyone stood up and shouted for the young student to run but he never and a bully grabbed him. The other students were shouting now for the bully to let him go. As the bully looked around at the crowd, they went quiet. None of them was a fighter and they didn't want to bring attention to themselves. The bullies hadn't seen Richard until he stood up. Although Richard had never been in trouble of any kind at university, he was also known by other bullies as someone not to bother with, no one knew why, not even Richard knew why, he just wasn't ever bothered by people like that. Richard had thought about it once, and he put it down to being quiet and not mixing with other people. It made bullies uncomfortable to see someone not being bothered by them and so they kept away from him, well that had been Richard's theory.

****

Chapter Three

Cora picked Catherine up late. When they arrived at the university car park, it was full, so they drove around looking for a place to park. They eventually found one at the other end of the campus. They parked up and decided to walk through the university rather than around it. They were walking down a hallway when a lot of noise started coming from one of the rooms. As they passed the doorway, Catherine saw two big students picking on a small one.

"Let's go in and help him, Cora," Catherine said, starting to go in. Cora grabbed her arm and stopped her.

"No way, babe, I know you can handle yourself but me," Cora said shaking her head, "I'm for lovin', not for fighting."

Catherine stopped trying to go in and turned around.

"All right but I'm not going to stand here and watch some poor kid get hit." Catherine started walking away with Cora following her but still looking in the room.

"Catherine, wait, there's the Love Machine at the back of the room."

This time, Catherine pulled Cora away from the room.

"We don't have time for you to get all flustered over an A.D.O.N.I.S." Catherine spelt the words out as Cora had done when they first saw him. She continued walking away, Cora mumbling something about never having any fun anymore.

The room went death silent when Richard stood up and walked up to the two bullies; he stood right in front of them.

"If you two don't leave him alone, you will have to start on me."

"Aw, Ricky we're only having some fun with him," the bully said.

Catherine's brain was trying to remember where it had heard that voice before, and then when she heard the name her body froze. Cora hadn't noticed that her friend had stopped walking. When she did, she turned to her and spoke.

"Catherine, what's wrong? You're shaking." Cora could see that she was starting to sweat and her face was going red, her eyes were going the same colour.

"Cora, oh Cora, what's short for Richard?" Catherine managed to stammer.

"Er, er, Rich, Richie, erm, Dick, Dickie, em, em Rick, em Ricky. That's all I think," Cora said.

"Oh God, Cora, that was his voice. Oh God," Catherine said as she turned around and ran back to the room.

When she got to the room, there was only the Love Machine there and he was letting the student pick his books up. The Love Machine had turned around to face the door when he heard running footsteps. Catherine stopped running when she reached the door. As soon as she saw him face to face, she knew it was Richard. She saw him smile at her, her legs went weak, she walked over to him and put her arms around him and her head on his chest and hugged him as hard as she could.

"Richard, I've missed you so much," she said and started to cry.

"Hello, Catherine," he said as he put one arm around her and stroked her head with his other hand.

When she heard him say her name, it seemed that all the lights that went out when he never showed up at the park, were put back on all at once, everything was bright and beautiful again.

Then Cora walked in.

"Well, I like that, I've been trying to get him for ages now, and you just decide that you want him and walk up to him and put your arms around him and hug him and that's that, I mean I saw him first you know." Cora was trying to sound hurt.

"No, you didn't, Cora. We met five years ago, didn't we, Richard?"

Cora's mouth dropped open because she could see the look on Catherine's face. She had known Catherine since they were tiny children and never had she seen her face beam like this. She was so happy for her; she wanted to give Richard a cuddle as well for making Catherine so happy.

"Catherine, you and Richard just stand here all right. I'll go because I don't think Richard will want me around while he explains to you why he never showed up at the park."

Catherine looked at Cora and knew immediately that she wanted to know and that wild horses wouldn't be able to drag her away from them.

"I know, let us ALL go over to the diner across the road and have a coffee. I'll even pay for it," Cora volunteered. Richard nodded.

As they sat down at a table, a waitress came over to them.

"Three coffees, please," Cora said.

"Why didn't you turn up at the park, Richard?" Catherine asked before Cora could. Catherine was sitting opposite Richard but she still held his hands in hers and Cora saw that she hadn't taken her eyes off him the whole time.

"I couldn't make it to the park because that night when I got home, my mother told me that we were moving out of the tenements and I couldn't let her move everything herself and I didn't know if you would really want to see me. I did go there the following Sunday but you weren't there so I guessed you had not bothered, you know…"

"I was there the following Sunday and a lot of Sundays after that, weren't we, Cora?"

Cora nodded her head then held a finger up as to interrupt whoever was going to speak next. The two of them looked at her and saw a look on her face that would have had John J. Rambo shaken in his boots.

"I promise not to lose my temper." She held her hand up. "But just answer me this," Cora continued. "What did you mean when you said, 'but I guess you had not bothered, you know'; what did you mean by that remark, don't let it be what I think you meant."

Richard felt Catherine's hand tighten on his.

"I meant, you know, Catherine coming from where she does and me coming from where I did, I just thought she was in some kind of shock still, that's why she asked to see me again…"

Cora held her finger up again, Cora slowly started to stand up, she put both her hands on the table, she leant forward until her face was close up to his.

"That's what I thought you meant." Her voice got louder with every word.

"You poor self-pitying idiot, that girl cried her fricking heart out for you every fricking night for six weeks."

Everyone in the diner stopped what they were doing and listened to Cora.

"Just because she comes from the Hill and you from the tenements means she can't fall in love with you? I'll tell you what you should do will I, you should go to the doctors and see if he can get rid of that serious case of class distinction that you have. I've had you rammed down my throat day and night for five years now and why, why, because you suffer from, from…from, ugggghhhhhhhhhh." Cora looked up at the ceiling then slowly she sat down again, her fists were white as she squeezed them together.

"All right, Cora, calm down, you're starting to get flustered," Catherine said.

"Flustered, flustered, fricking me, never," Cora said. The waitress came with their coffees.

"That was a lovely speech, dear, could I book you for the next time? I have an argument with my husband," she said and then walked off.

Catherine had taken hold of Richard's hand and had tightened her grip on it. She knew Cora was losing her temper and when she does, she really loses it and she didn't want Richard getting up and leaving.

Richard looked at Cora.

"I guess I had that coming, didn't I?" he said. He saw Cora nod her head. After that, the three of them talked all morning and afternoon. It was the first time that Richard had ever missed a class; he looked at his watch.

"It's five past four. I have to be going now my bus comes at ten pasts," he spoke.

"We'll give you a lift," Catherine said.

"Thanks, are you going past the projects across the river?" he asked them.

"Nope but we'll still give you a lift," Cora said, smiling, she had made her mind up that she liked Richard and that he was going to be good for Catherine. They all got into the car and Richard told them how to get to his house. They stopped outside of it and Richard got out, Catherine said to him.

"Richard, can I see you tonight please?" Catherine had wanted to ask him this all day but she had been afraid of him saying no.

"Do you still live on snob?" he was about to ask her, then remembered Cora's outburst.

"Yes." Catherine interrupted him while writing her address down and gave him it.

"Then I'll be there at about eight, okay?" He wanted to give her a kiss but was unsure, so he just smiled at her.

"Oh, Richard please do, I'll be waiting for you." Catherine wanted to kiss him so much.

"Oh God, will you two just kiss and get it over with? I won't watch," Cora said trying to look bored with them but fascinated with Catherine and her shyness.

Richard stood and watched them drive away. He had wanted to do what Cora had said, but, but he just couldn't do it, he wanted to, oh did he want to.

Tonight, I'll kiss her. He smiled as he went into the house, he put a CD on, cleaned the few plates they had used for breakfast. His mother usually only had a sandwich at work on Fridays so he made her a crispy salad, then he went and had his shower and a change of clothing, he looked at the clock.

Think I'll do a little revision. He took his books out and started to read the ones he wanted. He looked up from his book and saw how dark it was outside, then he looked at the clock on the wall.

Seven-o-clock. He jumped up out of the seat and went to the window to see if his mother was talking to anyone outside. The street was empty. He grabbed his coat and went outside. Although this area is not the tenements, it still had little bits of crime and panic was starting to build up inside of him. His mother, if late getting in would either phone him or she would be standing where he could see her talking with someone, and she had done neither of them. He knew which way she walked home and he knew she walked half the way with a Mrs Belmont but he didn't know where she lived so he ran all the way to the factory. He walked up to the security building and knocked on the window. The man inside opened the window and asked him what he wanted.

"My mother hasn't come home from work, is anyone working late in the typing pool please?"

The security man looked in his book.

"No, son, there's no one working late tonight."

"Could you tell me where Mrs Belmont lives, please, she walks half the way home with her?"

The security man looked in another book.

"Mrs Irene Belmont lives at two-one-three Redmond flats."

Richard thanked the security man and ran to the Redmond flats complex. They were a big complex and by the time Richard found the correct one, the sweat was running down his back. He knocked on the door, after climbing the three sets of stairs; he couldn't wait for the lift to come back down. A big man opened the door. He looked at Richard then started to close it again.

"I have no time for salesmen; my wife and her friend have had an accident." Richard stopped him from closing the door.

"I'm Richard Buckman, sir."

****

Chapter Four

When Cora dropped Catherine off, she ran straight into the house, throwing her coat at the stand, not looking to see if she had aimed correctly.

"Mom, Dad, I've found him and he is absolutely gorgeous," she shouted as she entered the main room. She couldn't hide her excitement. She just had to shout it out.

"And he's coming here tonight, oh Mom, he is gorgeous." Catherine's mother, Beverley, jumped up out of her chair just as her father, Alvin, came in from the garden.

"What's all the excitement about?" he said looking at his wife. Beverly shrugged her shoulders and went over to where Catherine was jumping around, she put her hands onto Catherine's shoulders and spoke.

"All right, Catherine, now slow down and tell us who you have met and who is so gorgeous that he has got you in such a state."

"I've found Richard, I've found Richard gorgeous Buckman, Mom, Dad, he talked to me and Cora all day, and he's coming here tonight."

Beverley told her to keep quiet until she made some coffee for them.

She came back in with the tray and they drank it while Catherine told them why he never turned up at the park. They all laughed when she told them about Cora losing it with him.

"But Cora told me that she really likes him now."

They could both see the excitement in her and they both loved seeing her like this. Alvin went back out into his green house.

"Oh Mom, he is gorgeous and just oozes sex appeal." Catherine put her hand over her mouth when she realised what she had said.

"A bit like your dad then," Beverly said laughing.

"Mom, if Dad was like him no wonder you fell for him," Catherine replied.

"Was, was, still is you mean," Her mother said.

"I'm going to have to find some clothes to put on," Catherine said as she got up off the sofa and went to the stairs. Beverly watched her daughter run up the left-hand side of stairs, then around the balcony, then out of sight as she went along the passageway to her room.

Alvin and Beverly had not always been rich. Beverly's parents were very rich and they had disowned her when they saw that she was in love with someone who they regarded as below their social standing.

Alvin was an engineer, which meant he got his hands dirty and that was totally against her parent's standards, as they put it to her. "We will never let a commoner marry into this family."

Alvin and Beverly met when Alvin was just trying to start his own business up.

The company he worked for went bust. Alvin went to the bank to see a manager and lucky for him, he saw a very sympathetic one who liked his idea and gave him the loan he needed. Alvin bought a small factory and some old machinery and then went about trying to get orders. It was on one of these trips in another county that he literally bumped into Beverly.

She had been talking to an uncle about some social function that they had attended and was leaving his office when Alvin tried to enter. Beverly knocked all of his plans and ideas out of his hands. Beverly had picked them all up for him and handed them back. Alvin went into the office. When he came back out, Beverly was still there.

"Did you get what you wanted?" she asked him.

"No, I'm afraid not. He said I had to leave them with a foreman, which means that he is not interested."

Beverly led him to another office and sat him down.

"Now tell me what you have got," she spoke. So, Alvin told her everything.

"Now you just wait here until I come back," she spoke. Alvin watched her go out; he liked what he saw. When she came back after half an hour, she sat down beside him and spoke.

"Uncle Thomas will be sending for more information and he will be putting in an order."

Alvin couldn't hide his delight and as he looked at his watch; he saw that he was going to be late for his bus to the train station to catch the train back to his state.

"Thank you, thank you, look I have to catch a bus, thank you again but I do have to go." As he was getting up from the seat, she looked at him and spoke.

"I'll give you a lift, let's go and have a coffee."

"Erm, I know this is the country of the motor car but I don't drive and I have to get to the train station. I don't live in this state and if I miss the train, it means I will have to find a hotel and stay the night, and then I will miss another appointment in another state."

"Well, I don't have anything to do for the next five days, so if you tell me where you are going, I'll drive."

And she did.

That was the start of her life with Alvin and the end of it with her parents. When they found out that she had been driving around the country with a commoner, they had blazing rows. Her parents had stopped her going out, even driving, so one night she slipped out of the house and drove to where Alvin lived. When he saw her standing in his doorway with a bag in her hand, he took her inside and asked her what was wrong. She told him that she had left home.

"So, what are we going to do now?" he asked.

"I know what I want to do," Beverly replied.

So, they both got back in the car and drove over the state line and got married with two strangers as witnesses. Their honeymoon was a slow drive back to Alvin's house.

Beverly worked just as hard as Alvin for the business. She would stay up all through the night producing flyers to send to other companies and she would drive Alvin all over the state and beyond. She drove him once to California. The first few years were slow to start but they could both see the work accumulating, they bought another factory, then another and another. Alvin has five factories in the state, seventeen factories in the country and six more in other parts of the world and in all, he employs over forty thousand people. Beverly is on the boards of countless charities. Although Alvin does not need to get involved with the day to day running of the company, he still likes to go down onto the factory floors of whatever factory he is in and talk to the people who work for him. The one thing he has said from the beginning was 'if you pay the best salaries, you get the best workers' and his workers are the best. When one of his secretaries went into labour with her first child and her husband was working down in Mexico for another company, he sent a private airplane down there to get him and he arrived at the same time as his son did.

It had taken Beverly and Alvin five years to have a child and they loved her so much. They were both dogmatic in their insistence that no matter how much money they had, they would never spoil or bring her up to think that she was better than anyone else. They would never tell her who to go out with or what to do and they both agree that they have done a wonderful job with her.

******

Chapter Five

"Have you got a car or do you want to go in mine?" Mr Belmont asked Richard, as they left the house.

"We'll go in yours if that is all right, sir," Richard replied.

They got into the car and Mr Belmont drove to the hospital in silence. The receptionist said they were on the second floor. They never waited for the lift but ran up the stairs. When they arrived at the ward, Mrs Belmont was sitting beside Richard's mothers' bed. Mrs Belmont stood up and flung her arms around her husband.

"I'm all right, I'm all right," she kept saying to her husband.

"It's Sharon, she has a broken leg. If she had not pushed me out of the way of the car, it could have been a lot worse for me." Mrs Belmont had never seen Richard before.

Richard was bent over his mother who was asleep.

"Sharon is all right. They had to put her out to set her leg. It's her son I'm worried about. The last thing she said to me before they put her under was to make sure her son was all right. Have you left him with one of your neighbours? I'll look after him if you have any trouble with babysitters, that's the least I can do for her after what she did for me, she saved my life."

Richard stood up straight and turned to Mr and Mrs Belmont.

"Please don't worry yourself about her son or a babysitter, Mrs Belmont. I'm her son."

Richard could see the surprise on both of their faces and Mr Belmont wanted to say something but Mrs Belmont got there first.

"But Sharon talks about you as if you are only ten or eleven years old…"

Richard smiled at her.

"I know, now please don't worry about me, as you can see, I'm old enough to look after myself."

Sharon made a noise and they all looked at her. She opened her eyes and saw all the smiling faces; she smiled back at them.

"Hello, Richard, could you give me a drink of water please."

Mrs Belmont handed Richard the glass of water. He handed it to Sharon and she drank it.

"Oh, that's better, my throat was like a desert," she said as she handed the glass back to Richard.

After half an hour, Mr and Mrs Belmont left the ward to go home. Richard moved closer to his mother. Sharon could see the relief on her son's face when they went.

"I know she talks a lot, doesn't she? But she is a good friend, Richard. She will sort everything out at work and will no doubt make it more dramatic than it really was." They both smiled at the thought of Mrs Belmont telling everyone at work what happened.

"So, Mom, are you going to tell me what happened, or do I have to go to the typing pool to find out off Mrs Belmont," Richard said. He could see that she didn't want to tell him as she was going to cry. He thought it would be better to tell him then she wouldn't feel so bad.

"It, It happened so fast, Richard. We were crossing the street, I, I saw the car coming and Irene didn't, I, I pushed her out of the path of it, I got hit, and…and ended up in here." Richard could see the tears forming in her eyes and her lips starting to quiver. He put his hand onto the side of her face and she snuggled into it.

"Mom, it's all right, you're fine, now stop worrying." His mother started crying; she ripped a piece of tissue and wiped her eyes with it.

"But what would have happened if it was worse. Oh Richard I'm sorry, please forgive me." She started to cry again. Richard sat on the bed and put his arms around her and squeezed her tightly.

"Mom, Mom, come on, it's not that serious. I'm almost twenty-one, anyway you will be out of here in a day or so," he said between kissing her on the brow.

Richard was still sitting with his arms around his mother when the doctor came into the ward. He let go of her and stood up when he saw that he was coming over to them.

"Hello, Sharon, now how do you feel? I told you it wouldn't hurt, didn't I?" They watched the doctor lift the chart off the bottom of the bed and write something on it, then he looked at Richard and spoke.

"Before you go, Mr Buckman, could I see you in my office please?" The doctor put the chart back in its place and walked away, smiling. Richard and his mother talked for a while until it was time for him to leave. He kissed her on the cheek and walked down the corridor to the doctor's office and knocked on the door.

"Come in, please."

Richard opened the door and entered the room.

"You wanted to see me, doctor?" he spoke.

"Yes, please take a seat, Mr Buckman," the doctor said pointing to the seat in front of his desk; he was looking at an x-ray that was hanging on his wall light. He flicked the switch off and sat down.

"Mr Buckman, has your wife ever complained of dizziness or breathlessness or a tight feeling in her chest?"

Richard was going to put him right on the 'wife' bit when the seriousness of the question hit him.

"Doctor, if you have anything to tell me, I would appreciate it if you just come out with it."

Richard saw the doctor trying to get himself comfortable in the chair.

"All right, Mr Buckman," he said standing back up and walking over to the wall light, he clicked the button, which lit it up and Richard saw that the x-ray hanging on it had his mother's name at the top.

"Whenever a car accident comes in here, we take x-rays of the injured parties, now before I go on, I have to tell you that at this moment, it is not at all serious, but" – the doctor seemed to be searching for the correct words – "but it could be. What we found was your wife has a tiny hole in her heart. Now the truth is, it will get worse but since we have found it at so early a stage, we can correct it…" The doctor saw Richard grasp the side of the table.

"Sorry, please sit back down, Mr Buckman." The doctor switched the light off and sat down as well.

"My father is one of the leading heart specialists in this country. I have been in touch with him. I told him what we have here and he has promised to come and check your wife over in two weeks' time." The doctor was just talking as far as Richard could make out, he couldn't understand what he was saying, his head was full of all the good times he and his mother had been through, his mind started from when they first met and went right up to now; he couldn't think or concentrate on anything.

"Now I must stipulate that your wife must have complete rest."

Richard looked at the doctor; he hadn't heard anything he had said, except for the complete rest.

"Have you told her?" Richard asked him.

The doctor knew Richard hadn't heard much so he repeated what he had said.

"Richard, you have to make sure your wife has complete rest after the operation, do you understand me?"

"Yes, doctor and I appreciate what you are doing for her but have you told her, are you going to keep her in here until you are ready to operate?"

"We will keep her here for another two days, just for tests. No, I have not told her yet, I was waiting to tell you first."

Richard and the doctor went back to the ward and told her what they had found, she admitted to the doctor that she was getting dizzy spells and all the other symptoms but had said nothing because she didn't want to worry her son. The doctor said that her husband would be more than capable to look after her son. Sharon looked at Richard in her 'Are you going to tell him' look. Richard turned to the doctor.

"Doctor, I'm her son," he spoke.

The doctor looked at both of them as he picked the chart up off the bottom of the bed again to check Sharon Buckman's age.

"Impossible, you're two years younger than me Sharon and, and, and…"

Richard walked home, he had never felt so lonely. His mother said it was all right, she knew something was wrong and she was glad they found it before it was too late. He didn't know if she really meant that or was, she just saying it for his sake. The doctor took some convincing about him being her son but what was really going through his head was, what is he going to do now. He obviously can't keep university up. He will have to find work, so that his mother will have the complete rest that she has to have without worrying about where the meals are coming from.

By the time he reached his home, he'd had a thousand ideas in his head and he had dismissed them one by one.

It was Saturday tomorrow, so I'll call at the university to see if anyone is in who can give me some advice.

He opened his front door and looked at his watch. It was eleven thirty, he wondered if he should try and telephone Catherine, then thought against it.

Now I think I have lost her this time. His mind told him. He made himself a cup of coffee and sat at the table. He wanted to go to bed but knew that sleep wouldn't come to him as his head was just buzzing around with things to do, things to try and do, and things he can't do. Then he thought of his mother lying in the hospital by herself.

Should I go back there and stay close to her, or would she worry about me. He looked at his hands; they were shaking. Then for some unknown reason, he started to cry.

****

Catherine was getting more and more excited as the pointers of the clock got closer to eight o' clock. She had showered, changed her clothes a hundred times. She had run up and down the stairs to and from her bedroom until her parents had told her to stop as they were going dizzy trying to keep tabs on her. When the pointers had gone to eight thirty and he had not arrived, her eyes started going red. Her mom and dad were trying to console her saying he might have got lost or something. By nine o' clock, she said she was going to bed and she wasn't really that bothered he never came.

Her mom and dad could hear her crying as she went up the stairs to bed, when they heard her bedroom door close.

Alvin jumped up out of his chair.

"Right, that is the second time that boy has done this to Catherine and I'm not going to let him get away with it."

Beverly put her hand on her husband's arm and squeezed it.

"Do you know that since Catherine mentioned his name, I've had the feeling that I have heard it before but for the life of me I can't remember where I've heard it?"

"I know, I'm sure I have heard it as well," Alvin replied trying to think where.

"Beverly, is Bob Simmons still at the university?" he asked her as he walked over to the telephone.

"Yes, I was talking to Anne, his wife, the other day and she told me he was now deputy head principal."

"Good," Alvin said as he went through the phone book for his number.

"Alvin you can't phone at this hour, why don't we sleep on it and see if the morning brings us any more answers."

They sat around talking about what had happened today and what they had planned for tomorrow. Beverly poured them each a drink of brandy and by the time they drank it, it was eleven o' clock.

"I think we'll go to bed now," Beverly said.

As they were walking up the stairs, Beverly stopped.

"I've got it Alvin; I know where we have heard the name before," she said going back down the stairs. Alvin following her.

"It's not Richard Buckman we know. It's Sharon Buckman; she is a typist at the factory across the river." Alvin's face lit up and he gave his wife a big hug.

"You're right, it is Sharon Buckman. I'll phone Susan and see if she will dig her files out for me tomorrow; she'll do anything if Catherine is involved, no matter what it is." He went over to the phone and dialled her number; he heard the phone being picked up.

"Hello Susan, Alvin here, look I know it's late but I really do need your help."

"Hello, sir. What is it you need?" a sleepy voice asked.

"Susan, I know it's Saturday tomorrow but could you go in the office and have Sharon Buckman's file on my desk for when I get in, please," he spoke.

"Sir, Sharon Buckman has worked for you for five years and two weeks, she is twenty-seven years old and is very good at her job, she came here after being recommended by her night school tutor and—"

"Wait, wait a minute Susan, I know you are a damn good secretary but I have thousands of workers and there is no way you can remember all of them like that."

"No sir, I got her file out tonight before I left work and read through it."

"And why did you do that, Susan?" Alvin asked her.

"Her friend, Irene Belmont called to say that she will not be in for work on Monday."

"Susan, why will she not be in on Monday?"

"Oh, I thought you knew that's why you were phoning me."

"Susan, why will she not be in on Monday?" Alvin repeated.

"Sharon Buckman was run over by a car on her way home from work this evening."

"My God Susan, is she all right?" Alvin said urgently.

"They have kept her in hospital overnight, Irene said she has a broken leg."

"What hospital is she in, Susan?" Alvin said as he saw Beverly put her hand over her mouth, he was also trying to reassure Beverly.

"Sharon is in the Central on Forty Fourth Street, sir."

"Thank you very much, Susan, I'm sorry for waking you up." Alvin put the phone down then immediately picked it back up and dialled the number for the hospital that Beverly had found in the phone book while Alvin talked to Susan.

"Hello, Central Hospital, how can I help you?" a woman's voice asked.

"Good evening, I'm enquiring about a person who was brought in earlier this evening, her name is Sharon Buckman."

"Please wait a minute, sir." Alvin heard the phone being put down and a keyboard being tapped, then the phone being picked up again.

"Yes sir, we do have a Sharon Buckman here, are you a relative?"

"No, I'm just…"

"I'm sorry, sir, but we cannot give out information unless you are a relative, I could buzz the duty doctor for you."

"Yes, please do that."

Alvin was about to put the phone down on the table when a quiet male voice said.

"Hello, Doctor Cunningham here, how can I help you?"

"Hello, Doctor Cunningham, this is Alvin De Charger here, I'm trying to find out how Sharon Buckman is."

"Sharon Buckman is doing fine, sir, there's no great urgency just yet so we are going to operate on Tuesday week, that is when we will have all the relevant staff at hand."

"Operate! I was told she had a broken leg and that you were just keeping her in overnight."

"Yes, sir, she does have a broken leg, when we took x-rays for other damage, we found that she has a small hole in her heart and—"

"A what?" Alvin shouted down the phone and immediately apologised.

"A hole in her heart." Doctor Cunningham was about to reassure Mr De Charger.

"Listen, do you know Henry T. Cunningham?" Alvin asked.

"Yes, he is my father, sir."

"Well, can you please get in touch with him and tell him I would very much appreciate it if he would consider doing the operation as soon as possible."

"Yes, sir," Doctor Cunningham replied.

"Thank you," Alvin said, as he put the phone down and looked at Beverly who was sitting on the sofa with a worried look on her face; she knew Henry Cunningham was the best heart specialist in the country and she did not really want to know why Alvin had mentioned his name.

Alvin went over to her and sat down next to her; he put his hand onto her hand and gave it a gentle squeeze.

"Sharon Buckman has a small hole in her heart but the doctor I have been speaking to is Henry's son and he is going to speak to his father, he says everything is going to be all right."

Beverly gave him a nervous smile.

The next morning, Alvin and Beverly were up and about early. Beverly had made them both a breakfast and coffees.

"Do you think it's still too early to phone Bob Davis, Beverly?"

"If you phone his home, he will know what to look for when he gets to the university."

Alvin dialled the number.

"Hello, Ann Davis here," the voice said.

"Hello Ann, Alvin De Charger here, could you get Bob for me please."

"Oh, Hello Alvin," she said before shouting for her husband.

"Hello Alvin what makes you phone me this early?" the familiar voice of an old friend asked.

"Bob, listen are you going to the university today?"

"Yes."

"Good, is there any chance you could pull Richard Buckman's file out for me and read it, then phone me and tell me what kind of boy he is please."

"Sure Alvin, is there anything specific I should be looking for?"

"No, no, I just need to know what kind of person he is, that's all," Alvin said.

"Well, that's not a problem Alvin, I'll do it as soon as I get there, okay?"

"I'll be at the factory across the river, Bob, phone me there when you can, thank you."

When Alvin arrived at the factory, the security man let him in. They smiled at each other as Alvin drove past him. He saw Susan's car parked in her own bay, he got out of the car and walked up the stairs on the outside of the building, he went inside at the second landing and walked through the empty desks of the typing pool. Susan could see that he was worried about something as she caught a slight frown on his face before he saw that Susan was watching him.

"I've put Sharon Buckman's file on your desk, sir," Susan said as he passed her.

"Thank you, Susan," he replied, then he stopped and turned around and looked at her, the smile coming back to his face, because he knew as well as she did what was going to happen now.

Susan had worked for him since almost from the beginning, she was very efficient and sometimes Alvin thought she could read his mind as all he needed to do was say, 'Susan where's the file on,' and she would have it in her hand, without him having to finish what he was saying.

"Susan, would you please stop calling me sir."

"Yes, sir," came the usual reply.

Alvin turned back around and, slightly shaking his head, walked into his private room. He shut the door, then he opened it again and spoke, "Susan, when Bob Davis calls put him straight through to me, please."

"Yes, sir," Susan replied as he closed the door. After half an hour, his phone rang.

"It's Bob Davis, sir."

"Thank you, Susan," Alvin replied.

"Hello Bob, have you got anything to tell me?"

"Yes, Alvin and it's all good. Richard Buckman is a model student; we are finding it hard to keep up with him. His studies include computers, which he is brilliant at and as a filler he is studying Advance Business Methods and he is finding those to easy. He has never been in any kind of trouble whatsoever, which is remarkable when you think that he was brought up by only one parent in the tenements."

"Well thank you, Bob, I owe you one, that's good news indeed."

Alvin pressed the intercom to Susan's desk.

"Yes, sir," Susan said.

"Susan, I do not want to be disturbed for an hour."

Alvin phoned Beverly and told her what Bob Davis had said, he could almost hear the sighs of relief coming out of her. After an hour, the intercom buzzed.

"Yes, Susan," Alvin said.

"It's Bob Davis again, sir."

"Hello again, Alvin. There's someone here who I think you might like to talk to."

Alvin heard the phone being passed to someone and a voice saying thank you, then.

"Hello. Richard Buckman here."

*****

Chapter Six

Richard left the house early; he was going to go to the university and see if anyone was there who could advise him on dropping out for a year and what he would have to do to get back into his studies when he returns. There was a hint of frost in the air as he fastened his coat up and clouds of breath formed as he exhaled. He had decided to walk as it would give him more time to think of something or some other way of coping but by the time he arrived at the university entrance, nothing new had formed. He went up to the reception and asked if there was a councillor in that he could see. The receptionist went into the office of Bob Davis, as he had just asked to see the files on Richard Buckman. Bob Davis came out and spoke.

"Richard, would you like to come through to my office please."

Richard followed Bob Davis through into his office.

"Sit down please, Richard."

Richard sat down, he felt a bit uncomfortable, he was about to drop out of university and Mr Davis was being so polite to him.

"What can I do for you, Richard?"

Richard told him what had happened to his mother and what he had decided to do. Bob Davis listened to him then picked up his phone and dialled a number.

"Before you make that decision, Richard, there is someone who I think would like to have a talk with you," Mr Davis said, then handed Richard the phone.

"Hello, Richard Buckman here."

"Hello Richard, this is Alvin De Charger. I know about your mother and I'm going to do everything I can for her and I would also like to meet you. What are you doing this afternoon?"

"Erm. Erm, after this meeting with Mr Davis, I'm going to the hospital to see my mother…"

"Would it be all right if I sent a car around to the hospital, say, say, about three-o-clock, it will bring you to my home, and then we can have a talk."

"Yes, sir," Richard replied.

"Good, now can you please put Bob Davis back on? Thank you."

Richard handed the phone back to Mr Davis; he sat in the chair quietly until Mr Davis put the phone back on the receiver.

"You certainly know some powerful people, Richard."

"Was that really Alvin De Charger?" Richard asked him.

On the way to the hospital, Richard was trying to remember all he could about Alvin De Charger. Schools and the universities use his story on how to overcome all obstacles that people come up against and how to make something of their lives. Richard's mother would praise him up even though she had never met him personally; she would say that he is the perfect boss.

He arrived at the hospital and went straight to the ward, when he saw that his mother wasn't in the bed, the panic he felt almost made him sick, he ran back down to the receptionist and asked her where his mother was although he was secretly dreading the answer. The receptionist gave him a smile and a look as if he was some kind of celebrity and she talk to him in a soft voice.

"Your mother has just come out of surgery and is recovering in the post-surgery unit on the third floor." The smile never left her face.

Richard ran up the stairs two at a time and along the corridor until he came to the ward, he saw Doctor Cunningham sitting at her bedside and breathed a sigh of relief. Richard walked over to him, while looking at his mother sleeping.

"You said she would have to wait until next Monday or Tuesday for the operation, doctor?"

The doctor stood up out of the chair.

"Yes. But that was before I knew you were a friend of Mr De Charger. Do you know what happened here at seven-o-clock this morning?"

Richard just looked at him and shrugged his shoulders then looked back at his mother.

"Well, I'll tell you, my father walked through those doors with all of his technical staff and they operated as soon as they were ready."

"How is she?" were the only words Richard said.

The doctor gave him a smile that said 'she is going to be all right'.

"I see you have no idea who my father is, Richard, do you? Let's go down to my office."

They went down to the second floor. Doctor Cunningham opened the door and let Richard walk in first. Doctor Cunningham gave a little yawn as Richard sat down in a chair.

"Sorry Richard, I've only had three hours sleep in thirty-six hours but honestly, you could have knocked me down with a feather when my father walked through those doors with his staff. I still think I dreamt it." Doctor Cunningham knew that Richard still had no idea just how important his father is.

"Let's see, how can I make you realise what it means to have my father here. He is the leading heart surgeon in America and he operated on your mother. Sharon is going to be just fine so you can at least stop worrying about her now. Now please tell me why you never said you were a friend of Mr De Charger." Doctor Cunningham could see Richard relaxing more and more as his words sank into him.

"I do not know Mr De Charger; my mother works in one of his factories," Richard said.

Richard was standing outside the hospital's main doors at three-o-clock. Doctor Cunningham had talked for an hour or so before he had to go and have a sleep and he reassured Richard that his mother would not be alone when she woke up and as he walked Richard to the doors, he told the receptionist that he must be told the minute Richard's mother showed signs of coming around.

Richard saw the big white Limousine coming up the driveway; it stopped right in front of him and the driver got out and walked around to where Richard was standing.

"Mr Buckman?" he spoke.

"Wah yes."

"Good, please." The driver indicated for Richard to get in the car. Richard got in and the driver closed the door then walked back around to his side. He got in and started the engine.

"I do hope your mother had a successful operation, sir."

"Yes, according to the doctor, she is going to be just fine, she was asleep when I left her," Richard replied wondering how many more people knew of it. "Where exactly are we going to?" Richard asked the driver.

"To Mr De Charger's home."

"And where is that?"

"Cloister Hill," came the reply.

Richard's heart skipped a beat when he heard the name. As soon as they got to the Hill, Richard scanned every inch of it to see if he could get a glimpse of Catherine and what he would do if he did. The whole area smelled of money; they passed some of the biggest houses Richard had ever seen in his life, some driveways went for about three hundred yards then they would turn and be covered by trees, so they could easily go further.

The car slowed down and did a quick turn right.

"This is where Mr and Mrs De Charger live, sir," the driver said as if he was a tour guide.

Richard felt a tightness in his throat as he looked at the house he was being driven to. It was huge with at least four floors and absolutely hundreds of windows. Ivy was growing up the front walls and was neatly cut above the second level of windows; it was intermingled with Honeysuckle. There was a sort of dug over trench around the house with rose bushes planted neatly, red, yellow, blue, purple, every colour that you can get in roses was planted there and it looked beautiful. The front lawn, which stretched from the wall at the roadside all the way to the house, was a lush green with statues of Greeks in familiar poses such as throwing the discus and throwing the javelin. When the car stopped and Richard got out, the smell of the Honeysuckle and the roses was very strong. The whole of the air smelled of them and he was sure the breath that was going into his mouth even tasted of it. He walked up the six steps to the big wooden door when the car drove away. He was disappointed that he never saw Catherine but he had made his mind up to ask Mr De Charger if he knew any one who lives on the Hill called Catherine. Richard rang the bell and turned back around to look at the Garden again, the size and beauty of it was something he would never forget.

****

When Catherine came down the stairs, Beverly could see that she'd had a restless night.

"How are you feeling now, Catherine?" Beverly could see even now Catherine was fighting to keep her tears in.

"I'm all right, Mom," Catherine replied after a short pause while she controlled herself.

"Well, I can tell you that Richard had a good reason for not turning up last night," Beverly said.

"Yes, Mom," Catherine replied as she went to the kitchen, it was in mid stride that what her mother said finally went into her brain and her brain screamed out at her to stop walking away.

Catherine stopped walking, one leg still off the ground, she slowly put it down, almost too scared to move it in case what she heard went away with the fright of a sudden movement. As her foot touched the ground, she swung around.

"Wha, what did you say?" Catherine stammered, hoping that she had heard correctly. Beverly was sitting on a sofa with a very big grin on her face.

"I said, Richard had a very good reason for not turning up here last night."

Catherine ran over to the sofa and jumped on it landing right next to her mother.

"What are you saying? Are you telling me you have seen him?" She grabbed her mother's arm just that little bit too tight and it left a red mark when she let go.

"Sorry, Mom, oh, how do you know, please don't tease me."

Beverly rubbed her arm and smiled at her daughter; she could see the change in her and she loved it.

"No, I have not spoken or seen him but your father has spoken to him, your father is on his way here now to tell you all about it and it seems Richard has really impressed him."

Catherine had felt as if the whole world hated her when she first came down the stairs but now, with the news that her father had actually spoken to Richard and liked him, now, now she felt as if the whole world loved her with all of its heart.

"Mom, tell me all you know please, please," Catherine pleaded.

"I honestly do not know anything, Catherine, your father is coming home to tell us both what he knows," Beverly lied; she had her fingers crossed down by her side. Catherine pretended not to see her cross them.

"Oh Catherine, there's a letter on the Davenport for you."

Catherine went over to the Davenport and picked the letter up, looking at the return address. Beverly saw Catherine's eyes light up even more.

Catherine read the short letter twice before she went over to her mother. She handed her the letter. Beverly took it noticing that Catherine's hands were shaking. Beverly read the letter twice as well, and then said in an excited voice.

"Catherine, when did you see Jonathon Kranz?"

"I've never seen him; all we know at drama is that he is doing a play at the theatre for one season we think he must have asked the university if they could forward some names." Catherine's heart was racing now.

"It says you have to go to an audition tomorrow, that's Sunday," Beverly said.

"Yes, Mom, Jonathon Kranz is noted for doing things different. I mean he is a world-famous stage director but as everyone who wants to be on the stage knows 'he likes to get back to the raw talent, just to get the stuffiness out of his head' and he does something like this."

Catherine was just about to start telling her mother of all of the stars he has discovered when Catherine saw a glint in her mother's eyes and a smile came to her face.

"Mom, you know him, don't you?" Catherine said in disbelief.

Beverley's smile got bigger.

"Yes, when I lived in the other life, my parents used to take me to see his plays every time he came to the city. He knew that his plays did nothing for me, and when he asked me why, I told him that it was a lot of garbage to pretend that everything has a happy ending, that's when he decided to try 'tragedies'. I'm not trying to say that I made him change direction, but…"

They heard the front door being opened. Catherine was up off the sofa and in the hallway before Beverly had time to move.

"Have you seen Richard, Dad?" Catherine almost shouted out.

Her father took his coat off and hung it on the stand. Catherine saw the smile on his face and knew it was good news.

"No but I have spoken to him," he said as they walked to the main room.

"I do not know how much your mother has told you, Catherine," he said looking at Beverly and seeing that she has her fingers crossed as she winked at him.

"But the reason he never showed up was his mother had an accident last night. She was hit by a car and ended up in hospital and as it has turned out, they have found that she also has a hole in her heart, which, if everything has gone well, she should be in the recovery unit by now." He looked at Beverly. Beverly was nodding her head. He continued, "I took the liberty of making a few telephone calls, and as I've said, everything should be fine with Sharon, that's

Richard's mother. Now let's have a cup of coffee." He said as he walked into the kitchen.

Catherine ran up the stairs removing her dressing gown as she went. When she was out of hearing distance, Alvin said to Beverly, "Richard is coming around here at about three thirty, so we have to keep her here."

Catherine came running down the stairs and into the main room. Alvin and Beverly looked at her as she was searching for something.

"What are you looking for, Catherine?" Beverly asked her.

"My car keys, where are my car keys?" Catherine asked.

"Where are you going?" her father said.

"To the hospital, I can't let Richard be there by himself, I have to go to him."

"To do what?" Beverly asked.

"To, to, to, to be beside him. Mom, Dad, I can't let him be there by himself, I have to be with him." They could both see the tears starting to wash down her face.

"Catherine, if your father thought it would make any difference, he would take you himself. I do not think it is a good idea, anyway you have something to tell your father, don't you?"

Beverly took the letter and waved it at Catherine just as Alvin came into the room with three cups of coffee.

"What's that?" he asked.

"It's something belonging to Catherine; she was just about to tell you."

Catherine walked over to her mother and took the letter. Catherine knew her mother was correct, as always, and being there with Richard might make it harder for him to talk to her or his mother. Catherine gave the letter to her father. Alvin opened it and read it, then looked at Beverly.

"Who is Jonathon Kranz?" he spoke.

Catherine's eyes widened as if in shock.

"Who is Jonathon Kranz, who is Jonathon Kranz…" she repeated. "Who is Jonathon Kranz, Jonathon Kranz is the best director of the stage in the world, and he wants me, me, to audition for one of his shows, that's who Jonathon Kranz is," Catherine said, pride just oozing out of her mouth.

"Your father would not know who he is, Catherine, he never takes me to the theatre. I used to love going there…" Beverly made it sound as if she really did miss going to the theatre. Just as Alvin was about to say something, the telephone started to ring. Beverly picked it up and asked who it was.

"Catherine, it's Cora."

"I'll take it up in my room, Mom," she said running up the stairs.

"How did you get on with the A.D.O.N.I.S. last night, is he still there with your ha ha ha ha ha." Cora knew that Catherine would be red as anything if he was there listening.

"He never showed up, Cora…" She was going to say why when all she heard from Cora was.

"HE WHAT! He never showed up, that dirty, lousy, snivelling, egotistical."

"No, no, no, Cora, his mother had an accident, they kept her in hospital overnight and when they took x-rays, they found out she also has a hole in her heart and they have operated on her today," Catherine said.

"You want me to go with you, babes?" Cora knew Catherine would be going to the hospital to see him.

"Mom and Dad say it would be best if I never went today, in case I make it awkward for Richard to talk to his mother while I'm there…"

"Well, I'll go with you tomorrow, okay?" Cora cut in.

"I can't go tomorrow either Cora, I'm…"

"You can't?" Cora cut her off again.

"No, I have to go to the theatre for an audition…" Catherine covered her ear from the noise as she heard Cora scream, then she slowly put the phone back to her ear.

"Cora, you almost deafened me there, it's no good shouting and yelling just yet. I might not get a part. Jonathon Kranz is different from an ordinary director."

"Don't you be so stupid girl, Jonathon Kranz will love you the minute he sets his eyes on you; you just promise me when you hit the big time, you don't forget your best friend." Cora started laughing.

"Cora, where I go, you go; we have done that all our lives and that's the way it's always going to be."

"What time do you want me at your house tomorrow then?" Cora asked.

"The audition is at ten-o-clock, so be here about nine, okay?"

"Okay. I'll get Tom to wake me." Cora oozed his name out as she always does.

Catherine started laughing at her.

"If Tom wants to come, he can but I would prefer him to stay outside until they were over."

"No, Catherine, Tom is here just now but he is going to New York tonight. I meant he will phone me at seven thirty to make sure I'm up in time."

"Hold on, Cora, Mom is shouting on me." Catherine put the phone down and went to the top of the stairs, she leant over the rail.

"Yes, Mom, what do you want?"

"Your father wants to have a word with you, Catherine," Beverly said.

"Okay. I'll just tell Cora I'll see her tomorrow," Catherine answered and went back into her room.

Catherine came down the stairs just as the doorbell rang.

"Get that, Catherine, will you please?" her mother asked.

Chapter Seven

Catherine went to the door and opened it. Richard heard the door open and turned around. When they saw each other, Richard smiled an amazing smile and Catherine just stood there with her mouth wide open.

"Hello Catherine, I'm here to see Mr De Charger, what are you doing here?" Richard said, as he was the first of the two of them to get over the surprise. Catherine was still standing with her mouth open. Then her feelings kicked in and she went to him, putting her arms around his shoulders and she whispered in his ear.

"Oh Richard, I thought I had lost you again."

Beverly came to the door.

"Are you going to introduce this man to me and your father, Catherine, or are you going to let him stand here in the cold?"

"Mom, this is Richard Buckman." Catherine got a tingle all over her body when she said his name. Beverly held out her hand and Richard shook it gently.

"At last, how is your mother, Richard?" Beverly asked.

Richard's head was doing somersaults. What was Catherine and her mother doing at Mr De Charger's? They walked through the hall and into the main room.

"Dad, this is Richard Buckman," Catherine said, and again she got those tingles.

This time, it was Richard's turn to stand with his mouth wide open as he watched Alvin De Charger get up out of his chair and walk towards him with his hand held out.

"Hello, Richard," Alvin De Charger said while shaking Richard's hand.

Richard could feel himself start to get nervous and he had to force himself not to.

"This is my beautiful wife, Beverly; I'm Alvin and I think you know my equally beautiful daughter Catherine. Now come over here and sit down and tell us about your mother and how she is doing."

"First. Are you hungry, Richard?" Beverly asked him.

Richard walked over to the sofa and sat down but he couldn't tell you how he walked there or anything because he felt as if he was in some kind of trance. After a minute, he said, "Yes, please. I've only had a sandwich at the hospital." Then he turned to Mr De Charger. "Sir. First of all, I would like to thank you for what you have done for my mother…"

Mr De Charger held up his hand to stop him from talking.

"Wait there, Richard. Like I said before, my wife is called Beverly and I'm called Alvin. I'm not sir nor is Beverly ma'am, and I have never had the chance to thank you for what you did for our daughter, now carry on."

"I'm sorry Alvin, my mother is doing really good. The doctor said that the operation was a success. She was still asleep when I was there but the doctor said that he will be with her when she wakes up and he is keeping a close eye on her."

After a small sandwich and an hour of talking, in which Catherine's eyes never left him, Beverly said, "Why don't the two of you go into the back garden while I make you something a bit more filling than a sandwich?" Catherine was up and out of the chair, taking Richard's hand and leading him through the house to the backyard. Catherine opened a door and they stepped straight into the summerhouse, a small door to the left would take them out into the cold. So Catherine led Richard down the middle of the summerhouse, which seemed to Richard that it went on for miles. As they got closer to the end, Catherine opened a door at the bottom and they ended up in the storm shelter. Catherine sat down as Richard did.

"It wasn't very nice being stood up twice, Richard," Catherine said in a hushed voice.

Richard turned to face her. He put his arm around her shoulder and squeezed gently until she was an inch away from him, then he kissed her softly on the lips.

Catherine felt her head leave her body. She could look down and see him kissing her, then her head came back and joined the rest of her body which was under attack by an electrical charge, the back of her neck was tingling, like she tingled when she said his name. She could feel the hair on the back of her head standing up. She was glad she was sitting down as she knew her legs would not hold her up as they were trembling, even her fingers were tingling. She could feel all of this with just a touch of his lips. Then he pulled his lips away.

"I…I…I'm sorry, Catherine, I shouldn't have done that, should I? I'm sorry."

Catherine just sat there; it took a while before her feelings all rushed back to where they should be. Then she said, "Richard, if you had not kissed me, then I would have kissed you, so please don't apologise, just kiss me again."

Richard put his arm back around her and kissed her again. And again, she could feel herself going through it all. Her emotions were being ravished. Her body was in turmoil. She could feel pieces of it falling away as she went limp to the touch of his lips. She closed her eyes and let it go with the flow of pure adrenaline that was rushing through her veins. She opened her eyes wide when she heard a moaning noise. She shut them again when she realised it was herself making the noise. She tried to stop it but found that she couldn't, so she just let her body go from one exotic feeling to another, until he stopped her. She could feel the pressure of his lips getting lighter and knew he was beginning to take his lips away from her. She wanted to pull him to her and never let go of him, she wanted to be found dead of old age like this, just the two of them. Kissing.

When she finally opened her eyes, she saw him looking into hers.

"I've wanted to do that since that first night, Catherine."

She put her arms around him and whispered, "Then why didn't you?" She opened her lips slightly and put them to his. Catherine had kissed people many times before but had never even touched half the feelings she was getting off Richard.

Catherine's mother shouted to them that there was some dinner ready. They got up off the bench and walked slowly back through the summerhouse. Their arms around each other's waists and Catherine with her head resting on Richard's shoulder. They separated when they reached the dining room. Richard sat down at the big table that must have been made for about thirty people. Catherine sat right opposite him. After about five minutes of eating, Alvin asked Richard, "Have you got your mind fixed on what you want to do after university, Richard?"

"Well si…Alvin. What I really want to do is teach children about computers. I already do a little at night times at a school and I love watching their faces when I show them something, then they do it and it works for them as it did me, their faces light up, it is incredible."

Beverly was watching Catherine, who never took her eyes off Richard and hardly touched a thing on her plate. Richard looked at his watch.

"Would it be all right if I went now? I have to go to the hospital but first I have to go home and change my clothes. If my mother sees me in the same clothes, she will worry that I'm not looking after myself." They all stood up and Richard looked at both Alvin and Beverly. "Once again, I must thank you for what you have done for my mother. I honestly do not know how I can repay you."

Alvin and Beverly waved his thanks aside.

"How are you going to get home, Richard?" Beverly asked him.

"I'll walk through the park; I know most of its pathways now and I'll catch a bus at the other side."

"Mom, Dad, I'll drive Richard home, then to the hospital if it's okay with you, Richard?"

Both her parents nodded their heads and smiled.

They walked along the hall and Catherine put her coat on. Beverly opened the door. Alvin shook Richard's hand, and then kissed his daughter on the cheek.

"Now you drive carefully, Catherine," Beverly said.

"Richard can drive if he wants to," Catherine said holding the keys in front of him.

"Sorry, I know how to get into the passenger side and that is my total knowledge of cars," Richard said holding up his hands. They could hear Alvin and Beverly laughing as they closed the door after they went out and Beverly shout 'déjà vu'. Catherine led Richard around to the back of the house. They could have gone through the house but it was more romantic to Catherine to walk this way. She put her arm through his and he squeezed it with his arm. She snuggled into him and he kissed her softly on the cheek, which shot a fire through Catherine's body. When they turned a corner, Richard saw a building with two double doors. Catherine pressed a button on the key holder and one set of the double doors opened. Richard stood outside while Catherine went in, then came out driving a British Mini car. She stopped and Richard got in.

"I never thought we would be able to get into such a small car," he spoke.

"Oh, Richard, I just love this car. It looks so small but as you see, the room you have when you're inside is just enough to make it comfortable and you never want to get out of it." Catherine wanted to feel Richard's knee as she went for the gear shifter but she never.

"What time do you have to be at the hospital?" Catherine asked him.

"Seven thirty about," he replied.

"We have time to go to Cora's, I have to pick something up, if it's all right with you, Richard, then we'll go straight to your house."

"If you think we have the time that's all right with me," Richard replied. Catherine drove along the driveway and out onto the road, it did not take them very long to get to Cora's. They got out and went up the steps then rang the bell. Cora opened a window and threw a key down to them; Richard caught it and gave it to Catherine.

"It's my key, I left it here the other night," she said as she opened the door. They were walking up the stairs when Tom, Cora's boyfriend, appeared at the top and asked them if they wanted a coffee.

"No thanks, Tom, I've just come to pick some things up…"

"Too late, I've already made it," Cora shouted from the kitchen, she came out and handed everyone a cup. Catherine watched Cora and saw a mischievous smile come to her face, as she said, "Tom, this is Richard, the person who has Catherine stuttering and flustering and puts her in such a state—"

"And Richard, this is Tom, the only person who can keep Miss Mouth Almighty's mouth shut." Catherine finished for her, giving Cora 'the stare'.

Richard took Tom's outstretched hand and shook it. Catherine went into another room.

"So," Cora said loud enough for Catherine to hear as she walked around Richard, looking at him from top to bottom. "So, you've finally got him, eh? After all of these years."

Tom was smiling at Richard's obvious discomfort, and said to him, "Take no notice, Richard. Cora is just getting Catherine back for all of the years of going on about you."

Catherine walked into the room that Cora had led them into.

"Cora, you leave him alone."

"I wasn't doing anything," Cora said innocently. Richard was trying not to show how embarrassed he was.

"Come on, Richard, I've got what I came for, let's get away from this den of inequity," Catherine looked at her watch.

"Yeah, it's only six-o-clock at night; we more than likely got Cora out of bed."

Anyone who heard them would think that they hated each other but as Tom knew what they were like, he just let them get on with it.

"We'll drink our coffee in the other room, Richard, it's quieter."

Richard watched Tom as they walked to another room, Richard saw that Tom had an air of confidence about him.

"I thought Cora was going to kill me in the diner. How long you been with Cora, Tom?" Richard asked him. Tom smiled.

"About three years, we met at a party. Don't get the wrong idea about Cora, Richard, she really is an angel as you will find out as you get to know her."

They heard the two women laughing; Catherine came into the room.

"Right Richard, let's go, Cora is feeling tired and wants to go to bed." Catherine started to laugh again.

Tom and Cora waved them off as Catherine drove away. When they arrived at Richard's house, he said, "I can't remember if I cleaned or not Catherine." Very red faced.

"That's not a problem, Richard, I'll clean up while you have a shower," she replied.

Richard opened the door and put his coat on the back of the sofa, then he went into the bathroom and switched the shower on. He came back into the living room and said to Catherine, "Catherine, you can put the television on or the CD player, whatever you want, okay? I'll not be long." Then he went back into the bathroom.

Catherine heard him getting into the shower and wondered what it would be like to join him. Then she went bright red at what she had just thought.

"Stop it girl or you will burn in hell."

She went to the CD player and looked at what he had; they were all by the same group. She picked one up and walked to the bathroom door.

"Richard, all your CDs are by the same group, and I haven't heard of them. Are they any good?"

"If you want to make a good impression on my mother, you had better not say anything bad about them." He laughed.

"But who are 'The Kinks'? I've never even heard of them," Catherine asked.

"To my mother, they are the greatest thing to come out of England. Put one on and listen to them."

Catherine put one on and by the time she had listened to the seventh song, she was a Kinks fan. Richard came out of the shower and went straight into his room. Catherine caught a glimpse of him with a towel around his waist as he went into the room and immediately went bright red again. When he came out of his room, he had put his jeans on but no top and was drying his hair with the towel. Catherine had to fight to control her will power and to stay seated or she might make a fool of herself with him but her mind was racing and she could feel her face getting hotter and flushed.

"They are pretty good," she said while trying not to look at him.

Oh, dear God girl, you're going to burn in hell for these thoughts. She was a trembling wreck, she held the CD cover up to try and keep her eyes away from him but she noticed she was shaking hopelessly, so she put her hand down.

"Yes, I like them as well," Richard said just as her hand brought the CD away from her eyes and he was standing right in front of her pulling his t-shirt down his chest, and as he pulled his hair out of the neck of the t-shirt, Catherine could not hold back anymore. She stood up and put her arms around his neck.

"Richard, kiss me please."

Richard put his arms around Catherine's waist and kissed her on the lips.

Catherine thought she was going to fall as she felt him pull her into his body. She could feel the power in his hands as they pulled at the small of her back. She was going to faint. She could see the blackness getting closer to her. She didn't want to faint, not when she was feeling like this, she wanted it all, she didn't want to miss one single emotion, she wanted more, she wanted him.

Richard please put your hands on the front of me, pleaseeeee. She felt herself going red again but this time, she couldn't care less. If she was going to lose her virginity, then so be it. Richard was the one she wanted to take it from her. She wanted to make it a gift to him, from her heart, from her head, from her body. She could see the two of them, playing with three children in a cornfield; she could see them growing old together.

Richard took his lips away from Catherine's and she came crashing back down to reality. She could feel her face absolutely burning with embarrassment. She had been willing to give her body up to Richard, her mind was now saying no but her body was still saying 'go for it'.

Her body was winning the fight.

"We'll have to go now, Catherine," Richard said as he switched the CD player off.

"Yes, yes, you're right, Richard, we'll have to go now." Catherine was so mixed up with all of her emotions fighting each other, she had forgotten why she was at Richard's house in the first place.

Catherine stopped the car at the main entrance of the hospital building.

"Richard, you go in from here. I'll park the car. It will give you time to have a private talk to your mother."

Richard smiled at her as he got out of the car and was about to close the door.

"Richard, I think I deserve a kiss for bringing you here, don't you?"

Richard closed his door and walked around to Catherine's side. Catherine lowered her window and Richard kissed her on the cheek.

"Is that it?" she said but she didn't know if he heard her as he was away, by the time she realised that that was all she was going to get, just for now.

Richard asked the receptionist what ward his mother was on.

"She's back on ward two, sir. Doctor Cunningham is with her at the minute."

"Thank you," Richard said and went to the ward. As he walked in, Doctor Cunningham was sitting on the side of her bed. He stood up and walked towards him.

"Your mother is going to be fine, Richard. I have just been keeping her company until you got here, and can I see you before you leave?"

"Okay," Richard said as he watched the doctor leave the ward, then turning back towards his mother, he had a big grin on his face.

"Mom, are you giving the doctor the hots?"

Sharon went bright red, and watched Richard pull two chairs over to the bed; he sat on one.

"Who's the other chair for?"

"She's parking the car."

"She, she, she, it can't be Irene, she can't drive."

"Mom, never mind, you will see her when she gets here. Now apart from the obvious, how do you feel?" he said as he looked at all the tubes going into her. She nodded her head.

"I feel fine, Richard, just fine."

The ward had nine beds in it, and each bed had at least two visitors, it was not loud but you could hear everyone talking in a kind of hushed voices. Richard had his back to the door. He could not see Catherine enter the ward but he knew something was happening as the whole ward went quiet. He watched his mother's face change and her mouth drop open. Richard turned around to look at what his mother and everyone else was looking at, then he turned back to his mother, a big smile on his face.

"I wondered what was keeping her," he spoke.

Catherine had changed her clothes, instead of the jeans and woolly jumper she had on when she left him at the main doors, she now had on a black skirt that left just enough to the imagination of the male mind, she had a black shirt on and with her waist length black hair, her black tights and stiletto heeled shoes, she was what every male thought, that Aphrodite, the Goddess of love, would look like if she was around today.

"God, isn't she gorgeous? Who has she come to see?" Sharon whispered to Richard. She watched Catherine walk to the bottom of her bed and stop, Sharon saw her smile as Richard pulled the chair for her to sit down.

"Mom, this is Catherine De Charger," he said with a big broad smile on his face.

"Oh, please tell your father that I will repay him for all he has done for me, I'm so grateful."

Catherine smiled back at her and Sharon saw her put her hand in Richard's.

"Mom, Catherine is not here to report your progress back to her father, she's with me."

"I'm his girlfriend," Catherine said it for the first time and just hoped Richard agreed. Sharon had to fight the tears back as she looked for the tissues to wipe her eyes.

"Richard, she is beautiful, how, who, how, did the two of you meet?" Sharon asked as she saw Catherine squeeze his hand and Richard squeezed hers back.

"We met just over five years ago, didn't we?" Catherine replied.

"You've been going out with each other for five years and I never knew?" Sharon said incredulously.

Catherine smiled at Sharon again.

"No, we met when he saved me," Catherine turned to Richard.

"You have never told her, have you?" she spoke.

"I'll go and see what the doctor wants me for okay," Richard said as he was feeling more and more uncomfortable. Sharon was wondering what Catherine was going on about. Catherine stood up then sat down in Richard's chair as it was closer to Sharon.

"Well, if Richard has not told you, I will," she said just loud enough for Richard to hear as he went down the ward.

Richard knocked on Doctor Cunningham's door and entered when he was asked to.

"Sit down, Richard, please." Richard sat down and was immediately put at easy with the tone of his voice. He watched as the doctor put two x-rays onto his light wall, the first was before the operation the second was after it.

"As you can see your mother's problem has been put right and she is going to be fine but now you must make sure that she is free from any kind of stress or work for as long as it takes to heal properly. I'll call around to your home when she is discharged from here in three weeks or so."

"She will be looked after, doctor, that I will guarantee," Richard said as he stood up to leave.

When he returned back to the ward, he could see the pride in his mother's face.

"Richard, why didn't you tell me?" his mother asked.

"Mom, that was the night you told me about moving from the tenements. I could not spoil that for you, could I?"

Sharon wiped another tear from her eyes when Catherine took his hand again.

"What did the doctor want you for?" Sharon hurriedly asked before she started to cry for real.

"Oh, he was asking my permission to date you."

Sharon went bright red.

"I know something is going on with you two," Richard said. Catherine laughed and Sharon wanted the bed to sink into the ground.

Catherine was quiet in the car going back to Richard's house. He knew something was on her mind.

"If you're having second thoughts about us, Catherine, I'll understand," Richard said quietly.

"Wha…Wha…what?" Catherine stammered as she stopped the car at the side of the road.

"Why would you say that?" She looked at him, a worried look on her face.

"You're all quiet and I can see that you're thinking hard," Richard said.

"No, no, it has nothing to do with us, it's nothing like that. What I'm trying to work out is that it is impossible for Sharon to be your mother. I mean there are all kinds of things going through my mind about it, and no matter what I think, Sharon cannot be your mother."

Richard burst out laugh, not so much at her question but more of relief at it not being what he thought it was.

"What's so funny? I don't think it's funny."

"Catherine, Sharon is my mother. I will not have anyone saying otherwise. She has looked after me since I was about five. She stopped me from starving to death, she kept me when no one else wanted me." Then he told Catherine how they met and how she did everything she could for him. By the time he had finished telling her, Catherine was almost crying; the sadness was crushing her heart and all she could say was.

"Oh, Richard." She put her arms around his shoulders and kissed him on the lips. They sat in the car hugging each other until they had to stop for the pins and needles they were starting to get. It was ten-o-clock when they finally got back to Richard's house. As they went inside, Catherine kissed Richard on the cheek as she passed him.

"What was that for?" he asked.

"I just wanted to kiss you, that is all. And I don't ever want you to say that again."

"Say what again?" he asked.

"That thing in the car, erm, erm, what was it again." Catherine pretended to think of the words. "Oh yes, erm, erm, if you're having second thoughts about us. Now please, Richard, listen to me, all right?" Catherine's voice was now deadly serious. "I have loved you from the first day we met. I will NEVER have second thoughts about going out with you, and I will always be in love with you. ALWAYS." She put her arms around his waist and her head on his chest. Then in a whisper, she said, "And I hope you feel the same way about me."

Richard put his hand under her chin and lifted her head upwards. He looked at how beautiful her face is and kissed her on the tip of her nose.

"And I will always love you, Catherine," he whispered.

"Is that all I get for poring my heart out to you? A kiss on the nose." Catherine opened her mouth.

Catherine knew right at that very minute what all the great lovers must have felt like when they kissed. How Cleopatra melted in the arms of Mark Anthony. How Grace Kelly was swept off her feet by the first kiss from Prince Ranier the Third of Monaco. How they must have been mesmerised by the taste of their love and how they gave up the secrets of their bodies, as she wanted to, if only he would ask her, she would give him it. She wanted Richard to ask for her body, everything she held sacred was his for the taking, everything. When he removed his lips from hers, it was like her lifeline to him had been severed. She wanted him to put back the feelings she had been getting. She was panting in anticipation, perspiration was covering her body, her face was flushed and her lips swollen, she wanted him so much, her whole body was screaming out for relief, to be set free from the strangle hold that was forming around her.

"Richard," she whispered when she had put her head back onto his chest and she was looking away from him.

"Yes," he replied. Even his voice sent her body into total submission.

"Can I stay the night with you here?" The moment she said the words, she knew she should not have. She felt his hands take hold of her shoulders and gently move her away from him; he looked into her eyes. She was sure he could see her heart and how hard it was beating.

"Catherine, I would love you to stay but your mother and father are putting a lot of trust in me and it wouldn't be right to break it, would it?"

The feeling of disappointment made her stomach knot up, she knew he was right but she had to ask him.

Richard could see that he had made her sad. He put his arms around her and squeezed her gently to him. She looked up at him again and opened her mouth slowly. He put his lips to hers again and they kissed wildly, slowly walking to his bedroom.

He stopped before they went in.

"Catherine, we can't." Richard thought he was losing his mind, here was the most beautiful woman he had ever met and he was refusing her.

"I, I, I know, Richard, I'm sorry." Catherine sat down on the sofa, she had to, her legs were shaking and they would not have kept her up much longer. Richard went and made them both a cup of coffee and they sat and talked. Catherine stood up and said she had better be going as it was getting late, and would he like to come over to her house tomorrow for dinner, he said yes.

"I'll pick you up about ten, then we can have a walk through the park before we eat, I'll phone Cora up and tell her not to bother coming over as I will not be going to the audition—"

"Wait," Richard said, stopping her in mid-sentence. "You can't cancel an audition just because of me."

"Yes, I can, I don't care about the theatre anymore, all I went is to be with you," she spoke.

"But Catherine, you can't. Please listen to me; you have not been going to Drama just to throw it away, not when you have the chance to be on stage at the theatre. Look, I'll be at the hospital until two-o-clock, if the audition is finished by then, you can come and pick me up, if you're not finished then I will be at the lake in the park waiting for you at five-o-clock. But I don't want you throwing this chance away, okay?"

"All right I promise I will give it my best shot." She smiled at him.

"Good," Richard said then looked at the clock. "It's getting really late; you should be heading home now, Catherine."

"Okay. I'll see you tomorrow, Richard." They walked to the door. Richard opened the door and as Catherine walked past him to go out, she put the palm of her hand on his cheek.

"I love you so much, Richard." Then her hand went to the back of his neck and she pulled his head to her and kissed his lips, her other arm went around his back and squeezed him closer. He put his arms around her and gave her the response she wanted.

When their lips parted, she was so flushed that she never felt the cold breeze that was blowing. Richard stood at the door and waved as she drove away. Catherine felt empty when her car turned out of his street and she couldn't see him in the rear-view mirror.

******

Chapter Eight

Cora rang the doorbell. Catherine opened the door then shouted back to her Parents.

"I'll see you later. I'll phone if I have a part. Goodbye." She saw her mam and dad waving from the bay window as Cora drove past. Catherine was deliberately quiet in the car. She knew Cora would be bursting to find out what happened with her and Richard. she never said a word for almost two miles. After four miles, Cora screamed.

"WELL, are you going to tell me or do I have to crash the car, I can't drive for thinking about what you have been up to with the Adonis?"

Catherine knew she wouldn't be able to hold her laughter in much longer but she was determined to make Cora wait.

"Nothing happened," Catherine said slowly.

Cora stopped the car and turned to Catherine.

"Look, if you don't tell me every little detail, I know you know I'm not a fighter but if you do not tell me, I'll take your head off."

"Ha Ha Ha. Oh Cora you should see your face. Curiosity killed the cat."

"Ah yes but satisfaction brought it back, now come on, I mean it. Every detail."

"Oh, all right then, after we left your place, we went to the hospital to visit his mother…" Catherine went quiet again, as she thought about what Richard had told her about their early life. Cora saw Catherine's bottom lip start to tremble.

"You have not had a fight already, have you?"

"No, Cora, you must know I love him too much to fight with him, just thinking about him makes me feel all warm inside." Catherine shivered as another bolt of electricity shot through her body.

"Well, why did you look sad for?"

"Okay but first you must promise not to tell anyone, not even Tom, about what I'm going to say next." Cora could see the seriousness of her words.

"I promise, I promise, now for God's sake, tell me." Cora made the sign of the cross, well some kind of sign.

Catherine told her what Richard had said about him and his mother. Cora started up the car again as Catherine told her. By the time they reached the theatre, Cora was almost crying.

"And you're saying that Sharon is no more than six years older than Richard and she brought him up all by herself now that is a woman I would love to get to know."

They went into the theatre. They asked a man who was standing reading a magazine where they had to go for the auditions. He pointed them through another set of doors which led them into the main hall. Catherine felt nervous as she and Cora walked down the aisle. Catherine handed her letter to a woman who was with a group of people and the woman went to a group of people who were sitting in the front row of seats. After talking to a man, she came back up to them.

"Jonathon wants you to come on the stage from the left, so if you go down there," she said pointing to a small doorway, "and you will read these lines." She handed Catherine part of a script. Catherine read the part she was going to say on stage as she walked to the small door; the first part was describing the situation. The second parts were the lines she had to say. When she finally came on to the stage, she did everything correctly and said her lines to perfection. The man sitting in the front row told the woman to tell Catherine she had to sit at the back and wait until he was finished so he could ask her some questions later.

Catherine and Cora walked up to the back and sat next to a man who by the look of it was making himself very comfortable as he had his hat and coat over the back of the chair in front of him and a tray of tea on the next seat.

"And what part are you two lovely ladies trying for?" he asked in a typical thespian voice.

"I'm not trying for any part but my friend here just wants to get anything, just so she can get the experience for when she breaks into the big time. Ouch…" Cora finished as Catherine elbowed her in the ribs.

"I'm sorry, sir but as you can tell my friend is somewhat of a fool, who thinks all I have to do is turn up at an audition and I will get it."

They saw the man smile as he nodded his head.

"Well from what I have just seen, your friend could be correct, you played Annabel beautifully, just how I have pictured her." Now it was Catherine's turn to smile at her very first complement in a professional theatre.

"Could you please indulge an old man's fantasy and give me your name?" he asked.

"Certainly, sir. My name is Catherine and this is Cora, my friend."

"Catherine what?" the man asked.

"Catherine Johnson," Catherine lied.

Cora almost fell off her seat. She was opened mouth, staring at Catherine.

"Why do you want to be called Johnson?" she asked her.

Catherine turned to Cora.

"Because it is your name and if I do get a part in the play, I don't want people coming to see it just because a De Charger is in it."

"How very gallant of you, my dear girl," he said as he stood up and started picking his hat and coat up.

"And what is your name sir?" Catherine asked.

"Oh. I'm sorry ladies." He took his hat back off. "My name is Jonathon Kranz."

Catherine and Cora were still in shock when they got to their car.

"What time is it, Cora? I have to meet Richard at two."

"Well, we better put the car in reverse and drive backwards because it is now four thirty." When the time sank into their heads, they both looked at each other in amazement; they just couldn't believe they had been in the theatre for almost six and a half hours. Cora drove the car towards the park.

"Wait, stop Cora, I knew I had forgotten something, my cell phone but there's a phone box. I have to phone Mom and Dad to tell them what happened and who we met."

After phoning her parents, they drove to the park and saw Richard sitting on a bench. He saw them coming and stood up. Catherine after getting out of the car, walked up to him and kissed him gently on the lips.

"Hi, Richard, how is your mother?" Cora said.

"She is doing fine; she was sitting up and wanted to get out of bed but the doctor wouldn't let her. I think I'm right about Doctor Cunningham. He was there when I went in and was going back to her when I came out." They saw a grin come to Richard's face.

"Now, how did you get on, Catherine?" he asked.

Catherine was getting those same funny feelings just standing beside him now. She told him what Jonathon Kranz had said.

"So, you think you might have a part, that's great," Richard replied and kissed her on the cheek.

Cora saw Catherine's body stiffen as soon as his lips touched her cheek.

WOW, that's some effect he has on you, girl, Cora thought.

"Well, I think it's time we went back to your place Catherine," Cora said.

Before you have an orgasm in the park.

Cora started to laugh at her own thoughts. Richard and Catherine looked at her quizzically; she just waved them away and took no notice.

Beverly and Alvin had prepared a cooked dinner for them all. Beverly was watching Catherine who was just playing with hers and taking the odd bite now and again. Catherine was too busy listening to Richard talking about Doctor Cunningham and his mother. Alvin said if he is anything like his father, he would make sure she is looked after just fine.

Cora was also watching Catherine but not what she was eating. Cora was watching Catherine's body language. Every time Richard touched Catherine with his arm, elbow or knee, Catherine would smile and her face light up. Cora had never seen Catherine in this way before, and she liked it.

"Richard," Beverly said, "has Catherine invited you to the annual Hill Ball?"

Richard looked at Beverly, then at Catherine again.

"No." There was total shock on Catherine's face as she answered her mother's question before Richard could.

"Oh, I forgot, Richard, you will come, won't you? It raises hundreds of thousands of dollars for City Charities, It's next Friday." Catherine had a pleading look in her eyes.

"Next Friday is the fifteenth of December, that's the day the hospital is having it's Christmas dance and I have already said to my mother I will be there," Richard replied, feeling he had let everyone down. "It's also the last day at university until after the new year, we always go across to the dinner on the campus. I honestly don't think I can make it." He put his head down just a little.

Cora watched Catherine and saw that she was almost crying.

"Is there any chance Catherine could go with you to the dinner, Richard?" Cora said.

"I was going to ask her if she would like to come to the dinner and the hospital dance."

Catherine looked at her mam and dad, who both nodded their heads. Cora saw Catherine's face change from a sad one to the happiest face Cora had seen in her life.

"Oh, Richard, I would love to come with you."

It was the smile that Richard gave Catherine that almost made Cora choke. Cora felt the electricity shoot through her body and she shivered. Now she knew what Catherine was going through. Cora had never ever been affected like that by a smile, not even with Tom.

WOW. Girl, hold on to that feeling for later, she thought.

The telephone rang and Alvin got up to answer it.

"Hello, yes, no she is with some friends at the moment. I can give her a message, yes, okay, I'm sure she will be there, yes. Goodbye and thank you." Alvin put the phone back down and went back to the table. He sat down and was about to put a forkful of potato into his mouth when he looks at the others who were all looking at him, waiting for him to say who it was. He put the fork down.

"Oh, by the way Catherine, you have a part in the play, you have to be there for nine-o-clock in the morning, that was Jonathon Kranz."

Cora gave out a squeal. Richard took her hand and squeezed it, Beverly and Alvin congratulated her.

Alvin, Beverly and Richard walked to the main room. He was asking Richard to stay the night in a guest bedroom and Richard said yes. Cora and Catherine had volunteered to clear the table, when Richard, Beverly and Alvin were out of hearing distance, Cora said, "Catherine, I feel heart sorry for you, girl."

Catherine looked at her friend quizzically.

"Why?"

"Weeeeell. You're twenty-one and a virgin and you are going out with the sexiest man I have ever seen and that includes Tom. I could see how it affects you whenever he touched you accidentally. And, and, oh my God that smile he gave you at the table, God. Catherine, I almost had an orgasm. I was praying Tom would phone and say he was at home waiting for me. Catherine you must be going through hell, shear hell, girl."

"I am. Believe me, I am," Catherine replied.

The next morning, Cora drove Richard to the university. Catherine gave him a kiss as he left the car. Then Cora and Catherine drove to the theatre. Jonathon Kranz was waiting in the foyer.

"I told you I would be seeing you again, please enter." His thespian voice boomed off all the walls. There were about forty people already there rushing around doing their work as if they were ants. They never had to be told anything as it was Jonathon Kranz's own team. They worked only for him and they would have it no other way. Jonathon asked a woman to give Catherine a script to read. Catherine looked at it, then gave Cora a quick look at it. Cora's mouth dropped open. Catherine went over to the woman and said that she had given her the wrong script; the woman said no she hadn't.

Catherine went over to Jonathon Kranz.

"I have been given the wrong script, Mr Kranz," she said, quietly as if she would get the woman into trouble if she said it loudly.

Jonathon took the script off her and looked at it.

"No, you have not, my dear." He handed it back to her.

"But…but this is for the lead role. I auditioned for a small part; you already had the people for the lead rolls."

"Look, my dear. I know you have no experience of big theatre." His voice getting louder and louder and it sounded like he was reading from something like Shakespeare. "But ask anyone here," he said with outstretched arms. "Who is the greatest creator in the history of this planet?"

"God is." Came the reply from everyone who had been busy but had stopped what they were doing. By now, Jonathon was in the centre of the stage with his arms up in the air.

"And, whom am I?" His voice was at it loudest.

"GOD." Came the reply. Everyone could see the grin on his face as he looked at Catherine.

"So, there you have it, my dear, if I say I want you to be my leading lady, then you will be my leading lady, now go over there and learn your part." He turned on the heels of his feet and started speaking to someone else.

Catherine was trying to figure out if she had just made a fool of herself or if she should be proud of the fact that she was now an important part of a Jonathon Kranz production.

The first day was a 'just to get to know' day as Catherine and Cora watched Jonathon putting all the other people in their places and when he wanted this or that doing. But what Catherine and Cora did not know was that Jonathon was also watching them, and he liked what he saw.

Cora would read the lines of the other characters and Catherine would feed off her. He could see that she was enjoying doing it, and it was not just for the work that she had accepted the part. By the end of the week, Catherine knew her lines and all she had to do was polish them up a little. Cora asked Catherine why sometimes she was a little hesitant. Catherine had said it was because she could see hundreds of faces looking at her and it worried her, she might fumble her lines. Cora had a word with Jonathon in secret about it, he winked at Cora, and then he stopped everyone from doing what they were doing and told them all to sit in the front rows of the seats. Catherine was about to go down the stairs to the rows of seats.

"Not you, my dear, please stay on the stage and read the first five pages of scene two."

Catherine stood in front of them all and did exactly what was asked of her. When she had finished, they all stood up and gave her a round of applause. Jonathon went up onto the stage and took her hand and kissed the back of it.

"My dear, that was just the way I had imagined it to be, thank you."

After that, Catherine never had one bit of nervousness.

Catherine and Cora would pick Richard up at the university and they would either drive to one of their houses, have a bite to eat, then Richard and Catherine would get changed and go to the hospital to see his mother, who was recovering just like Doctor Cunningham had said she would. But on Friday, Catherine had special permission to leave early so that she could go to the university. Cora went straight home as Tom was on Christmas leave and he was waiting for her at home.

Catherine arrived at the diner before Richard and she sat in the same seat she had when they had first come in after meeting again. Catherine was remembering that day and smiling to herself until Richard and the other students arrived.

The diner made a lot of money from the students over the year, and as always, the owner would put something special on for them at Christmas time. This year it was big roast Turkey. The owner knew that most students would be going home for Christmas but some would be staying and finding it hard to eat as well as they should so when a student asked for a sandwich to take out, that student knew he was going to get enough to feed him for a few days. After eating everything, the owner said the Jukebox was free and they could dance for as long as they wanted to. Catherine and Richard sat in their corner and Catherine snuggled up to him with her arm around his waist and Richard's arm over her shoulder as they watched the students dancing and enjoying themselves. Catherine had never felt so warm and content in all her life, she looked out of the window.

"Oh Richard, it's snowing," she said as she cuddled right into him. A student put 'Santa Claus is coming to town' on the jukebox and Catherine felt Richard pull her closer to him.

They left the diner and drove to the hospital; the snow was still falling gently. Catherine drove straight to the car park and went to the furthest corner, she switched the engine off and turned to him.

"Richard, I want to kiss you before we go in." She put her arm around the back of his head and pulled him to her. She could feel the heat off her body as his lips got closer and closer to his. When they made contact, it was all she could do not to scream out. They both opened their mouths as their tongues searched for each other's and they danced together like two lovers silhouetted in the sunset, their kiss lasted for five minutes, neither of them wanted it to end. Catherine wanted to feel Richard's hands on her body. She wanted that so much, oh so much. When they finally got out of the car, the snow was still falling. Richard opened his big coat and let Catherine put her arm around his waist as he pulled her into him.

"Oh Richard, I love you so much," Catherine whispered in his ear as they entered the hospital. The party was being held in the main hall that was just a door further on from where Richard went up the stairs to his mother's ward. As he and Catherine were about to go up, Doctor Cunningham came out of the hall.

"Hello, Richard, Catherine," he said holding his hand out to shake theirs.

Richard shook his first and spoke, "I'm going straight up to see my mother okay, doctor."

"There's no need to go up there then," he said, pointing through the window to a table in the hall. Richard and Catherine turned to where he was pointing; his mother was sitting there at the table. They went over to her.

"Mom, what are you doing down here?"

"Awww, come on, Richard, do you think I would miss a party. David and I have been wanting to tell you but I thought it would be a nice surprise for you to see me like this."

"Mom, you look as lovely as ever." Then looking at Catherine then back to his mother he said.

"Who is David?"

They could see Sharon going red faced as a grin appeared, so she changed the subject.

"Now come on, tell me what kind of day you have had."

"I'll go for the coffees," Richard said, Catherine sat down next to Sharon and told her how, if she could she would relive it every day.

"Sharon, it has been perfect in every way and Richard is really wonderful." Catherine took the tissue off Sharon to wipe her eyes as the thought of how good it has been started to get the better of her.

"I'm sorry, it's just at this moment my life just cannot get any better, Sharon, I'm so in love with Richard."

"Catherine, Catherine stop it please or you will have me going all soft and weeping. There's something I want to tell you before Richard comes back."

Catherine wiped her eyes. Sharon made sure Catherine was ready to hear her news.

"Doctor Cunningham, erm, erm, David, has asked me to go to California, to his father's house just to make sure I get the complete rest that I need. It seems David is going into heart research at an institute in San Bernardino and he wants me to go with him."

Catherine could tell that Sharon wanted to go but would just as easy not go if Richard said no.

"Sharon. Richard knows that something is going on with you and the doctor and I'm sure that if it's in your best interest, he'll gave you his blessings, and I'll make sure Richard is all right at this end."

Sharon put her hand up against Catherine's cheek and softly rubbed it.

"I know you will, Catherine, and I can see how much you love him."

Richard came back with two cups of coffee and sat down at the table.

"The doctor said you will have to do without Mom," Richard said smiling as he saw his mother looking over his shoulder at where the doctor was standing. "And he said he will only give you the best Californian fruit juice when the two of you go there."

This time, it was Sharon's turn to reach for the box of tissues as her tears started to fall. Doctor Cunningham went around to where Sharon was sitting and put his hands on her shoulders. Richard pushed a cup of coffee to Catherine and whispered loud-ish so that all at the table could hear.

"Mom, you go and enjoy yourself and get better." He kissed her on the cheek.

Doctor Cunningham, David. Told them all about his father's house and how well Sharon would be looked after; he would not be more than three miles away from Sharon at any time.

When they left the hospital, the snow had stopped falling but lay on the ground like a beautiful undisturbed pure white carpet. They walked over to the car which was covered in snow. Richard was about to wipe it off when Catherine stopped him.

"No, Richard, leave it on for now. You have not been in a car that is covered in snow, have you?"

Catherine opened the door and they both got in; they sat there in silence for a few minutes.

"Everything is so muffled," he said finally.

"Yes and no one can see us either," Catherine said as she put her arm around him and kissed him again and again and again. It took them half an hour to drive away from the hospital. She drove to Richard's house and it seemed as if the heavens had decided to let all the snow fall at once. She stopped the car outside his house and they both ran to the door, by the time Richard had found his keys, Catherine was shivering. He finally opened it and Catherine said, "Richard put your arms around me, I'm freezing." As she walked into the house. Richard walked over to her and saw the grin on her face as she opened her mouth and closed her eyes to wait for the kiss.

Richard went into his mother's room and took a dressing gown that was hanging behind her door.

"Catherine, you go and have a shower, okay? Here is a dressing gown, I'll phone your parents and tell them your here," he said handing her it.

"No, Richard, you go in the shower first and I'll phone my parents." She took the dressing gown off him and smiled.

Could this be it? Her mind screamed out.

Richard went into his bedroom and took his clothes off. Catherine was trying not to look at his door and imagine what was behind it as she picked the phone up. Then he came out and walked to the bathroom with a towel around him. Catherine's legs almost gave way when she saw him.

"Hello Mom, look, I'm at Richard's house, the snow is falling heavy now, would it be all right if I stayed here, please?"

"Yes, of course it will be all right, we do not want you driving on a night like this, have you enjoyed yourself, Catherine?"

"Oh Mom, today has been the best day of my life." Then she told her what it had been like.

"All right, Catherine, that is enough you will get me dreaming of the days when me and your father were like that, we still are but keep it to yourself, ha ha ha."

"All right, Mom, I'll let you get away to the ball, love you and Dad, bye."

Catherine put the phone down and wondered if she should go into the shower, then she felt her face going red.

You are going to burn in hell, Catherine, have no doubt about it.

Richard came out of the bathroom and Catherine gave out a small sigh and had to sit down, her heart was pounding in her breast. Richard smiled at her as he walked past her, going to the fire to switch it on. Catherine wanted so much to feel his legs as they went past her, so close she felt a breeze off them. Richard then went to the CD player.

"Are there any particular songs that you like?" he asked her.

Catherine couldn't keep her eyes off him. He had bent over to switch the fire on. His bathrobe had opened a little to show his chest. It was a small bathrobe which was tied loosely in the middle. His chest and his legs were just as you would imagine a Greek god's would be like. Catherine just stopped herself from jumping on him and making mad passionate love to him.

"I think I had better go in the shower, Richard, just put anything you want on." Catherine got up from the sofa and almost ran to the bathroom; she just about ripped her clothes off and got in the shower while it was still cold.
Oh thank God.

She just looked up and let the water run down her body, cooling it down, taking all the feelings she had and could hardly cope with.

What is wrong with you, girl, now stop being silly, go out there and take him, nooooo. Her other part of her mind screamed.

That is not the way to do it, if it is going to happen tonight, then Richard will make it happen, not you, you hussy. Catherine wanted to laugh at her thoughts but it was too serious. By now, the water was a lovely warm cascade. She stood in it for a few minutes then got out and dried herself. She came out of the bathroom drying her hair. Sharon's dressing gown was a nice fit if just a tiny bit small.

"Oh, I like this song, Richard, all day and night, I think it's called."

"All day and all of the night." Richard corrected her. The room was now nice and warm. Richard had made them both a coffee and they were sitting on the sofa talking. By the time the Kinks started singing 'Lola', they were both sound asleep. Richard still sitting up and Catherine lying along the sofa with her head on his lap.

Richard was first to wake up. He looked at Catherine as she lay there, still on his lap as if she had not moved a muscle all night. She looked so peaceful. He lifted her head up gently and slid out from under her. He put a cushion under her head and went into the kitchen. He made himself a cup of coffee, then sat in the chair and drank it, looking at Catherine and thinking how lucky he is.

"Catherine, Catherine, it's time you got up," he whispered in her ear and softly kissed her cheek. Catherine turned her face a little and opened one eye and smiled. Catherine took the cup of coffee that he had made her and sipped it, then she screwed her eyes tight shut and opened them wide again. Something was niggling her, then it hit her full in the face.

I fell asleep, I, I, I fell asleep, I have just spent the night with the sexiest man in the world and I fell asleep. She didn't know if she should laugh or cry, they had been on the sofa together in bathrobes and they had fallen asleep.

Cora got out of the car and walked up to the door and started banging on it, then she bent down and shouted through the letterbox.

"Come on, I know you're in there, come on, Catherine. Put that poor man down, girl, we have to be at the theatre in half an hour. Richard put Catherine's bra back on her, now that is disgusting…"

Richard opened the door while Cora was still shouting through the letterbox.

"Ha, ha, ha Cora, how did you know Catherine was here?" Richard smiled at her.

"Catherine, that man of yours is smiling at me tell him not to, girl, and be quick about it or we might fall out, ooohhhh Catherine…"

Catherine came to the door laughing. She kissed Richard as she passed him.

"I'll see you tonight at my house, Richard."

They got in the car and drove away. Catherine looking out of the back window until they turned a corner.

******

Chapter Nine

Jonathon Kranz got everyone together in front of the stage. There were about fifty pairs of eyes watching him walk to the centre of the stage with a smile on his face. The ones who had worked with him before knew what was going on as they had been through it all with him and they loved it.

"I" – He raised his arms upwards to just about level with his chest – "I have an announcement to make." His arms got higher and his voice went deeper. "I have an announcement to make. I know that we do not open until the new year." Now he was in full Shakespearian voice. "But I have been asked to put on a taster for charity, the day before Christmas Eve. Thank you." He stood and watched the new members of his Company, their faces always amused him.

Catherine's legs felt weak. Cora was over the moon.

"Now you can strut your stuff, Catherine," she said as she hugged her.

"You'll be great, I know you will. Oh God, I love you, Catherine."

Catherine was feeling funny inside, outside she could feel the electricity in the air as her arms and legs started to feel like a million pins and needles were jabbing at her.

"Cora, suppose I freeze on stage—"

"Don't be so silly, Catherine, you are a natural and I love you for it, now come on, be more positive." Cora stopped hugging her and they walked to a quiet corner.

The whole cast were running all over the place as Jonathon Kranz walked over to Catherine and Cora.

"This is the part of producing a play that I like the most, Catherine, now you just stand here and watch everything come together. Oh, and Cora, I want you to be Catherine's personal makeup."

Then he walked away to some other people.

Catherine looked at Cora, who was standing with her mouth wide open.

"Now that's a first," Catherine said as if in shock.

"What is?" Cora replied.

"You with your mouth open and nothing coming out of it."

The whole city had been waiting for the opening of the first Jonathon Kranz production to be staged in it for twenty years, and when the invitations went out, not one was returned.

The theatre was packed full, not one seat was empty for the charity show. Beverly and Alvin, Richard and Tom were there. Sharon and David had flown in from California. Sharon had a beautiful suntan and she was looking one hundred percent fit. Richard could not believe how good she looked. Catherine's mom and dad had not told him that she had been invited and when he saw her, he almost died of shock. They were all sitting in the box at the right of the stage. When the lights went down and the music started, all of the talking stopped. When Catherine came onto the stage, Beverly and Alvin were almost crying. Richard was mesmerised by her beauty. Sharon and everyone else were stunned by Catherine's performance. There had been no publicity whatsoever about what the play was about. Jonathon had everyone reading different parts of scripts so that no one could put it together. All anyone knew was that Jonathon Kranz was producing the play. When the play finished, there was not a dry eye in the theatre, everyone thought that the man was the main character and it was not until the second last scene that they realised it was Catherine's character that was the star and it was being built up slowly, and when they finally did realise it, she died. When the curtain fell, there was a stunned silence and you could hear a pin drop on a pillow. Men and women were crying quietly so that they would not make a noise while Catherine lay dead. When the curtain came back up to show the whole cast standing on the stage, people finally realised it was over and they could let out their breath, then they burst into applause. Catherine had to stand on the stage for twenty minutes while the audience stood and shouted for her and the applause just kept coming. In the end, she had to walk off stage, because they would have stayed there all-night clapping. Backstage everyone was jumping up and down and screaming and hugging anyone who was close enough to hug.

Cora had her arms around Beverly and Alvin until she saw Tom, then made one big leap into his arms and she was crying. Jonathon Kranz was waiting at the side of the stage while Catherine was taking the applause. When she came off, he kissed her on the forehead and spoke, "You will not be with us for very long, my dear, not when the studios get word of you. The only piece of advice I will give you is. Always enjoy what you do." He left Catherine standing there wondering what he meant as he went down the stairs back stage, then Catherine went down.

She saw Richard standing by her dressing room door and ran to him, other cast members patted her as she went past them. Richard took hold of her and gave her a little peck on the nose.

"What did you think, Richard?" she asked.

"Catherine, you were fantastic, your mother never stopped crying and your father tried his best to hide his tears but in the end he couldn't. My mother never blinked once, she just stared at you. When it ended, she made one lunge for the tissues before they were all gone."

The two of them entered the dressing room and they all clapped her and kissed her and hugged her. Richard got his mother in a corner and quietly asked her when they were going back to California. David came over just as he asked her when her airplane was going back.

"There should be a one in two hours' time," Sharon said. They could both see the disappointment on his face, then David said.

"But as we're staying at Alvin and Beverly's house for the Christmas, we'll let it go."

Richard's delight was obvious as he put his arms around his mother and gently gave her a hug.

"Well, I couldn't leave you at Christmas, could I? I mean without warning Catherine about you." Everyone heard what she said and were waiting for her to tell all, when Cora came in with Tom.

"The car is here," she spoke.

Alvin had ordered the biggest stretch limousine he could find to take them all back to the house. When they arrived home, Beverly showed them all into the lounge/bar that Alvin had made. She went straight behind 'The Starlight Blue' Counter and produced bottles of Whiskey, Brandy, Vodka, Rum, soft drinks. Little umbrellas, cherries, everything that a bar called 'The Starlight Blue' which was on the coast of California would have, everyone made their own drinks and went and sat down at the round tables that 'The Starlight Blue' bar had. Alvin stood up and announced a toast to Catherine and Cora; they all drank to it and started talking and laughing. Beverly asked them all to be quiet while Sharon explained what she meant in the theatre. Sharon looked at her son and smiled.

"Should I, Richard?"

"Well, after saying that in the theatre, I don't think you will get out of here alive if you don't," Richard replied. Then he whispered to Catherine. She nodded her head and they both left the room and went and got their coats. Catherine called back to them that they were just going out for a walk to get some fresh air. They closed the door after them. Catherine put her arm through his and her head on his shoulder and they walked down the driveway.

It was cold but they never felt it. Their breath left their mouths in big white clouds and it was beginning to snow again. The driveway had hidden lights and there were lights up in the trees that hung over the drive which turned the snowflakes a very pale blue. It was so quiet that the only sound they could hear was the sound of snow being crunched under their feet. They were both watching the snowflakes fluttering to the ground but deep in their own thoughts.

"What time is it, Richard?" Catherine broke the silence. Richard looked at his watch.

"Nearly quarter past two," he said. Catherine pulled him to the side of the driveway, then told him to watch down at the house. Richard stared at the house.

"What are we looking for?" he whispered, why he didn't know but he did.

"Ssshhhhh, get ready, here he comes."

Just then, Richard saw a black thing flying down towards them, his mouth dropped open in amazement as the biggest bird he had ever seen flew over their heads and was away in the distance before he could see it properly. As it had passed over him, he saw it changing colours with the lights that were shining on it.

"What was that?" he said incredulously.

"That was Barney, the owl, he lives somewhere down the back of the house. He's been with us for about twelve years now, and every morning between half two and three, he goes for a fly down here and comes back at about six." Catherine felt his body tremble and pulled herself into him.

"Sorry, Richard, I didn't mean for you to get a fright." She gave him a squeeze.

"No, it wasn't that, I just got a flash through my mind, that if I had gone to another university, we would still not have met." This time, it was Richard's turn to hug Catherine. They walked further down the driveway in silence then Catherine asked.

"What was your mother going to tell us about you and Christmas, I know that was why you asked me out here, wasn't it?"

"No. But it was partly that, the main reason I brought you out here was so that we could be alone." Then he stopped talking and walking and turned to her, he cupped her chin in his hand and kissed her softly on the lips. When Catherine's body had come back to her, she mentally checked to see if her legs could hold her up.

"Ohhhhh, Richard," she whispered to him, "I love you."

"Catherine, can I ask you something, something I need to know." Richard's voice was slow.

Catherine said he could ask her anything that he wanted to and she will answer.

"Okay. I know we have not known each other for very long—"

Catherine put her hand up to his mouth to stop him from talking anymore.

"I've known you for more than five years, Richard." She took her hand away from his mouth.

Richard took her hand and kissed it before she took it away.

"What I'm trying to say is…is…is that I love you so much." Richard stopped talking and started to try and think how to say it properly. "I don't know how to put this, Catherine, do you want us to be together for always or is this thing, we're going through just a 'thing' and it will end sometime., Maybe, next week…month…or year even."

Catherine looked at him, her face deadly serious, she was frightened to hear what he was trying to say.

"I mean, Catherine, what does the most beautiful woman in the world, who has everything she could ever want, want with someone like me."

The relief Catherine felt was enormous. For a brief second, she thought he was going to say that they were finished, that what they had was not going to last, that this was all a dream, a dream turning into a nightmare. The hair on the back of her head was tingling her legs were still shaking but it was relief because her thoughts had been wrong.

"Richard, yes, I do have everything I could ever want, and you're standing right in front of me. I want us to last forever, let me try and tell you what you mean to me and how much I love you…"

They started to walk again.

"I want you so much, that when you say goodnight, I feel I want to cry. Even falling asleep on your sofa made me sad, because I didn't know if I fell asleep first. I wanted to fall asleep with you, not before or after but WITH you. This walk, I want it to last until eternity, I want us to walk hand in hand or with my arms around you." All the time she was talking, she was taking side looks at him, making sure he was listening.

"When I go to bed at nights, I can't go to sleep until I have thought about every single thing we have done since we met, when I wake up you're the first thing on my mind and you stay there all day. Oh Richard, can't you see the love in my eyes that I have for you." They were at the end of the driveway when she finished talking. Catherine manoeuvred Richard to the side of the entrance wall just where the gates hinges were. She opened her coat for him to put his arms inside and around her. She closed her eyes and kissed him on the mouth, forcing his lips apart with her tongue. His hands were pulling at her back and she started to moan aloud in pure pleasure and she couldn't care if anyone heard her or not. She was with her man and she wanted him to know that was all that mattered. Her hands were on the sides of his face as she kissed him. She felt a burning inside her stomach. Her hands went behind his neck and she squeezed him so tight that she thought she would choke him. She felt his left hand move to her waist, then up until it touched her breast. At that very moment, her body was transported to another place that she had never been to before, she was floating around somewhere, she could feel his hands on her, not hard or rough but soft and gentle, his lips kissing her, his body pushing into her but all the time, flying, arms outstretched, flying, her hair wasn't blowing and she could feel no wind but she was flying.

The snow was falling in slow motion as she opened her eyes to make sure that she was with Richard and that it was not a dream, then she closed them again. She was still flying.

She looked down and saw a beach. Then she was laying on the sand. The rays of the sun warming her body. She turned her head and saw Richard beside her talking, and she was laughing, there was no sound, just Richard talking to her and her laughing. She could feel something pressing on her, and it was a nice feeling, not heavy, just a warm pressure. She couldn't move any part of her body. She could feel her heart pounding away inside her. It started to get faster as the pressure started to move around her body. Her heart was now beating so hard she thought that it might frighten Richard, so she tried to slow it down but it went faster and faster, the pressure started to ease, then it stopped altogether. She saw the pressure flying up in the air. She jumped up and shouted at it to come back, to come back and stay with her but it just flew up and up.

Catherine opened her eyes. Richard was still here. She looked behind him and saw the snow falling properly. It was no longer in slow motion. She felt a tightness around her stomach and looked down at it, she saw Richard tying the belt of her coat. She looked back up at Richard, unable to focus her mind.

Howl. How can I be here when I was on a beach with Richard, HOW? HOW? She couldn't figure out what was wrong, why was she here and not on the beach? Why were her legs feeling so weak? She saw Richard look at her, then put his hand to her face just below her eye and wipe away a tear that had fell. She felt Richard's hand lifting her chin upwards.

"Catherine, why are you crying? I'm sorry I will not do that again…"

"Wha…Wha…Richard, what are you saying, do what?"

"Put my hand on your breast, I'm so sorry," Richard said.

Is that all you did, is that all you did, oh my God Richard, what will happen to me when we go further.

"Richard, it has nothing to do with that, well it does but not the way you think." She smiled.

"Richard, I'm so happy being with you. I never want this to end."

Richard smiled at her and gave her a hug as she put her arm through his.

"Let's go back to the house before we look like a pair of snowmen." He said as another shudder went through Catherine's body at his touch. They started to walk back up the driveway.

"What time is it, Richard?"

"Half three."

Catherine was going to stop walking in shock at the time but just managed to keep going. She didn't want to startle Richard.

How can it be that time, they had been on the beach all day, oh my God, what is wrong with me. Her mind was doing somersaults; it seemed so real on the beach.

It was real, her mind told her. She looked at all the snow on her and Richard and began to laugh. Richard looked at her in a quizzical manner.

"Take no notice of me, Richard, I'm just in love." Then she cuddled into him and they walked back in silent thought.

Chapter Ten

The next morning, all Catherine could think off was the night before. She stood up at the breakfast table and asked if anyone wanted more coffee and was glad, they all did.

"Right, Cora, come on I need some help." Catherine and Cora went into the kitchen and she told Cora what had happened. Catherine could see the envy in Cora's face.

"Catherine, you've got one up on me, babes, I've never been anywhere like that. Tom is the only one for me but as far as taking me anywhere, all we've been to is the bedroom." Cora tried to make a joke of it but it fell flat. Catherine looked at her and shook her head.

"Cora, I mean it, I was on a beach, first I was flying, then I was on a beach, it had soft sand and a beautiful light blue water, almost a pink colour in the end, and the heat was lovely and comfortable, how can you explain that, Cora?"

"Catherine, you're in love and when you're in love you can go anywhere you want to, your only limit is your imagination."

"But Cora, it was so real, so real."

"So is love, babes, so is love," Cora said as she picked up the cups and left the kitchen.

After breakfast, they all went into the lounge. Alvin was talking to David about what kind of research he was going to do. Beverly was talking to Sharon and she knew that if Sharon had not got the invite to the theatre, she would still have been here, because Beverly could tell that Sharon didn't want to leave Richard again.

"We have been together for so long, Beverly. Whenever things started to get me down, he would look at me, just look at me, and I would be all right again and when he had difficulties, I would help him." Beverly handed Sharon a tissue.

"Sharon, believe me. Catherine will not let anything happen to Richard, that I can promise you, just look at them now."

They both looked over to them and saw Catherine smiling at everything Richard said.

"Now what we want is for you to get back to full health," Beverly whispered to her.

Cora and Tom had gone for a walk in the gardens. The snow had stopped falling and the rays of the sun had started to melt it. Catherine had asked them if they wanted to go to 'sound city'. Cora said that they would call in later. Richard asked her what 'sound city' was. Catherine took his hand and led him to a room that he had not been in before. Catherine turned the key to lock the door.

"I don't think you should do that, Catherine," he spoke. Catherine turned the key back.

"All right," she replied.

Richard looked around the room. It had a few shelves with books on them; there was some kind of cabinet at one wall. In the centre of the ceiling was a big crystal ball hanging, there were four lights in each corner. Catherine pressed a button that was on the wall next to the door and the main lights went dim. Janet Jackson started to sing and when the main lights finally went out, the four corner lights came on and the beams hit the crystal ball, which started to turn, throwing small dots of light everywhere. Richard stood there fascinated by everything, then he saw Catherine slowly making her way over to him.

"It puts my CD player to shame," he spoke.

"Richard, don't be silly, I'm just sorry we don't have any Kinks music to play."

Catherine moved closer and closer to him, then she leant forward.

"Kiss me, Richard," she said in her most provocative way and closed her eyes. She had practiced for hours in front of the mirror, and she had walked in so many different ways that she had forgotten which was the best. In the end, she had decided to just let the moment take her wherever it went.

Richard gave her a light kiss on the cheek and pulled away before she could open her eyes. When she did open them, she saw him smiling at her.

"Awww, is that all I get." She put her arms around his waist and started to move slowly with the music, pulling him in towards her. Richard put his arms over her shoulders and they danced like that.

Catherine put her head onto his chest. She felt so warm and safe in his arms, she could have easily stayed like this for the rest of her life, the feelings she was getting, even just dancing with him, were unbelievable. Her body started to tingle and her heart skipped a few beats when he moved his hand. Then before she could think straight, he had put his hand on her hair and was smoothing it, her body went limp again, her brain was screaming for him to touch her again in the same place just as he had done last night but as his hand started to smooth her hair again and again, she drifted into another dream. She was just about to watch him take his shirt off when Cora and Tom came into the room.

"My, that was easy," Cora said.

"I thought Catherine would have had the door locked." Cora saw Richard smile.

"Oh Tom, she wanted to but I think Richard must have stopped her and now she is cursing us for being here now." Cora knew she was correct because she could see Catherine's shoulders going up and down as she laughed.

"God, girl, do you ever shut up, no wonder Tom has to keep going away to have his ears plugged."

Catherine left the room to get them all some coffee, when she had closed the door, Richard said.

"I know it's a bit late but do you have any idea what I could give Catherine for Christmas."

Tom burst into a coughing fit. Cora was hitting him on the back trying not to laugh.

"Yes, I know of something you could give her and she would love it…but a gift." Cora had her finger at the side of her face and she was looking at the ceiling. Tom was almost on his knees.

"Nope I just have not got a clue." Then she clicked her fingers.

"Ah, yes I do know, Rosewood's; they have a pair of western boots that she just loves."

Richard looked at the floor and pulled a face that said, 'not a chance'.

Catherine came back into the room with the coffees. She knew that something had happened because Tom was still recovering from his coughing fit but no one said anything so they drank their coffees and had a talk, then Catherine took the cup's back to the kitchen, as soon as Catherine was back out, Cora said, "What's wrong, you asked, I told you."

"Rosewood's is the most expensive shop in the state. I could never pay for a box of tissues never mind a pair of boots from there."

Tom told Cora to go and help Catherine. Cora saw the wink Tom gave her and left.

"Listen Richard. Catherine is a very good friend of me and Cora, and we like you one hell of a lot as well, so look, now don't take offense okay, here take this, you can give me it back whenever you want." Tom handed Richard a roll of money.

"And I don't want you to say no."

Richard looked at the roll of money; he unfolded it. Richard's eyes almost popped out of his head.

"Tom, there's nearly five hundred dollars here; there's no way I'm taking this."

"Look I said I don't want to hear 'no'. Now put it in your pocket and we'll go and find the girls. Then we'll go to the mall to see if we can get them for you."

"Tom, how can you go around carrying so much money?"

"Uncle Sam says I have to, so I do what Uncle Sam says," Tom replied casually.

"Uncle Sam, as in the Government Uncle Sam?" Richard asked. Tom nodded his head.

"Tom, what line of work are you in, that's if you don't mind me asking you?"

"Sure, I don't mind telling you, I'm a bodyguard."

"Bodyguard, as in movie star's bodyguard," Richard said.

"Sometimes but mainly the president."

Richard stopped dead. He was going to say something but he couldn't. It took a while before he could move again.

"You, mean the President of the United States…"

"Of America," Tom finished for him.

"Now that is cleared up, let's go and do some shopping," Tom said. They closed the door of 'sound city' as they went out.

The shopping mall was a huge complex about three miles outside of the city. Richard had never been to it before. Cora parked the car and they got out and took the lift down to the main walkway, when they left the lift Catherine took hold of Richard's hand tightly.

"We're going this way, Catherine," Cora said as she led Tom down a different walkway.

"See you outside Emilio's in about an hour, okay?" Catherine and Richard watched Cora and Tom disappear into the crowds.

"Come on, Richard, let's go to the soda shop before we walk around. This is where most of my friends hang out. Now if you feel uncomfortable, tell me and we'll leave all right."

They entered and a few people said 'hello' to Catherine and a few of the females said 'hi' to Richard. They found an empty pair of seats and sat down. Catherine got back up and went to the counter for their coffees. When she got backm there was a girl in her seat.

"God, Amelia, you must have slithered under the seat to get here without me seeing you."

Amelia took no notice of her as she purred at Richard.

"Catherine darling where ever did you find him?" she said in a hushed voice. "Are you not going to introduce me?" She held a hand towards Richard.

"Amelia, this is Richard, Richard, this is Amelia, the local tramp." At which, both girls started to laugh. Catherine put the coffees on the table and sat next to Richard. Amelia still had not even glanced at Catherine.

"Richard, I know I have no chance of taking you away from little miss Aphrodite here but if ever you fancy a wild night, pleaseeeeeeeee, give me a call." Amelia cooed at Richard.

"Yeah, Richard, you'll find her name and number on every phone box in the city. Now move yourself, babe, me and Richard want a quiet word," Catherine said. Amelia smiled at Richard and still totally ignored Catherine as she got up out of the seat and went back to her own.

"That girl tries it on with every new man that comes into this place. Cora was going to rip her eyes out when she tried it on with Tom."

Richard smiled at Catherine.

"She is a nice looker," he said jokingly, just before Catherine elbowed him in the ribs. Richard put his hand on Catherine's knee and gave it a little squeeze, which almost sent her into orbit.

"Richard, what do you want off me for Christmas?" Catherine asked him.

"Well according to what Cora has said, I want the same as you but I think we should wait for a while." He smiled at her and she went red.

They sat and talked and drank their coffees, a few of Catherine's friends came over and said 'hi' then went away. They stood up to leave and as they went past Amelia, she said could she have a word with Catherine in private. Catherine walked to the door with Richard then said.

"Richard, stay here, I'll see what the Hussy wants," she said it with a smile on her face.

Catherine walked back to where Amelia was sitting and sat down.

"What is it, Amelia?"

"Robert was looking for you at the Ball the other night and when someone said you had a new boyfriend, he wasn't pleased."

Catherine sat up straight, then leant forward towards Amelia.

"You tell Robert, that I'm not his, nor will I ever be or want to be." Catherine hissed at Amelia.

"No problem, Catherine."

Catherine got up out of the seat and walked out of the 'Soda Shop'. Richard could see that she was not her usual happy self.

"What's wrong, Catherine?" he asked.

"Oh, just some person has ideas that he has a right to be with me, because he thinks we should be together but to be honest, I can't stand his egotistical way, I even don't like speaking to him when we pass. He's unbearable." She shivered as she thought of him. She put her arm through his and the smile came back to her face.

They walked past 'Rosewood's' window and Catherine gave out a disappointed sigh when she saw that the pair of boots she had wanted were not there anymore. They saw Cora and Tom coming out at the same time Cora and Tom saw them. Cora took Catherine's arm and led her straight back into the shop.

"I hate shopping with Tom, he moans all the time. Come on, Catherine, let's blitz the place."

Tom handed Richard a package. Richard felt it.

"It's the boots," Tom said winking at Richard.

"But you gave me the money to buy them," Richard said.

"So, buy something else for Catherine, now come on, you're going to watch something that you will very rarely ever see again. Two of the most beautiful girls in the world going shopping, and in a fun mood, so just watch if they see a counter staff man looking bored, they will have him ripping his hair out by the time they're finished."

So, Tom and Richard followed them into the shop.

When the car stopped outside Catherine's house, the trunk of the car was full. Catherine had gotten a bit anxious when Richard had went missing for half an hour. Tom had not even noticed he had gone but when he showed up again, both Cora and Tom saw the relief that oozed out of Catherine; she had told them what Amelia had said about Robert looking for her.

"I don't think Richard would have that much trouble with that pig headed fool." The disgust in Tom's voice made it evident that he never liked him.

"Yes but if he is with his friends…" Cora had tried to stop herself from saying it, and wished she had of when she saw the look on Catherine's face. Everyone had expected the worst but when Richard came around a corner as if nothing was wrong, they all gave out a sigh.

They unloaded the car. Tom carrying the bulk of the wrapped gifts, the snow had mostly melted and the sun was shining up from the wet ground which dazzled the eyes and when Richard went up the stairs he couldn't see for the glare and walked straight into the side of the door that Catherine had left open. Tom collapsed in a laughing fit, dropping the gifts as he tried to land softly on his knees. Catherine and Cora turned around and came back out to see what was wrong, they saw Richard holding his eye and Tom on his knees unable to get up for laughing, the gifts were scattered all over.

"It's a good thing there is no glass in there, you, you, you laughing hippo, you," Cora said to Tom, they could see when he lifted his head up to look at Cora that the tears were streaming down his face.

"He'll be no good tonight, that will last for a week," Cora said, pretending to be annoyed but couldn't quite pull it off as she started to laugh.

Catherine took Richard's hand away from his eye and she kissed it lightly.

"There you are." She kissed his hand as she put it back on his eye.

Tom had been right, it had been an experience watching Catherine and Cora shopping. They had waited until a man behind a counter was standing doing nothing, they split up, one going as far to the right of the man, the other going to the far left of him, then they would, both at the same time, ask him for help but in the most provocative voice they had, then they would tease and tantalise him until he started to sweat. They would pick the skimpiest garment on the racks and put it up to their bodies and ask him if it looked okay, by the time they had finished, he was a wreck and was glad for them to go.

"Mom, we're back," Catherine shouted.

"Yes, I heard." Beverly had been preparing the evening meal and she was drying her hands.

"Richard, your mother and David have gone to see a friend of his, they will be back later. Catherine, your dad is in the backyard doing some repotting, okay?" Beverly was trying to see what they had bought but Catherine kept them out of view.

"We're going up stairs to wrap some of them for under the tree, Mom, all right," Catherine said as she started walking to the stairs.

Tom and Cora shared the same room whenever they stayed over at Catherine's and they went in. Richard was walking along the landing to his room and Catherine was just in front of him going to her room. Catherine heard his footsteps had stopped and she looked around just as he went into his room, she walked back to his door and knocked, Richard opened it.

"Yes," he said with that smile on his face that had damaged so many women's hearts when he was younger.

"You can come along to my room you know, Richard; it is not out of bounds," Catherine said.

Richard closed his door and followed her to her room. He just had time to put his arms around her as she ran to him and kissed him full on the lips, both of them falling on the bed. Catherine was on top of him with her arms around him, her lips were crushed to his. She knew she loved him more than anything in the world, she had never ever made the first move to kiss a boy, never but with Richard, all she ever seems to want to do is kiss him, and other things.

Hush your mouth, you hussy. Her brain screamed at her, she wanted to laugh at her thoughts, how her 'good side, fights against her bad side' which is happening more and more.

"Richard, I love you so much," she whispered as her hand went up the inside of his t-shirt and slid across his chest.

"Oh Richard, so much, sooooooooo much." She could feel herself starting to cry.

"Oh. Soooooooooooooo much, Richard, I never want us to fall out, I want us to be together for the rest of our lives." The two of them fell asleep in each other's arm.

****

Chapter Eleven

Christmas and New Year went by. Sharon and David had gone back to California, leaving quite a few tears on the tissues that Beverly had handed to her as she said her 'good-byes'. The show was opening in two days' time and Catherine and Cora had been working hard to get everything just right. The Theatre was a place of organised pandemonium, people were running around carrying props, backgrounds were being lifted into place high up by wires so when they were needed all the stage managers had to do was press a button and they would be down and ready, trapdoors were being tested and the actors would be reading their lines, some out loud, some quietly. Whenever Richard could get there, he would stand at the back and just marvel at the, what looked to him, the sheer madness of it all, he would watch Catherine go through certain scenes with Phillip Ward, the leading man. He knew there were three scenes where she had to kiss him, he didn't like it but as Catherine told him, "Sometimes, although from the seats it looks like we do but sometimes our lips don't touch."

When Jonathon Kranz called a halt to the day's rehearsals, Richard, Catherine and Cora would go to a dinner for a coffee, before going to either Catherine's or Cora's house, then after a few hours of talking and Catherine kissing him, she would drive Richard home.

Ten minutes before the curtains went up, Jonathon Kranz got the cast onto the stage behind the curtains.

"Now, as everyone knows by the accolades we received after the charity show, people are going to expect nothing less of us but I want more from you, now ladies and gentlemen let's put on the show." The hair on the back of Catherine's head started to tingle.

The curtains went up and all of the talking in the audience stopped. When Catherine came onto the stage, she could hear their intake of breath and she could see out of the corner of her eyes, her mom and dad and Richard sitting in the presidential box. When it came to the final scene and Catherine was laying on the floor with her head in Phillip Ward's arms, she could hear people crying, then when she said her last line.

"Mark, my darling, I can see the angels coming for me..." Then she died. The music never started as what would have happened; there was just silence. Jonathon watched the audience then after two minutes gave the signal to drop the curtain. When it closed, there was still silence and Jonathon was jumping around with his thumbs up in the air, the cast waited and waited to hear the applause but none came. Jonathon knew that this would happen and he rushed every one of the casts on the stage, he gave the signal to raise the curtain and the whole place erupted, the applause was so loud that the walls were shaking. In all of his years as a producer, he had never experienced anything like it, as the cast left the stage, the audience started to shout for Catherine to come back on, when she did the audience went wild, flowers were being thrown at her from all angles. Catherine had to stand there for half an hour, then they still shouted for her to stay when she decided that it was time to walk off. By the time Richard and her mom and dad got back stage, everyone was kissing and hugging the nearest to them, some were jumping up and down with excitement, some were laughing, some were crying. Richard saw Cora with her arms around Catherine, they were laughing and crying and kissing each other on the cheeks. Catherine saw them and ran to them.

"Was it as good as the first show?" she asked them.

"I was too busy watching your mom and dad fighting over the tissues, awwwww Catherine you were fantastic." He kissed her full on the lips as he lifted her up in the air.

Catherine looked at her parents' eyes and knew that they had been crying. Richard put her down and her mom put her arms over Catherine's shoulders and started to cry again, which started her dad off crying again, tissues were all over the place as everyone was laughing tears or crying them, they all knew they had a huge hit on their hands. Richard saw Cora's mouth drop open and she stared at the door, he turned to see what she had seen and he saw Tom standing there. Cora gave out one of her best screams when she saw him and ran up to him and jumped into his open arms.

"I just managed to get to see the last scene," he said to her as they kissed.

Jonathon Kranz stood on a chair and announced to the cast and their families that there was a convoy of taxi's outside to take everyone to a party he has organised at the hotel he is staying at.

They were all at the same table at the party and a bottle of Champagne was on every table in a chill bucket when they had arrived. Cora asked Tom to dance, Catherine asked Richard and they all got up and went onto the dance floor. Cora whispered into Tom's ear.

"I want you to keep an eye on Catherine, okay?"

"Why?" he asked.

"Because I have been watching Phillip Ward and I think he is going to make a play for her." Cora saw Tom wink at her and nod his head.

The party looked as if it was going to go on forever, so Richard said, "I have to go now, I have to be up early tomorrow for classes." He looked at his watch.

"No, I have to be up early today." He corrected himself.

"We'll have to go as well, Catherine," Beverly said.

Catherine stood up and was taking her coat off the back of her seat.

"No Catherine, you stay here and enjoy yourself, you've earned it." Richard stopped her.

"No, I'll go home as well," she spoke.

"No, you stay and enjoy it, please," Richard said.

"Are you sure, Richard?"

"Yes." He kissed her on the forehead.

Alvin and Beverly dropped him off outside of his house and drove away.

Catherine and Tom were talking while Cora was watching Phillip Ward; he was drinking far too much. He came over to their table and asked Catherine if she would like to dance, there was a slow record playing and as Catherine never suspected anything, she said yes.

Cora looked at Tom.

"Get ready, I may be wrong but just in case."

The dance floor was full of people enjoying themselves, most were couples dancing and it was hard for Cora to watch Catherine and to see if Phillip Ward was going to do what Cora thought. But Tom was trained in this kind of thing, he had to keep an eye on the president while trying not to look anxious, his eyes never left Catherine's face and when he saw the look of shock on her face, he was up and out of his seat in a flash. To the people who were dancing alongside of them it looked as if Tom and Phillip were old friends as Tom had his arm over Phillip's shoulder, what they couldn't see was Tom's other hand closing Phillips's wind pipe. Tom put his face right up to Phillip's and whispered to him, "If you do not go and sit down somewhere, I will snap your neck." All the time,

Tom was talking and looking at Phillip, Tom had this smile of pure satisfaction on his face. Phillip Ward walked away breathing a sigh of relief and gulping for air. Tom took Catherine's hand and began to dance with her as if nothing happened. When they went back to their seats, Catherine was still shaking. Cora had a smile on her face.

"He's good, isn't he, Catherine?" Cora said, winking at Tom.

"Good, he could have killed him and no one would have known. I wonder what made Phillip go like that, did I do anything, or say something, or what?" They could see that Catherine was honestly wondering why he did it.

"Because he can see your beauty," Tom said in a mythical eastern voice as he kissed the back of her hand.

"He tried to kiss me…" Catherine said, smiling at Tom but not really hearing the fun in his voice. Jonathon Kranz had seen what had happened and he came over to Catherine's table and sat down.

"Now that is something you never see every day," he said quietly.

"What is?" Cora replied, not knowing he had seen it all.

"Someone squeezing the life out of someone else on a dance floor and the music not stopping." Then he laughed and somehow put Catherine at ease, which took the tension that had been building up, out of the air.

"I will have a word with Phillip and, Catherine, I promise you he will be the perfect gentleman after this." Jonathon stood up and started to walk away, then as if he had another thought, he turned back around and came back to the table.

"And sir, please remind me to never get on your bad side." Then he walked away in the direction of Phillip Ward. They watched him as he started speaking to Phillip, then Jonathon left him. Phillip came over to the table; he didn't try to sit down.

"Catherine. I'm sorry for what I did, it will not happen again." He turned around and walked away, not even glancing at Tom.

In the taxi going home, Catherine asked them not to say anything about what happened to Richard. They agreed and Catherine got out of the taxi and went into the house. Cora waited until Catherine was inside then she told the driver to go to Gillbridge Heights.

Catherine could hear her mother shouting up the stairs to pick the phone up. After waiting to get her head and eyes woken up, she picked it up.

"He…he…Hello."

"How was the party?" It was Richard's voice. She sat straight up and was immediately wide-awake.

"Not too good once you left, when can I see you again?"

"Tonight, I'll try and get to the show before it starts, if not, I will definitely be there before it ends. I have just phoned you to ask if you have seen the morning papers?"

"No, I haven't, what time is it?"

"It's a quarter to two in the afternoon. Have I woken you up? I'm sorry if I have."

"No, you have not, so stop apologising."

"Well, I'm sorry anyway, look I have to go, okay? See you tonight, I love you, Catherine."

"And I love you, Richard." She heard the phone being put down. Catherine got out of bed and put her dressing gown on and went down stairs.

"Mom, that was Richard, he said have I seen the morning papers, what's in them?"

Her mother had them all laid out on the table. Catherine looked at the headings only at first and she was amazed. She couldn't believe that every one of the critics liked the play. Not one of them had a bad word for it and they all said that Catherine was a shining star which out shone the brightest in the skies, one even said she was the greatest person to die on stage since Julius Caesar.

A couple of critics said that they had never experienced anything like it in the fifty years of theatre they had been reporting, one said he couldn't write properly as he was still crying when he got home. Catherine looked at her mother, who had gone quiet and saw that she was crying. Catherine put her arm around her and gave her a hug.

"Oh, Mom please don't, you'll start me off as well."

The phone rang and Beverly picked it up.

"Hello."

"Beverly, is Catherine there?"

"It's Cora." Beverly handed Catherine the phone and went into the kitchen. Even from there, she could hear Cora squealing.

"Catherine, put the phone down and turn your TV onto channel twelve, now." Catherine put the phone down and went to the TV and switched it on. "Mom, Cora says we have to look at the TV."

Beverly came out of the kitchen as the advertisements were finishing.

The anchorman was talking about the play to someone, the camera swung to the man he was talking to and there sitting in a chair was Jonathon Kranz.

"Jonathon, is the show as good as all the critics say it is? I know you are the producer, but, as everyone who knows you or has read your remarks on past productions, you do not pull your punches, and what can you tell the people out there about the leading lady, erm, erm, Catherine Johnson."

"First, let me tell you that every show I do is full of people and that is the secret about the show, it is not just one person, the whole cast is one of the most professional that I have ever worked with, and so, without divulging to much about the story, as you have just reported, ALL the critics liked it, so that must tell you that it is good." Jonathon breathed in deeply, then carried on.

"So obviously the show is a winner and as for the leading lady, Catherine Johnson, what can anyone who saw her last night say but that she is a natural Thespian." Jonathon was building up his voice.

"Yes but where did you find her, what other productions has she appeared in?" The TV researchers had hunted high and low for something Catherine Johnson had appeared in and yet they could find nothing.

"That, sir, is my secret. I had to scour the country until I found the woman that I wanted." Jonathon was now in his most perfect Thespian voice.

The TV company cut to another story.

The telephone rang again and Catherine picked it up.

"Hello," she said.

"Hello darling, how are you today, has your mother shown you the newspapers?"

"Oh Dad, I knew the show was good but not one critic criticised it and Jonathon Kranz has just been on the TV talking about the show."

"Catherine everything that has been written about the show by the critics is correct, now is your mother there?"

Catherine handed the phone to her mother.

The second show was just as good as the first and as the week went on the show was getting more and more publicity, tickets for it were going at double, sometimes triple their prices. Sharon phoned from California to say she had read about it in their newspaper and it mentioned that the star of the show is none other than Catherine Johnson.

Everyone knew that there was a big meeting of theatre management with Jonathon Kranz and they knew it would be about extending the run of the show, because after the first month, it was now the biggest ever.

It was now in its second month and it was still at full capacity, news of the meeting with management and Jonathon was slowly leaking out. How he had told them that he was signed to do a year and that was all he could do as he had other commitments to keep.

Catherine and Cora entered the theatre to do another performance. Jonathon was waiting for them at the stage door.

"Would you please come into my office? I wish to have a word with the two of you," he said smiling at them. They looked at each other, then followed him into his office.

"As you know, this show has beating every box office ever," he said, showing them to the two seats he had put out for them to sit down on, they walking around his desk, he sat down.

"And, as you know I have some very special friends in the entertainment business, who are coming here for tonight's performance and one of them is none other than Milton Ebbstein."

Catherine and Cora looked at each other and they both took deep breaths at the name.

"So, by the look on your faces, you know the name. Cora, you are a good makeup artist and you know what makes Catherine's face happy or sad but I think you should also act as her agent—"

"Why would Catherine need an agent, and why me?" Cora interrupted him.

"Because you are her friend and from what I know, you have been friends for a very long time, you know what Catherine likes, and more importantly dislikes."

"Yes but why would I need an agent in the first place?" Catherine asked him.

"Because Milton Ebbstein has been making discreet enquiries about you. Do not get me wrong, Catherine, he is a good man and believe me, he will stick to any agreement he makes with you."

"It seems that you already know that I will sign a contract…"

"No Catherine, you NEVER sign anything without going over it with a fine-tooth comb. If it states that a contract says you have to er, er, er, stay in a forty-foot camper at location shoots, you say you want a fifty-foot camper, if it states you have to wear a certain thing and you feel uncomfortable in it, you tell them to go away and come back when they have re-written the contract. Cora, let me give you a little advice. Never take the first offer. Well, that's all I have to say on the matter but please feel free to ask me anything at any time. Now let's get on with the show."

Catherine had done, what had become the normal thing after each performance, her twenty-minute ovation of standing on the stage while the audience went wild with their applause. Cora was sitting with two strangers when Catherine walked into her dressing room. Jonathon Kranz was sitting in the corner behind the door. Catherine only noticed him when she shut the door. The two strangers stood up when she entered.

"Catherine," Cora said, "this is Milton Ebbstein."

Milton Ebbstein walked over to Catherine and shook her hand.

"My dear, that was one hell of a show you put on tonight. This man is with me," he said, pointing to the other man.

"I'm sure Jonathon told you I would be here tonight. I will not beat about the bush. I want you to do two or three movies for K.P. studios. I'm not going to ask you to sign anything yet, all I want to know is will you consider it."

Catherine nodded her head. Jonathon opened the door for them to leave. Catherine saw Richard standing leaning on the far wall.

"Richard, what are you doing standing there? Why haven't you come in?"

He gave her a gentle kiss on the lips then tapped them lightly with his finger.

"I heard you had guests so I didn't want to interrupt anything that was going on." He smiled at Cora and Jonathon as he entered the dressing room. "I didn't mean that the way it sounded," he said apologetically. Catherine put her arms over his shoulders and gave him a hug.

"Richard, those two gentlemen were from K.P. studios and they wanted to know if I will do two or three movies for them."

Richard's eyes went wide open and he looked at Cora. She nodded her head. He put his arms around Catherine and lifted her up off the ground and kissed her on the lips again.

After leaving Cora at her house, Catherine and Richard drove onto Catherine's house. Her mom and dad were still up, so she told them what had happened.

"Is that what you want to do, Catherine?" her mother said.

"What do you mean?" Catherine asked.

"Well, if you are going to do movies, you have to go on location, me and your father would miss you but I'm sure you would miss Richard more."

Catherine put her hand to her mouth.

"Oh, I never thought about that, well that is the end of my movie career," she said smiling, which no one believed.

"Catherine, there is no way you can say no to a movie career. You have to at least try it, if you don't like it, okay, stay on the stage but at least try it first," Richard said. Catherine turned to her father.

"Dad, what do you think I should do?"

"I think Richard has a point, Catherine, try it and if you don't like it, go back on stage."

"Okay but nothing is going to happen until the show runs its full season," Catherine said.

Chapter Twelve

Richard always slept in the master guest bedroom at weekends and on Saturdays, he would go to the university to do extra studying while Catherine slept. She would come to the university to pick him up when she woke up, then they would go down to the valley where it was quiet and peaceful, it was where Catherine was teaching Richard to drive.

Richard was working on a computer when Mr Davis came into the room with a man Richard had never seen before.

"Richard, this is Mr Smithson, would it be all right if he had a word or two with you? He is something of a computer man himself."

Mr Smithson held out his hand and Richard shook it. Richard looked at his watch.

"Sure but you will have to be quick; my girlfriend should be here soon."

Mr Smithson looked at Mr Davis. Richard saw Mr Davis nod his head and leave the room.

"Listen, son, how fast can you find, identify and kill a virus in a computer without touching the files in the computer?" Mr Smithson said in a deep Texan voice. Mr Smithson saw the frown on Richard's face but pretended that he had not.

"If you knew about computers, then you would know that it depended on how strong the virus was and what kind of computer it was attacking," Richard replied without looking at him.

"Could you find it and get rid of it without damaging the files in the computer?"

"What time scale are we talking about here?" Richard asked.

Richard saw the look that Mr Smithson put on his face, it was a 'Should I tell him or should I not' look.

"Okay, the virus we are talking about attacks whole buildings, it gets into a computer and has been known to lay dormant for up to six weeks, then it goes hell for leather and hits every computer in the building, wrecking them completely."

Richard looked at Mr Smithson now. He had never heard of a virus that stopped for up to six weeks before.

"And it just lays there doing nothing for up to six weeks, that's pretty hard to believe."

"Why?" Mr Smithson said.

"Because a virus is not a real thing. It can't just go into a computer and do nothing, look, although computer people talk about virus as real living things, they are not, and if the virus is not moving then it is no good, the people who put viruses into computers want to see it working, they get a kick out of watching it move around the world and if it does not move, they don't get their kick. So, although you say it lays dormant, I doubt that very much."

"Could you wait here for one moment please?" And before Richard could answer, Mr Smithson had left the room.

After twenty minutes, he returned.

"I have been instructed to give you as much information as I can and to give you this." The door opened behind Mr Smithson and a man came in pushing a trolley with boxes on it. Richard watched as the man just walked around the room unplugging all of the computers, even the one Richard was working with, then he started to unpack what was in the boxes, all the time Mr Smithson was talking.

"We know that this computer has got the virus that I have been talking about. When we set it up, we will load it with data. What we want to know is how long it will take you to find the virus and to kill it and retrieve all the data, undamaged."

Richard walked over to where the man was putting everything together, he looked at the keyboard and saw that it was not the usual 'qwerty' keyboard; this keyboard had symbols on it instead of letters.

Richard sat down on a chair and looked at his watch.

"You're wasting your time, Mr Smithson. My girlfriend will be here any minute now, so I will be going…"

"She will not be coming; we phoned her home and explained what we are doing here."

Richard was up and off his chair before Mr Smithson had a chance to say anything else.

"Who the hell do you think you are? I have gone along with your silly question and answer game. I know you don't know anything about computers but I went along with it, now you say you have stopped my girlfriend from coming to see me."

"Like I have said, I have been instructed to give you as much information as you need." Mr Smithson put his hand into his inside pocket and pulled out a wallet and opened it like they do on the police shows on the television.

"My name is Martin Smithson and I work for The Central Intelligence Agency and we want you to do what you can to help us."

Richard fell back into his chair, his mouth wide open, he wanted to say something but all that would come out was C.I.A. then he looked at the keyboard.

"It's Chinese," Mr Smithson said.

"The whole computer is Chinese. I've been instructed to let you have this mobile phone, it is linked to a person in England who is doing the same thing as you but over there for M.I.

The two of you can talk for as long as you like if you're having problems." Mr Smithson finished talking and the other man had finished doing what he was doing and had left.

Richard looked at his watch again.

"Look, Mr Smithson, it is past four, it will take a lot of hours to do this, I think we should start in the morning." Richard watched Mr Smithson pull a chair over to a far corner of the room.

"Yeah, you are probably correct but you have to start now, oh, and don't mind me, I have been told I don't snore. You don't have to dial on the mobile, just press the 'on' button and it will connect you to England." With that said, Richard saw Mr Smithson sit down and put his feet up on the table and looked as if he went straight to sleep.

Richard had to find out if the person in England had found anything. He picked the mobile up and pressed the 'on' button, no sooner had he put it to his ear when he heard.

"Yo there, is that the Yank computer repair centre?" said a voice that was English in as far as Richard could understand one or two words.

"What?" Richard answered nervously.

"Yo Yank, how's it hanging?"

"What, I'm sorry. I'm supposed to be talking to someone in England."

"Yeah, you are Yank." Came the voice again.

"What, I'm sorry I can't understand what you are saying."

"That's okay, Yank, we have the same problem with our own lot, I'm a 'Geordie', okay, I'll talk slowly for you." Then there was a silence, then he started talking again.

"Are, you, the, Yank, who, is, doing, the, computer, thing."

"Yes," Richard said relieved.

"Good, how, far, have, you, got."

"That's why I phoned you, to find out how far you are."

"I'm, frightened, to, touch, anything, in, case, it, ain't, the, right, button."

"Same here." Richard confirmed.

"I'll tell you what, pal, why don't we make a paper copy of our keyboards and put it over the keyboard in front of us, and see what happens when we type, okay?"

Alvin and Beverly were planning their forth coming trip to Texas when the phone rang Alvin picked the phone up.

"Hello," he spoke.

"Hello Alvin, Bob Davis here." There was a long pause.

"Alvin, I have been given this number for you to phone, all I know is that you have to phone it, okay? That's all I can say."

Alvin dialled the number Bob Davis gave him.

"Hello," a pleasant woman's voice said.

"Hello, I have been given this number to phone and—"

"Could I please have your name?" the woman interrupted him.

"Yes, of course, it's Alvin De Charger," Alvin said.

"Thank you, Mr De Charger, please can you wait one minute while I put you through."

Alvin could hear her talking to someone, then the phone made a noise as if it was connecting to a facsimile machine, he pulled the phone away from his ear until he couldn't hear the noise.

"Hello Mr De Charger," a man's voice said.

"Yes," Alvin replied.

"This is the Presidents chief Secretary; I'm putting you through to him now."

Alvin could hear the phone ringing, he indicated for Beverly to pick up the hall phone.

Beverley put the phone to her ear just in time to hear.

"Hello Alvin, Barack Obama here. I know it's only a trivial thing but the C.I.A. insisted on this when they found out who you were, what it is, is that a foreign government has ask for our help with a computer problem that they are having, something to do with a virus, so we are testing people over here, it is very important, what it is, we are testing someone that your daughter knows. The C.I.A. do not want him distracted so they asked me to talk to you to show you just how important it really is."

"Yes, sir, could you tell me who this person is, so that I can tell Catherine?" Alvin asked.

"Certainly Alvin, his name is Richard Buckman. And now if it is all right with you, Alvin, I would like to finish my lunch with the English Prime Minster. Thank you."

Alvin and Beverly heard the receiver being put down, they held theirs for a few extra seconds as they wondered if this had really happened. Beverly put hers down and walked into the room and took Alvin's out of his hand and put that down as well.

When Catherine came down the stairs, she knew something was just not right. Beverly told her what happened exactly as it had. Catherine thought they were playing a joke on her.

"You're trying to tell me that Barack, the President of the United States of America, Obama, phoned you, to tell me, not to pick Richard up from university because he is working for the C.I.A.," Catherine said incredulously.

"We know it sounds unbelievable but he did," Alvin said.

"So, did he say when I could go and pick him up?" Catherine would have laughed if it was not hurting her so much.

"He never said," Beverly replied.

"But, if the C.I.A. is involved, it means we cannot say anything to anyone, which means Cora."

Catherine knew that keeping a secret or anything from Cora would be hard, very hard indeed. When Cora picked her up to go to the theatre, she had to pretend that everything was normal and that she had just left Richard.

"We'll have you managed to bed him yet?" Core said.

Catherine went bright red but said nothing.

"I take that as a 'no' or is it the red face of embarrassment." Cora was looking at her as she drove.

"No, to both of your questions." Catherine snapped at her.

Cora slowed the car down, then pulled into the side and stopped.

"Okay, so what could have happened, I know, the two of you have had an argument and you have stormed out of the house but now you are regretting it, so you're going to take it out on me. That's why you're snapping like a crocodile with toothache and you've a face on you like you have just woken up and thought it was Friday instead of it being Monday."

"It's Saturday fool." Catherine barked at her.

"I know it's Saturday, misery, so come on, tell me."

"I can't."

"You WHAT!" Cora couldn't believe what she had just heard.

"You can't, you can't, oh, I know what's happened, the stardom is going to your head and now we can't speak to each other."

"Oh Cora, I, I can't." Catherine was almost crying now.

When Cora saw how upset Catherine was, she put her arm around her and squeezed her.

"All right, Catherine, I'll not go on at you about it but you and Richard have not had a fight, have you?"

"No Cora, you of all people should know I could never have a fight with him," Catherine said while wiping her eyes.

"Okay, babe," Cora said as she started the car up again and they drove away. "If it's that much of a secret, I'll not pester you anymore," Cora said.

"I want to tell you, but, I, can't," Catherine replied.

All through that night's performance, Catherine kept looking for Richard, no one noticed her looking. When the show finished and she had taken the ovations, she ran to her dressing room praying that he had been let in through the backstage door, she felt like crying when she only saw Cora waiting for her. Where she usually changed her clothes, all laughing and smiling, then leaving straight away, Cora saw her sullen looks and how she would just take her shoes off then sit for five minutes looking at the floor then put her other shoes on.

"Catherine, look, you're starting to worry me. I've never seen you like this and whatever it is that you can't tell me, well, you're going to or I'm going to tell your mom and dad that you're making yourself ill," Cora said after seeing Catherine's bottom lip start to quiver. Catherine went to her and started to cry on Cora's shoulder.

"Cora, I have not seen Richard today, I mean, all day, and he hasn't come here tonight," Catherine said between sobs.

Cora patted her on the back.

"Okay, tell me what's wrong, you say you haven't been fighting, so it can't be that, ohhhh, he wanted in your panties and you wouldn't let him."

"No Cora, you know I would do anything for him."

Cora stood there; her mouth wide open.

"Catherine, I know you said you would do whatever he wanted to do but I always thought you were joking. Catherine, you have kept your virginity intact for twenty-one years and now you are telling me you would just lose it if he asked you?" Cora was lost for words now, she hugged Catherine as hard as she could, for the first time in her life, Cora was frightened for Catherine.

"Do you know the reason why he has not come tonight?"

Catherine nodded her head.

"And you know that the reason he has given you is the truth?"

Catherine nodded her head again.

"Well all you have to do is wait," Cora said. Cora hated seeing Catherine like this, they had known each other from the start of their lives. Catherine was always there for her and she had always been there for Catherine. Catherine was the gentlest person Cora had ever known and she was so sad inside whenever Catherine was sad.

"Cora, I can't wait. I have to see him. When I don't see him, I feel empty inside, as if all of the feeling I have been having are just in my mind, that he doesn't exist," Catherine said in between sobs.

"All right, girl, if that is how you feel, get dressed and we'll go to his house and see him."

"He's not at his house, he's at the university."

"What, at this time of night?"

Catherine was trying to put her clothes on.

"And I have been told that I can't even go and see him."

"What, by the university, they do not have that kind of authority to keep two people apart."

"No, not the university. It was Barack Obama."

"And who the hell is Barack Obama when he's around. Oh!"

Cora said when she realised who the only Barack Obama she had heard of came into her mind.

"Barack, president, Obama?"

Catherine nodded her head, she wanted to tell her but stopped herself, she was so frustrated she started to shake.

"Catherine, Catherine, take it easy, I know what it's like. Tom works for the same man and sometimes I feel like killing him myself for taking Tom away for so long but I also know that we have great home comings."

Catherine looked at Cora and she could see that Cora was remembering some of the homecomings.

"Yes, I know but Richard is in the same city as me and I still can't see him."

"No, well we'll see about that, come on, get dressed."

Catherine put the rest of her clothes on in record time. Then they were in the car and heading for the university. As they pulled into the car parking bays, a security patrolman came up to them. They could see that he was ready to meet most kinds of trouble as he had a hand covering the top of a gun holster. They saw him relax when he looked inside and saw Catherine and Cora and not a bunch of young troublemakers.

"It's a bit early for classes, ain't it? The building won't open for another eight hours." They saw him smile at his own joke.

Cora got out of the car and stood with her hands on her hips. Cora was dressed in the tiniest of miniskirts and with her long legs and high stilettos; she looked as if she had come straight from a raunchy video shoot. The security man had just been watching MTV on one of the monitors and he would have sworn that he had just seen her on the show.

Cora walked up to him, slowly and over exaggerating the swing of her hips.

"Listen, wise guy, my friend left her books in her locker earlier today and we need them to look some stuff up because we have a retest to do."

"Yeah, what part of the building do you want to be in?" the security man asked.

"Biology, we're in the biology class." Cora knew from where they were now, they would have to walk all the way through the university to get to the biology rooms and if Richard was here, not that Cora thought he was telling Catherine lies, she just found it hard to believe, then they would see where he was.

He led them through the main entrance, then through the gymnasium, up the stairs and along the second floor.

"We can't go through the computer building, there's something going on."

"Oh," Cora said, winking at Catherine but trying to sound uninterested. Catherine could feel her legs turning to jelly as she was finding it hard to move.

They reached the biology rooms and as luck was on their side; there was a row of lockers outside the rooms. Cora was in front of Catherine, as they got closer to the lockers, she was already looking for a locker with a 'C' in the initials.

"Here it is, Catherine, where's your paper with the combination numbers on." Cora looked at the security man.

"We're new here and still have not memorised them."

The security man wasn't that interested and he turned and looked out of the windows overlooking the grass and other buildings.

Cora could see panic building up in Catherine's face and it looked as if Catherine was ready to turn and run.

"Don't tell me that you have left it on the table back home," Cora said.

Catherine stood there with her hands outstretched showing Cora she had nothing in them. Cora turned to the security man.

"Look I'm very sorry for this but my stupid friend here has forgotten to bring the numbers with her, so we will have to wait until we come back at the correct time after all."

"That's no trouble, it has been nice walking through here with two beautiful girls and it has made a nice change to what we usually have to do." He led them back through the building and as they got in their car, he said, "I hope you do well in your tests."

"Eh, yeah, thank you," Cora said and drove out of the parking bays.

"Well girl, we know where he is; now it's up to us to get there," Cora said as she turned the car into a side street and parked up. Catherine was almost too frightened to ask the next question but knew she had to.

"What are we going to do now, Cora?"

Cora turned to Catherine. Catherine saw the gleam in her eyes.

"When we went through the gym, I slipped a catch off a window." They both got out of the car and started to walk back to the university. They found the open window and climbed inside, then made it to the computer building.

"I was told I couldn't disrupt his work." Catherine reminded Cora in a very low whisper.

They were outside a room that had lights on inside. Cora looked down the hallway; she went down and came back with a couple of chairs.

"Well, we ain't going to disrupt his work; we'll just sit here until he comes out." They sat down on the chairs, sitting right opposite the computer room door and waited. The hallway had small emergency lights on that threw light in small nooks and crannies, so it was not as dark as if there were no lights on at all. Down the hallway, about fifty yards from where they were sitting there was a group of lockers, and the small lights cast a shadow over them, every now and again, the shadow looked as if it moved, and as they couldn't make any noise, the silence made it even more eerie. Cora had noticed the shadow at first, although she knew it was just her imagination, it was beginning to get the better of her. She looked at her watch again. It was exactly a half an hour since she last looked at it but she knew she had to look at it, to take her mind off the shadow. The one thing Cora really hated was horror movies and believe me, this shadow that had caught her imagination was a horror movie in the making. She was sure it was getting closer to her. She wanted to tell Catherine about it but she couldn't, she didn't want to frighten her as well. Catherine had noticed the shadow as well but didn't want to frighten Cora.

"What time is it now, Cora?" Catherine asked after watching her look at her watch. Cora turned to Catherine so that she could whisper the time but Cora saw that Catherine was looking down the hallway, a coldness crept up and down Cora's back as her mind conjured up all kinds of monsters. She was just about to fight back at the panic that was threatening to take over her when the door was thrown open and a man stood in the light.

Cora almost fell out of her chair and Catherine was ready to scream the place down as they heard him say.

"What are you doing here, who are you, you should not be here?"

Cora looked at him, her temper starting to build up after being told that she shouldn't be here.

"This is America. I can be where the hell I like," she shouted back at him, more with relief that he wasn't an axe murder or monster from the shadows.

"And who the friggin' hell are you to keep a girl waiting all of this time to see her boyfriend, eh?" Cora was now in full flow, after taking a quick glance down the hallway.

Richard heard the shouting and walked to the door. When he saw Cora giving the C.I.A. man a tongue-lashing, he leant on the doorpost and looked at Catherine.

"Even in this darkness you're beautiful," he said and went over to her and kissed her on the cheek.

"What are you doing here?" Richard asked her.

"I'll tell you what we are doing here, will I, will I. Your girl was making herself ill with worry."

Cora's temper had still not receded, then turning back to the C.I.A. man she said, "And if you think for one minute, you're going to get us arrested, I'll give you such a kick in your reproductive system, your eyeballs will hit the floor before you do."

"He will not get you arrested, will you, Mr Smithson?"

"They are not allowed into the room, we can go down to the security room and talk there but I must lock up here first. If anyone finds out about this, it's my head." He turned to lock the door.

"Wait, I was on the phone, I'll have to tell him I'll be back soon." Richard went into the room and picked the mobile up.

"Hello, English, are you still there?"

"Yeah, Yank, what was all of that racket, it sounded like a fight?"

"No, it was my girlfriend and her friend, look I'll have to switch off for a while. Is that all right with you?"

"No problem, Yank. While you're gone, I'll see what I can come up with okay, Ta-Ra." Richard heard the mobile go dead and he put it down then went back to the door.

"Okay, you can lock it now. I know I'm dying for a cup of coffee."

They walked along the hallway as Mr Smithson locked the door.

"How long is this going to go on for, Richard?" Cora asked.

"To be honest, I don't know but English is a wizard with computers."

"English, who's English?" Catherine asked him.

"I don't know who he is but he knows what to do with computers."

"I hope you are not talking about what you're doing, Richard?" Mr Smithson shouted from down the hallway as he tried to catch them up.

"No Mr Smithson, we're not," Richard shouted over his shoulder.

"So, who is this English?" Cora asked, never a one to let a small thing like the mighty C.I.A. worry her.

"I told you, I don't know who he is except that he lives in England."

"England?" Catherine and Cora said at the same time.

"Yes, he is doing the same as me but for their security people."

Mr Smithson was in front of them when they reached the security room. He went in and asked the two security men if they would go and do their rounds so that they could have a cup of coffee. After talking for half an hour, Mr Smithson looked at his watch.

"It's time we got back, Richard."

"Yeah, okay, Catherine, I do have to go back and start again."

"How long will this take, Richard, will I see you today, will you be at the theatre tonight?"

"Catherine, I don't know, all I do know is that it is very important that I do get it finished as soon as possible."

"All right I understand." She gave him a kiss on the lips.

"I promise I will not bother you again," she said it so sadly that Richard's heart started to crumble.

"Catherine, don't say it like that, please. You can bother me as much as you like." Then turning to Mr Smithson. "Look, if you don't give her the number for the mobile, I promise you I will not do another thing on the computers."

Mr Smithson huffed and puffed but knew he would have to do what Richard asked.

"Okay," he said as he wrote the number down and gave the paper to Catherine.

"It is still not the same as seeing you." She knew she was pushing her luck.

"No way," Mr Smithson shouted.

"If the two of you come anywhere near here again, I will have you arrested."

The three of them burst out laughing at Mr Smithson's discomfort.

When Catherine and Cora left them, Mr Smithson said, "You know you are a very lucky person to have those two beautiful women looking after you."

"Yeah," Richard said, then pressing the mobile on again.

"Hello, Yank, glad to have you back in the world of cyber space." Came the now familiar voice.

******

Chapter Thirteen

Cora decided to stay at Catherine's house that night as it was really late. Beverly asked them what time they came in last night as she had stayed up until late.

"It was about three in the morning wasn't it, Catherine," Cora said.

"Yes, we went to see Richard," Catherine said as she watched her mother's face. Beverly almost dropped the letters she was carrying.

"Catherine, you were told not go, they told you what was happening."

"Beverly, honest, Catherine was making herself sick with worrying about him, so I thought it would be best to get her to see him, oh I know I'm not supposed to know but anyone who knows Catherine knew that something was wrong with her. Anyway, Mr C.I.A. was rather nice about it."

"Yes, after you threatened to kick him in his reproductive system."

Beverly burst out laughing.

"You threatened the C.I.A."

"Well, he nearly frightened us to death, didn't he, Catherine?"

Beverly was shocked at first as they told her what they had done but she saw the look on their faces and she just had to laugh.

"Come on, Catherine, let's go into the garden," Cora asked her.

"Okay," Catherine replied. They went out through the green house and down to the storm shelter.

"Right, Catherine, now tell me again about you and your virginity and how you want to get rid of it."

Catherine went bright red.

"What's there to tell?" Catherine tried to sound normal but knew she couldn't hide anything from Cora.

"What's there to tell! What's there to tell? You tell me that it was rubbish, that's what you have to tell me. It was rubbish okay, now you tell me that babes, please." Cora saw the sadness in her friend's eyes so she softened her voice.

"Catherine, look, it might be with Richard that you lose your virginity but you have always said you were going to wait until you got married."

"Cora, Richard is the one I'm going to marry."

"Okay but please wait until you are married, Catherine. Catherine, you have something that everyone like me wishes they had…"

"Cora, it is all right for you to say that but what if he wanted to do it and I wouldn't let him and he finished with me."

"If he finished with you because you wouldn't open your legs for him, then he is not worth spitting on."

"Cora, I love him so much."

"I know you do, babe, but turning into a little hussy is not the way to keep him, take it from someone who knows." Cora put her arms around Catherine and gave her a big hug.

"Cora, when did you realise that Tom was the man for you?" Catherine asked her.

"Who says he is?" Cora replied looking as if butter wouldn't melt in her mouth.

"You've been going out with him for three years now, Cora, all the others lasted no more than a month or two."

Cora smiled a happy smile, not a forced smile or a smile that was supposed to let people think she was happy but a smile that told you she was really happy.

"I knew Tom was different when he never tried to get into my panties on the first date, or the second, or the third, or even the damn forth and in the end, as it was driving me crazy, I dragged him into my house and practically ravished him." She laughed. Catherine saw that she was remembering the time as her smile went right across her face.

"That's what is happening to me. I keep thinking something must be wrong with me, I mean that night when I stayed at his house all night, there was just the two of us, we were even in bath robes, do you know, we never did anything."

"Yes but you must have gone to bed with him and did some heavy petting?"

Cora's jaw dropped open when Catherine shook her head.

"Nothing happened Cora, oh we kissed but that was it," Catherine replied.

"Is he homosexual?" Cora asked.

"No," Catherine shouted at her.

"All right, babe, it's just I find that hard to believe that's all, he must have tried then, didn't he?"

"No," Catherine replied. Cora could sense the sadness in her friend's voice.

"Good God, Catherine, you have someone who wants you and not for what's between your legs. Listen, babe, you have a good one there but it still doesn't mean you have to turn into a hussy or let him blackmail you—"

"I don't think Richard would do that, Cora." Catherine interrupted her.

"Neither do I but just in case we have him wrong, don't do it, okay?"

Cora and Catherine were on their way to the theatre. Catherine had not used the phone number Mr C.I.A. had given her and it was burning a hole in her pocket.

"Do you think I should phone him, Cora?" Catherine asked her.

"If you want to, then do it when we get to the theatre," Cora replied.

Catherine nodded her head; she was feeling much better after their little talk. Cora had put her mind at ease as she always did.

When they arrived at the theatre, Jonathon was waiting for them at the door.

"Step into my room please." After the three of them sat down, he said. "It seems that the show has made an impact." Jonathon smiled.

"And other states want to see it. I'm being pressured to take it on the road. And Milton Ebbstein has been on the phone to me spitting blood because he cannot find out where you live, Catherine." He was now laughing loudly.

"I want the two of you to think it over. I will take the show on the road but but only if you two come with it. I don't know what other commitments you have after this run is finished but I will ask you to think it over carefully. Now go and get ready."

Catherine and Cora went to their room deep in their own thoughts of what Jonathon had just told them. Cora started to get Catherine's costumes ready for the changes she needs to make and then she started to put Catherine's make up on, they never spoke about what Jonathon said, Catherine was leaving that up to Cora.

"Should I phone Richard?"

"Yeah, go on, it will give you a boost."

Catherine dialled the number.

"Hello." The voice was Mr C.I.A.

"Is Richard there please?"

Catherine could hear Mr C.I.A. talking to Richard.

"Hello, Catherine, how is everything, are you getting ready to go on now?" Richard's voice was beautiful to hear and Catherine all most swooned at it.

"Oh, it is so good to hear your voice, Richard, are you almost finished now?"

"It will not be long now, Catherine, that's a promise, me and English think we have it nailed."

"Have you been there all of the time?"

"Yeah."

"What are you having to eat, are you getting any sleep?" Her voice was full of concern.

"Well, that's the down side. I've never had a wink of sleep but for eating, all I have to do is ask Mr Smithson and he gets it delivered. It feels good to know that you are still thinking of me, Catherine."

"Richard, I think of you all of the time," Catherine replied.

"And that is the bloody truth." Richard heard Cora shout in the background. He started to laugh, which made Catherine laugh.

"Oh, Richard there's my two-minute call, I will have to go."

"All right, Catherine, goodbye and it will not be long now, I love you. Bye."

Catherine went on stage and did her best performance yet. She had everyone in tears. When she came off the stage, the whole of the cast was applauding her as well as the audience, and when she went into her dressing room, Cora was even wiping her eyes.

"God Catherine, you damn well broke my heart that time. I have seen every performance you have done but that time you yanked my heart strings out and crumpled them up and put them back upside down. If you go on stage like that tomorrow, then I will not be watching you, I just could not go through that again."

"It did feel good, Cora."

Cora answered the door when someone knocked on it. Jonathon walked into the room; Cora could see that he had just finished rubbing his eyes as well.

"Catherine, there are some people here who want to see you." He sniffled. Catherine was looking at Cora, who had not moved from the doorway.

"All right but you will have to lift Cora out of the way if whoever it is wants to come in," Catherine said trying to fasten the strap on her jeans. When she had done it, she looked up and saw Christian Slater and his sister Helen. Catherine's mouth dropped open and she froze.

"He has that effect on people," Helen said smiling. He took hold of Catherine's hand and shook it.

"Thank you. That must be the best show I have seen for a very long, long time," he spoke.

Then he and his sister left the room. Cora went over to Catherine and grabbed her hand.

"Let me have a feel," Cora said, rubbing Catherine's palm.

"He touched me Cora…Cora, he touched me."

"Yes, I know, I saw him do it, oh Tom, where are you when I need you the most, oh Catherine I think I'm going to faint." Cora pretended to swoon and fall into a chair.

They had to keep telling each other that he had been in their dressing room and he had spoken to them, even driving home they kept saying that it did happen and it wasn't their imaginations, it did happen.

Catherine had phoned Richard twice and still he could not give her a time that he would be finished.

"Richard, I'm going crazy here waiting for you. It's been three days now."

"And so am I. Catherine, we are doing what we can. Just when we think we have it, it goes to some other place. English has smashed three monitors, believe me, I know how he feels."

"Richard, I'M going crazy for you, not some stupid computer."

"I know, Catherine. I'm just trying to make a joke of this madness."

"Richard, this is not funny. I miss you so much," Catherine said slowly.

"Catherine, I will be with you again. I just have to do this, please understand."

"I do understand how important it is, Richard, but I do not want to rely on memories of you, I want to see you, be able to touch you, to kiss you—"

"Catherine, I have to go. English thinks he has found something, goodbye." She heard the phone clicking off before she could say goodbye back to him. Catherine put the phone down and whispered 'goodbye Richard' then she fell asleep crying.

The next morning, Beverly saw the red marks around Catherine's eyes.

"Catherine, you look as if you have been crying?" Beverly watched her daughter going through the motions of trying to look all right but Beverly knew there was something wrong with her.

"Oh Mom, why can't everything be the way it was. Before I started doing the show, everything was fine, I was doing drama, I had Richard and everything was great, now I have to decide if I want to go on tour, or make a few movies and now I can't even see Richard."

Beverly took hold of Catherine's hand and led her to the sofa, then she went and made them a coffee each and sat down beside her.

"Catherine, one thing you must realise is that life is very strange and when it is good, then you have to remember all of it in your mind, so that you can look back and smile at the good times, because life has a tendency to throw stuff at you that turns everything upside down and more often than not, it also gives you a slap in the face for good measure. When I met your father, I was very lucky to pick a good man. Yes, we had it hard but we had each other to give each of us a pick me up. If we were feeling down, we would look at the good times but there were a few times where I would just burst out in tears but your father was there to hold me, to squeeze me gently and to reassure me. When he had to go away on long trips and for some reason, I could not go with him, the telephone was the only way we could talk to each other at night times and he always said the right things, things like, how much he loved me, and that this would be the last time that he would be away. Oh, we both knew that he would have to go away again but to just hear him saying it made me feel great and it built me up for the next day…"

"Mom, when Richard is not with me, I have this horrible feeling that he is trying to avoid me, that he doesn't really want to be with me, and it makes my body feel strange and empty and sometimes I have even felt like I want to be sick."

"Oh, Catherine that is not true, me and your father can see how much he loves you. We have seen how he looks at you and how he likes to feel your hand in his, how, if you're talking to Cora and he is talking to Tom, his eyes never leave you and we can see the pride he has in you. Catherine, take my word for it, he is a man just like your father is. But you have to let him do what he is doing. In his mind, he is doing it all for you." Catherine had put her clothes on and she and her mother were waiting at the main door for Cora to come and pick her up to go to the theatre. Cora drove into the driveway and waved to Beverly as Catherine got into the car and they drove out again.

"Well, babes, what kind of mood are you in today?"

"A bit better than I woke up." Catherine smiled at her.

"Okay, let's give the audience another tear jerker then."

They did and the audience would not let Catherine go off the stage, they just kept clapping and shouting for her. When she finally managed to get off after thirty minutes of standing in front of them and she went into her dressing room Cora was still crying.

"Catherine, please, you're going to have to stop this, it's killing me. I just can't go through this every night. Catherine, you're draining me."

There was a knock on the door, Cora opened it and in walked Jonathon.

"Catherine, you must be the most extraordinary person. How can you not be affected by that performance, even I used up a full box of tissues tonight." He gave her a kiss on the forehead and was about to leave when he turned back towards them.

"Oh, by the way, there was a kind of cryptic message left for you." He pulled a piece of paper out of his pocket and handed it to her then he left. Catherine unfolded it and read it. Cora saw the smile that came to Catherine face.

"Well, what does it say?" Cora said.

Catherine read it again and again. Her smile was filling the room.

"I'm at my house. Oh Cora, it's Richard, he is at his house."

"What?" Cora said.

"It's Richard, he has finished doing the computer thing and he is waiting for me at his house. Come on, let's get changed and get over there."

Cora must have broken the speed limit on every road getting to Richard's house. When they got there, Cora refused to go in.

"Look babe, if it was me, I wouldn't like people there with me, so you just go in and show him how much you have missed him." Catherine waved to Cora as she drove away. The anticipation was almost choking her as she put the key into the lock; she opened the door and went in. Richard was sitting at the table with a small light on. Catherine went to the switch to turn the main light on.

"Catherine, don't, please," Richard said. Catherine threw her coat off and went over to him. When he turned his face to look at her, she had to put her hand up to her mouth to stop herself from screaming. His face was battered and bleeding. She ran to the light switch and turned it on. She was shaking as she went back to him. His face was cut and his right eye was starting to swell, there was blood coming out of his nose and his lips were much fatter than they should have been with droplets of blood coming out of them. His shirt was ripped to shreds and she could see bruises forming on his chest.

"Richard, what happened, have you been to the hospital?"

"No," he said as a bolt of pain shot through him.

Catherine went to the phone and dialled Cora's mobile number.

"Yeah, you've reached me, now make it interesting or I'll put it down again," Cora's voice said.

"Cora, come back to Richard's now please, he has been in an accident."

Cora swung the car around. She knew there was no traffic on the roads at this time but that didn't really matter as she would have done the same in a rush hour if Catherine had phoned her in the same voice she had screamed at her then. She was back at Richard's house almost at the same time Catherine had put the phone back down. Catherine had opened the door so she could come straight in. When Cora saw him, she was shocked at his injuries. The two of them lifted Richard up and slowly walked him to the car. The hospital took x-rays and cleaned him up. His face looked worse than it was and after the blood was wiped away, the swelling did not look as bad but he had a few cuts about his body, so they strapped him up. There were no bones broken. He was in pain because he was bruised inside. When he was explaining to a doctor what had happened, both Catherine and Cora saw the quizzical look he gave Richard. Cora saw the doctor looking at a big bruise on his shoulder. Cora thought it reminded her of a footprint, then just as she thought of it, she turned away so that Catherine wouldn't see the shock on her face. The hospital let him go home as soon as they had checked the x-rays again for broken bones and they were sure he did not have any.

They were sitting at the table drinking the coffees that Catherine had made for them, when Cora asked him.

"Are you sure you don't know what happened?"

Richard looked at Cora, and saw that Cora was staring deep into his face. He knew she was looking for a trace of a lie and he knew that he would not be able to tell her a lie without her knowing, so he took a slow deep breath and spoke.

"Okay, promise me you will not say anything to anyone about this." He saw them nodding and Catherine looking puzzled.

"Why?" Catherine asked.

"Because he has not been telling us the truth, Catherine, he was not hit by a car, were you Richard? I saw the look the doctor gave you in the hospital when you told him you were hit by a car."

Richard gave out a long sigh.

"I was not hit by a car. When we were talking last night, Catherine, English tried something new on the computer, anyway it took us in another direction and we finally found out how to kill the virus. We spent a couple of hours finding it and killing it, then I thought I would surprise you when you got back to your house. I wanted to be there when you opened the door, so I was walking through the park when I came up against some people who knew you. One of them mentioned that I should get back in the drains where I came from. Another mentioned that I was only your pet and that one day, I will bite the hand that is feeding me and you will throw me back in the garbage where I belong, that never bothered me, names never have but one of them, I think he was called Robert, threw a punch at me. Then I knew it was going to get rough, so I started punching and kicking anyone who came near me but in the end, they got the better of me, and got me on the ground and started kicking me…"

Catherine got out of her chair and shouted, "First thing in the morning, I'm going around to his house and I'm going to tell—"

"Catherine, I asked you not to tell anyone, and I mean anyone."

"You're not going to let them get away with this, are you?" Cora said angrily.

"Yes, for the moment," Richard answered her.

The two of them fussed over Richard, making him comfortable, getting him coffee and a blanket to cover him when he went onto the sofa.

"Okay, do you want me to stay the night here or should I go home and leave you two love birds to get on with your lives," Cora said as she finished another cup of coffee.

"We'll be all right, Cora," Catherine said with a smile on her face that told Cora 'This is what I want, me and him alone'.

Cora leant forward and kissed Richard on the forehead and whispered to him.

"Don't you dare break this girl's heart."

Catherine walked Cora to the door and watched as she drove out of the street, she closed the door and came back into the room. Catherine switched the CD player on and a Kinks record started to play, then she sat down on the sofa beside Richard.

"Richard, I have something to tell you." Catherine hesitated.

"Jonathon has asked me and Cora if we want to go on the road with the show, he said he would only do it if we agreed."

Catherine saw the smile come to Richard's face.

"That is great news, Catherine, with Jonathon with you, it will mean you will be in all of the biggest theatres in the country."

"Yes but it will also mean that we'll be apart for…for…for—"

"Catherine, I will try and get to some of your shows, it will not be too bad, I find it hard to be without you as much as you do without me."

"Oh, Richard, do you, do you honestly miss me?" Catherine had never felt so much in love as she did now. Richard took hold of her arm and pulled her slowly towards him, he kissed her softly on the lips.

A bolt of pain shot through his body as he pulled her to him. Catherine pulled away from him until the pain had gone, then she knelt on the floor right beside his face.

"There, now you don't have to pull me." And kissed him.

"Richard, I love you so much, I don't think I could be away from you for a few hours, never mind a few days." She saw him wince as he tried to smile. She put a finger to his lips. He lay down and with Catherine sitting on the floor, it wasn't long until they both fell asleep again.

The telephone woke her up, as she put her elbow on the side of the sofa, she tapped Richard.

"Sorry, I'm just going to answer the phone," she whispered.

"Hello."

"It's only me, babe. How's the invalid."

"Cora, what time is it?"

"Ten fifteen, babes, I want to know if you've seen the papers?"

"No, you have just woke us up, why, what do they say."

"Well, it seems that you have signed to K.P. Studios to do three movies."

"What! Cora, you're my agent, have you signed anything?"

"Nope, now can I do the agent thing and tell them where they can stick their stories, this will cost Mr Milton Ebbstein."

Catherine could hear Cora laughing.

"Yes but no bad language, please," Catherine said, she heard Cora laughing louder.

"Okay, babe, now, with you staying with Richard all night on your lonesomes and him being in such a bad state, I hope you let him go straight to sleep and you didn't do what you said you would do if he asked you to do it."

"Cora, what are you going on about?"

"You're still a you know what?"

This time, it was Catherine's turn to laugh.

"Cora, we fell asleep on the sofa again."

"That's a good girl, see you later then, bye." Catherine heard the phone being put down. She felt good to know that her best friend was so concerned about her. While she was talking to Cora, she was watching Richard getting up off the sofa and walking to the kitchen. He came back with two cups of coffee. They both went and sat at the table.

"That was Cora, she says the newspapers have said that I have signed a three-movie deal with K.P. Studios, she was just making sure that I had not before she tells them off for telling lies." Richard smiled and spoke.

"Then I feel pity for the person who picks the phone up at the newspaper offices." They both started laughing. Richard felt all right after he'd had a night's sleep, he still had a little pain now and again shooting through him when he moved certain ways but he was all right otherwise.

"Richard, you don't have to go to the university today, do you?"

"NO, they gave me the rest of the week off. Mr Smithson says I have to go to the bank and see how much they have put in for me. If it is not enough, I have to phone a number and tell them."

"Right, Richard, can I have a shower please?" Catherine asked him.

"Catherine, you don't have to ask, you can do anything you wish in here. While you're in the shower, I'll make us some breakfast."

"No, you have a shower first, Richard, and I'll make your breakfast," Catherine said.

"Okay," Richard replied and got up and walked slowly to the bedroom.

Catherine put the CD player back on and was singing 'Dedicated follower of fashion' while cooking the breakfast. She was putting the breakfast on the table when Richard came out of the shower with just a towel around his waist. Although he had some bruises on his chest and back and shoulders, she still went weak at the knees when she saw him like this, he came into the room and sat at the table.

"Catherine, this smells beautiful," Richard said looking at it.

She had to sit down fast or she would have fell over; she just couldn't take her eyes or mind off his body.

"Richard, please tell me the truth, do you honestly not realise what you look like dressed like that."

She saw him going red with embarrassment.

"You don't, do you? You honestly have no idea what you look like, do you?" she said in amazement.

"I'm, I'm sorry if I have embarrassed you, Catherine. I'll go and put some clothes on."

She took hold of his hand.

"You honestly have no idea, do you, no idea of what you're doing to me, and no, you are not embarrassing me, far from it actually. Oh, never mind, just sit down and eat your breakfast. How are the pains now that you have had a shower?"

"It's not hurting as much now," he spoke.

Catherine ate her breakfast, then told Richard to just sit here and to not move a muscle. Catherine got up out of the chair and went into the shower humming 'All day and all of the night'.

When she came back out of the shower, all she had on her body was a towel around her waist as Richard had, she walked up to Richard, and took his hand and led him into the bedroom…

They came back out of the bedroom at three-o-clock, their bodies were dripping in sweat, it looked as if they were covered in oil. Catherine had been thrown from one fantastic place to another nonstop. She never wanted it to end. She had been to the heavens and back then she had gone straight to the knife edges of her emotions as Richard took her body. She was breathless and she tingled all over. She now knew what it felt to have a million volts of electricity shooting through her body. The hair on the back of her head was still standing up, her arms and face and neck were all aching and her legs felt so weak she was almost afraid to stand up. They both went back into the shower. Catherine was now more than ever convinced that they were together for the rest of their lives. They got dressed and went for a bus to take them into the city. All the time Catherine had her arm through Richard's and was whispering in his ear how much she loved him. They got off the bus and walked the short distance to the bank. Richard put his card into the machine and pressed for a balance to come up.

"Five thousand dollars," he said as he looked at Catherine.

"Do you want to go and have something to eat?" Richard asked Catherine.

"No, let's just go back to your place," Catherine replied with a glint in her eyes.

"All right," Richard said.

"Richard, I'm going to show you how much I have missed you."

Cora knocked on the door. Catherine opened it and Cora knew immediately that they had been to bed.

"Catherine, you said you would wait, oh girl I really hope you knew what you were doing," Cora said with a hint of sadness. Catherine took Cora's hand and led her to the table.

"Now you just sit here and watch, then you tell me that you could have resisted."

Richard was having another shower.

"But, but, you said—"

"Cora, just do what I have said all right, just sit and watch, then tell me it was wrong."

Just then, Richard came out of the shower room and walked into the room where they were, all he had on was a towel around his waist, his hair hung to his shoulders and he had a big smile on his face, that is, until he noticed Cora sitting there. Catherine could hear Cora breathing in deeply.

"Friggin' helllllllllll. Richard, please cover yourself up."

Richard turned around and walked fast into the bedroom.

"There, now you tell me that you could have resisted that," Catherine said proudly.

Cora was busy wafting her face.

"Catherine, how have you lasted this long; it must have been killing you waiting for him to take you in there?"

Catherine was smiling as she was shaking her head.

"I took him in." She purred.

Chapter Fourteen

Catherine wanted Richard to come to the theatre with them but he wouldn't until his face at least, went back to normal.

"I'll see you tomorrow, Catherine, but you will have to come here. I do not want your parents seeing me like this and asking me questions."

"Richard, after what you have done to Catherine, she will be here more than you," Cora said laughing at her own little joke. The two of them watched Richard going bright red.

"Well, why don't I come here after the show?" Catherine said seriously. Cora giggled and Richard went a deeper red.

"No, I have a bit of reading to catch up on, now go, or you are going to be late."

Cora went out to the car and Catherine went to Richard.

"Kiss me," she spoke.

He put his arms around her and kissed her on the lips, Catherine's tongue went in search of his and she pulled him tightly into her as they met.

"Oh, Richard, I love you so much," she whispered when their lips had parted. Richard closed the door after they had turned the corner and was out of sight; he went to the phone and dialled his mother's number.

"Hello."

"Hello, David, is my mother there?"

"Richard, hello, she was getting worried about you. She has tried to phone you three times. She is doing fine, oh, here she is now." Richard could hear David teasing her.

"Richard, where have you been for the last three days? I have tried to phone you but nothing. In the end, I had to phone Beverly and Alvin. All they would say was you were doing something for the university."

"Yes, I was, and they put five thousand dollars in my bank account for doing it."

"How much?" Sharon asked again.

"Five thousand dollars."

"Richard, people don't go putting five thousand dollars in other people's accounts, what were you doing?"

"Mom, believe me when I say I can't tell you just yet, anyway, enough about me, how are you and the doc getting on?"

"Oh Richard, it is beautiful out here. I just wish you were here with me. At weekends, David takes me horse riding. Last weekend, we packed a tent and went up into the hills—"

"Mom, are you telling me you went camping?" He heard her laughing.

"Yes, and it was wonderful."

"So, any idea when you're going to have a name change?"

"What do you mean, Richard?"

"From Buckman to Cunningham."

"Well, it's funny you should mention that. I think he is trying to build the courage up to ask me but he is just that little bit short at the moment. How are you and Catherine doing, we read that she has signed to do a few movies?"

"Mom, that's a load of garbage but she is thinking about it. Up to now she is going on tour with the show, so she might be in California for a few days."

"Richard, I miss you so much. I feel so empty not having you here with me. You are doing all right; you would tell me if anything is wrong, wouldn't you?"

"Mom, I'm doing just fine. Oh and Catherine just loves your CDs." Richard heard her laughing again.

"Mom, I will have to go now, okay? I have some reading to catch up on."

"All right, Richard, I love you, goodbye."

"I love you too, Mom, goodbye and look after yourself, goodbye." He put the phone down, he felt a bit empty as well. He shook the feeling out of him and went and made himself a cup of coffee as he sat down with a book the phone started to ring again.

"Hello."

"Hi, Yank." Came a voice he was more than enough familiar with.

"English, how the hell did you get my home number?" Richard said in amazement.

"Aw, it's simple when you have a computer. Listen, did your people put any money in your bank account?"

"Yes, they put five thousand dollars in my account, why?"

"Oh, I'm just naturally suspicious. Where I come from, no one gives you anything if they can help it, whether you've earned it or not."

"That's just what my mother has told me, what do you think is going on?"

"I don't know, Yank, but a word of warning, don't say anything to anyone. Now how are you and that Amazon woman you have getting on?"

"Amazon woman, what do you mean?"

"Well as you were doing the same as me, you must have had some big men standing behind you, and all the shouting I heard, she must be an Amazon to not be frightened of them."

"Oh, you mean all the shouting and fighting sounds you heard, we're doing okay English, she has just left here to do a show."

"She's an actress?"

"Yes, and a good one as well, they are trying to get her to sign for a few movies," Richard said proudly.

"Well, when she does and the two of you come over here for a first showing, don't forget me, I'll come down to the capital, then we'll put faces to our voices."

"You have a definite yes on that, English."

"I'll have to go now, Yank, okay? They don't know I'm phoning America, they think I'm doing an E.T. anyway I have to go to the Sol so goodbye, Yank, been nice talking to you again."

"Wait, what is the Sol?" Richard asked.

"Stadium of Light, man, see you, bye." Richard heard the phone go dead. He put his down and smiled. He started to read his books but after two hours his side started to hurt him. He put his book down and walked around the room a little. It eased the pain, so he decided to go for a little walk outside. He opened the door and felt the warmish air. The weather was starting to get ready for the summer although it was a while before it would start to get hot. Most of the time, there would be days where the warm air would surprise the people and this was one of them. He walked along the street; the streetlights gave off a yellow glow and now and again a breeze would blow the leaves on the trees, that was the only movement in the street, he remembered the streets around the tenements and the noise, that would last for twenty-four hours a day, seven days a week. He tried to think what time it would be in England. He looked at his watch; it was eleven-o-clock. England was about five or six hours in front of them, which meant that English was up and at university at five in the morning. It was a funny time to be at university but after being with English, Richard knew that nothing was as it seemed with him. Richard thought about it.

If English is five or six hours ahead of him, then he had been talking to someone who was in his future. That made Richard laugh, before Richard realised it, he had walked to the city. There were people going here and there, he knew Catherine would be finished at the theatre and would be home now. But as he was near it he decided to walk there anyway, then he would walk back home. He crossed the street and looked at the big poster with a picture of Catherine on it. He never looked at Catherine; he was looking at the flash across the poster proclaiming that Friday night's show would be the last for two weeks for Catherine and that Debra Daniels would be standing in for her.

Tomorrow was her last night for two weeks. Richard wondered why she had not said anything to him about it. He turned around and walked home a different way. He went along what was commonly known as 'Restaurant Boulevard' as it was full of cafés and restaurants some very high-class ones, and some for the likes of workers and steel men that were helping to build up the city centre. He looked in the windows of some as he passed, he could see people enjoying their meals and laughing.

One day, Catherine, I will bring you here, he thought.

The walk had tired him more than he thought it would, and as he sat on his sofa, he fell asleep.

He thought he could hear Catherine whispering in his ear. At first, he couldn't make it out what she was saying, then as he listened more and more, she became clearer.

"Richard, what are you doing on the sofa?" He smiled without opening his eyes, her voice was so close to him, he didn't want to wake up, he just wanted to lay here and listen to her voice.

"Catherine, don't wake me, just let me listen to your voice, keep talking."

"What are you doing sleeping on the sofa?" Catherine asked him again. She saw the smile come back onto his face, then she realised he was still asleep. Catherine put the two cups of coffee that she had made on the table and went back to him. She knelt on the floor and started to kiss his face, just little kisses, then she nibbled at his ear, then his neck, then back to his face, all the time kissing him soft and gentle, she started to say his name.

"Richard, I love you." Then she would kiss him a few times then say it again.

"Richard, I love you." She kissed his eyelids, then she felt them open, she moved away from him and saw his smile appear again.

"Mmmmmmm, Catherine, that is a beautiful way to wake me up."

"What are you doing sleeping on the sofa, Richard?" she asked again, while still giving him little kisses around his mouth. He sat up and Catherine got up and gave him one of the cups of coffee that she had made.

"I went for a walk last night and when I got back, I remember sitting down on here, then I must have fell asleep."

"Why didn't you phone me? I would have come over here," Catherine said.

"I walked to the theatre and back."

"That's almost four miles, Richard," Catherine said startled.

"That must have been how I was so tired when I got back. Catherine, I was having a lovely dream about you."

"Aw, were you, were you dreaming of us?" She put her cup on the floor and kissed him on the cheek.

"Was I being nice to you?" she asked in that purring voice, she gave him her best innocent smile she could.

"You have a very wicked smile, don't you?" He laughed.

"And just as it was going to get exciting, you woke me up." He finished.

"Well, drink your coffee and we'll see if we can turn your dream into reality," she said, looking at the bedroom door.

"Catherine?" Richard said.

"Yes." She looked at him as his voice had turned to a serious voice.

"Why didn't you tell me that tonight is your last night for two weeks?"

"I never knew myself until last night when we got to the theatre. I have told you that Jonathon is being pressured to take the show on tour?" Catherine waited for his answer.

Richard nodded his head as he sipped at his coffee.

"Well, he does not really want to as he has commitments with other projects and Jonathon is noted for keeping promises. Anyway, the people who are pressuring him are big in the theatre world, and Jonathon has told them that he will pull the plug on the whole show if they try to make him do something that he doesn't want to do. They all know that I have been offered a movie contract and by letting me have two weeks off, is Jonathon's way of showing the big people that I'm considering the contract and he will not use his influence on me to stay with the show, which will make the big people nervous. So, he told me last night that I and Cora have a two-week holiday." Catherine kissed him again.

"And, and I have something planed for us, do you think you can get two weeks off from the university?" Catherine had that glint in her eye again.

"Why?" Richard asked.

"Mom and Dad are going to the show tonight, then they are flying down to Texas. They will be gone for a week and they want you to stay at the house with me."

Catherine almost fainted when he smiled at her. She had never seen him smile like that. She went warm all over.

"I could pick you up after seeing them off at the airport, then we will have a whole week together, by ourselves, no disturbances," Catherine whispered the last two words in his ear. She got up off the sofa and took the two empty cups into the kitchen then she walked over to him and gently pulled him up off the sofa and then walked him to the bedroom.

"I'll have to go to the university and let them know I will not be in for at least one week," Richard said.

"Phone them when I have finished with you," Catherine said in a determined voice. She had closed the bedroom door. Richard was taking his t-shirt off. Catherine had her blouse off and had just loosened her bra strap when the doorbell rang.

Richard stopped doing what he was doing and spoke, "I have to find out who it is, Catherine."

Catherine had finished taking her clothes off and was in the bed.

"Well, hurry up," she spoke. Richard went to the door and opened it.

"Hi, Richard, I phoned Catherine's and her mother said she was here, I hope I'm not disturbing anything," Cora said, raising her voice on the last four words while covering her mouth pretending to stop herself from laughing.

Catherine came out of the bedroom fastening the last button on her blouse and with a very red face.

"Impeccable timing, as usual," Catherine mumbled. Giving Cora the look of death.

"Oh Catherine," Cora said matter-of-factly while leaning on the doorpost, "you've forgot to put your bra on."

Catherine stopped and gaped at herself then turned around and ran back into the bedroom, when she came back out, she was redder than ever.

"What time is it?" she asked.

"Six thirty," Richard said.

"God, I didn't know it was so late." Catherine was too embarrassed to look Cora in the face.

"That's pretty obvious, babe," Cora said.

Catherine gave Richard a kiss on the cheek and told him to be ready for her coming back here tonight. Then they got in the car and Cora gave a loud laugh as they drove away.

"Godm girl, you're twenty-one, it has got nothing to do with me what you and Richard get up to in his house, so why all of the red face."

"Because it is what you're thinking we have done, that's why I'm all flustered."

"So," Cora said.

"So, you're wrong, that's so. You stopped us before we even started." Then Catherine told Cora of her plans for the whole of next week. Cora was green with envy as Tom was away again.

Catherine saw the look on Cora's face.

"You can stay as well, Cora; I'm sure Richard wouldn't mind you there."

"Yeah, babe, but you would kill me in my sleep."

They both burst out laughing.

"No, Cora, you know you can stay with us any time you want to," Catherine told her.

"Yes, I know, babe, but I think I'll go to 'Noo York' to see my parents, thanks anyway."

Catherine had just finished putting her first costume on when Jonathon knocked at their dressing room door and walked in.

"Catherine, Cora, have you given any more thought on Milton Ebbstein's offer?"

They looked at each other, then back to Jonathon.

"What offer?" they both said together.

"The letter I left on the dressing table on Monday that was from Milton."

Catherine and Cora both went to the dressing table and looked on it and around it, then Catherine put her hand to her mouth.

"Cora, look in the trash bin, will you? I remember putting paper in there."

Cora picked up the bin and tipped it onto the floor, she bent down and went through the papers, then she stood up holding an unopened letter and a big smile on her face. She handed the letter to Catherine, who refused to take it, saying as she was her agent, she should open all of her correspondence. Cora opened the letter. Catherine watched Cora's face for a clue of what was inside the letter, she saw Cora's jaw drop and her eyes go wide open.

"Well, what does he say?" Catherine tried not to sound excited.

"He…He…he definitely wants you to do two or three movies for his studios. The first one is to be a movie of this show, with as many of the original cast you wish to have. The second is to be a movie of your choice, and, if you wish to do a third one, then that will be a movie of your choice as well. And, and, and he is prepared to pay you Five and a half Million Dollars a movie, he also promises that he will not put any pressure whatsoever onto you, all you have to do is phone him and tell him you will sign when the show has done it's full run."

Catherine had sat down when Cora said how much he would pay her, the two of them looked at Jonathon, who was chuckling in his seat.

"What are you so happy for Jonathon, if Catherine signs, you will not be able to take the show on the road?"

Jonathon pulled a cigar out of a pocket and smiled as he slid it under his nose.

"That my dear, Cora, is the only way I can get the big theatre people off my back, they would not dare threaten K.P. Studios." His smile got bigger and bigger. Cora stared at him.

"Are you saying you have been talking to Milton Ebbstein behind our backs?"

"All I'm saying is that I had a word with him about how much he wanted Catherine on his books, and that she has a very tough agent and he would have to make it worth her while to get her to sign. I told him that you are at this very moment talking to one or two other people and they know that you are getting fifteen percent of anything Catherine gets."

"Wait a minute, are you saying I get fifteen percent of five and a half million dollars?"

Jonathon nodded his head.

"That's if Catherine is prepared to give you fifteen percent."

Cora looked at Catherine, who twisted her face a little.

"I suppose I could manage it," Catherine said as her twisty face turned into a big smile.

"Fifteen percent of five and a half million dollars, that's, that's six hundred and forty-five thousand dollars."

"That's the kind of agent you want, Catherine, one who works out what they get before anyone else." He laughed at his own joke. Cora was sitting stunned.

The show was still pulling full crowds and making everyone cry. People were coming back time and time again to see it and to see Catherine who, as one person told a television network camera team that were doing a news channel program, that Catherine was the best he had ever seen, some critics were still shouting Catherine's name from the roofs. As this was the last show, she would be doing for two weeks, the audience would not let her leave the stage. Catherine lifted her arms in the air and the audience went quiet, she walked to the edge of the stage and said to them.

"Thank you for making this such a good show and thank you for making my debut on stage such a nice one. I know the newspapers have said I have signed a deal with a movie studio. I have promised I will look at what they have to offer me but I have also promised Jonathon Kranz that I will see out my run with this show here, I always keep my promises." The applause was deafening. Catherine raised her arms again and it went quiet.

"Now please show your appreciation to the rest of this fantastic cast, Thank you."

The cast walked back on stage and the noise was tremendous. Catherine joined in with the audience in applauding them.

Catherine and Cora went to the airport with Alvin and Beverly. They kissed and said goodbyes. Alvin went to the departures and booked him and Beverly in. He came back to Catherine and Cora and spoke.

"One thing I have learned in life Catherine is, when you have time to relax, make the most of it." Then he lifted the cases and went in through the departure doors. Beverly gave them both a kiss.

"And make sure Richard enjoys it as well," she said as she winked at them before she went in through the departure doors. Cora looked at Catherine and laughed at the embarrassment on her face.

"Wha…Wha…What did she mean by that?" Catherine stuttered. Cora was now hurting her side with laughing.

"Oh babe, everyone can see that you and Richard have been at it like a pair of bunny rabbits."

"How, how can anyone know?" Catherine hoped that Cora was joking.

"Little things, like the vacant look in your eyes whenever his name is mentioned but the best is the bright red face whenever you think of it, Miss Bunny Rabbit."

"I don't," Catherine said as she and Cora waved at her parents walking across the tarmac.

"You do, Miss Bunny Rabbit," Cora said.

"I don't," Catherine said again.

"You are, Miss Bunny Rabbit." Cora could hardly speak now as she was laughing so much at Catherine's red face.

Catherine drove them back to the theatre and Cora got into her own car, they said their goodbyes and Cora drove away. Catherine drove to Richard's house. She had her own key now and she let herself in the house, Richard was just making a cup of coffee when she shouted hello. He stopped making it and gave her a big hug, after a kiss he said.

"How was the show?"

"Richard, they would not let me leave the stage, oh, and have I got something to tell you but it will wait until you finish making the coffee," Catherine said as she took her coat and shoes off and sat down on the sofa. Richard came into the room with the coffees and sat beside her. Catherine curled her legs up under herself and leant against him.

"Can you remember Milton Ebbstein?"

"Yes, he is the one who wants you to sign for K.P. Studios, isn't he?"

"He wants me to do three movies for him."

"Have you made your mind up yet if you are going to do them or not?"

"No, me and Cora are still thinking about it. But do you know how much he wants to pay me for each movie?"

"Since you haven't told me yet, no, I don't know."

"Well, he is going to give me five and a half million dollars a movie." She saw the amazed look on Richard's face.

"Oh Richard, everything in my life is so perfect now, I love you," she said, and kissed him.

"Catherine, do you want to go to your house tonight or in the morning."

"Well, if we go to my house now, it will mean driving there and we'll end up in bed." She looked at Richard's bedroom door.

"So why don't we cut out the driving and just go to your bedroom, we'll go to my house in the morning." She took Richard's hand and they both walked into the bedroom.

Catherine was lying beside him, listening to his breathing. The sun was high up in the sky, the rays off it lit the room, she looked at him, he was still sleeping, she turned on her side so she was facing him, she brushed his hair away from his face and kissed him lightly on the cheek. She rested her head on her arm and thought about last night. How the muscles in her arms and legs were paining her and she wondered if she would ever get the same feelings. Her lips felt as if they were swollen. She touched them with her finger and her body quivered and she gave out a little moan. She moved her face closer to his and she started to kiss him on the cheek gently so as not to wake him. She started to kiss down his cheek until she was at his neck, then across his chest and up the other side, around his chin, over his nose, she kissed each eye, then his forehead and back down to his mouth. She paused just above his mouth. She opened her mouth then slowly put it to his, soft and gentle at first but as she felt his arms going around her body and pulling her on top of him, her kissing started to get more and more passionate.

An hour later, Catherine got out of bed and went into the shower. Richard went and made them a coffee each and he sat at the table until she came out. She walked towards him with just a towel around her waist and a one on her head.

"Catherine, have you got no shame?" he said to her.

"You never said that last night," she replied. She bent down and kissed him on the lips. "Are we going back into your bedroom?" she asked him with a grin on her face.

"No but tonight we'll go into your bedroom."

The thought of being in her own bedroom with Richard made her body start to tingle and she felt bolts of electricity running through her veins as her body prepared itself for another night of love.

Richard went into the shower as Catherine put her clothes on. It was almost one-o-clock when they were finally dressed.

"What shall we do until tonight?" Catherine asked him.

Richard stood in front of her and kissed the tip of her nose.

"Has my face gone back to normal?"

Catherine put her hand onto his cheek.

"Richard, your face is beautiful." She kissed his cheek. "Your eyes are perfect." She kissed each eye. "Your lips are so soft and tender." She kissed first his top lip, then the bottom lip.

He put his arms around her and pulled her to him, she wrapped her arms around his neck and their lips melted into each other's.

"Why don't we stay here?" she murmured through their kiss.

"Because we can't stay in bed for the rest of our lives," he replied.

"I could, if you would," she said smiling at him.

"Let's go for a walk, to cool us off."

"I'm happy with the way we are." She tightened her grip around his neck, their lips had still not parted.

"Catherine, you're going to give me a heart attack." He laughed when their lips did part.

"Richard, I'm going to make love to you all through the night." She sighed.

It was warm outside, so Catherine never bothered putting her coat on as they went for a walk. It was the first time Catherine had been here except to go to Richard's house, so she had never really seen the projects buildings except for his house, they were all built in the style of John F. Kennedy's American Dream, and they all had small front tidy grassed yards, some had roses growing around their borders. Catherine had her jeans on and a small pink blouse. Her jeans fitted her perfectly and her blouse only had the one clasp on it in the middle, her long black hair hung down to almost touch her waist. Richard had his jeans on and a t-shirt, they walked around slowly, just taking their time, hand in hand, as lovers would. A woman who was walking towards them stopped and stared at them, Catherine felt a bit uneasy but all the woman did was fish in her bag for a pen and a bit paper.

"Catherine, Catherine Johnson, is that really you?"

Catherine smiled at her.

"Please, please sign this for me." She was almost begging her.

Catherine took the pen and paper off her and started to put her name.

"Do you want a message?" Catherine asked her.

"Catherine, put anything you want on it," the woman said. Catherine wrote, 'Thank you, lots of love, Catherine Johnson'.

The sun was nice and warm, Catherine took hold of Richard's hand again as they walked down another street, they both noticed people staring at them.

"Richard, are these people looking at us, or am I getting paranoid."

"They are looking at you, and to be quite honest, I don't blame them." Richard was trying to stop her from panicking.

"Richard, let's start going back. I'm starting to get nervous. I never thought anyone would recognise me without my makeup on." He felt her hand tighten around his.

"Catherine most of these people don't know who you are; they are looking at your beauty."

"Oh Richard," she said and gave him a kiss.

"What was that for?" he asked her.

"Do I need an excuse to kiss you now, anyway it was for saying that, a girl likes to be complimented and I love it when you compliment me and do other things to me." He saw the twinkle in her eye and he smiled at her.

"Richard, let's go to my house now." She put her hand in his back pocket and nipped him, they walked back to his house and he locked up, then they drove to Catherine's house. Just before they went down the driveway, she stopped the car and got out, went to the mailbox, she took all of the mail out and then she drove to the house.

Catherine threw her keys onto the Chesterman and started to take her blouse off.

"Catherine, not yet," Richard said.

She looked at him; the hurt in her eyes was for real.

"All right but you tell me the minute you want to take me to bed, and don't be afraid to say so."

He grabbed her around the waist and kissed her.

"Okay, let's go up the stairs." He smiled at her.

The week went by so fast that Catherine and Richard got a shock when Beverly phoned them from the airport to say they were on their way home now. Catherine was standing at the door when the car came down the drive and her mom and dad got out, paid the driver then came into the house. Richard had made everyone a cup of coffee.

"How was it, Mom?" Catherine asked.

"It was good. Your father had to go down to Galveston so I went over to see Maria Perez for a few days."

"How is she? I have not seen her since I was small," Catherine said.

"She is fine and her daughters are all up and are at college. Oh, I bought you these." Beverly handed Catherine a bag and Richard a bag. "I hope they are your size, Richard." Beverly saw Richard's eyes light up when he looked in the bag and saw the pair of real Texas Cowhand boots.

"Come on Richard, let's try them on," Catherine said and they went into the lounge.

Alvin opened the letters that had been on the Chesterman all week, just as Catherine and Richard came back into the room, wearing the boots and a big broad smile.

"It looks like we got back just in time, Beverly, we have been invited to Rebecca Whyte's twenty first birthday party at the Hall tonight."

Catherine had the look of death on her face when she heard her father.

"Is it just for you, Dad, and not for me and Richard?" she asked.

"No, it is for all of us, including a friend, which will mean Richard."

"Well, we are not going," Catherine said sharply.

"Why?" Beverly asked.

"Because we are not going, I don't want to go." The distress in Catherine's voice made Beverly suspicious.

"Catherine, you know we have to go, it is tradition," her father said.

"Well, I'm not going and neither is Richard." Catherine walked out of the main room and into the lounge. Richard followed her.

"Catherine, you're upsetting your parents, why do you not want to go?" he asked her.

"Because Rebecca has a brother called Robert," Catherine said, just as her parents came into the room.

"Oh, thee Robert," Richard said.

"Yes, Thee Robert." Catherine turned around and saw her mother standing there looking puzzled. Beverly heard the tone in her voice when she had said that. Catherine had to do some quick thinking or she might ask a difficult question.

"And I don't want him making trouble for Richard, just because he is going out with me."

"Catherine, Robert would not cause trouble with Richard," Beverly said.

"Well, I think he might so I'm not going to give him the chance," Catherine replied.

"If it makes you feel any better, I will not leave you two alone all night," her father said.

Catherine had finally given in to her mother and father and agreed to go.

******

Chapter Fifteen

They entered the hall. Catherine had her arm through Richard's and she was pressed right into him. Alvin and Beverly were looking for Rebecca, to wish her happy birthday. Catherine and Richard were looking for Robert. As soon as Rebecca saw them, she came over to them. Alvin and Beverly kissed her. Richard smiled but Catherine ignored her. Rebecca seemed not to notice the snub Catherine gave her.

"Hi, Catherine," Rebecca said.

"Hi, is Robert here?" Catherine said still not looking at her but looking around the crowd that was in the hall.

"Yes, he's over there with some of his friends," Rebecca said pointing to a corner away from them.

"Is this the person everyone is talking about; he certainly looks nice," Rebecca said looking at Richard up and down. Catherine pulled him in closer to her.

"Yes, and he is staying mine."

"Do you want me to tell Robert you're here?" Rebecca said, still unaware of Catherine's coldness towards her.

"No." Catherine snapped back at her. Rebecca went to greet some other guests who had just arrived.

"Mom, Dad. It will be all right, there are far too many people here. Robert will not start trouble now. You can go and join your friends."

When her parents left them, Richard looked at her and saw the frightened look on her face.

"Catherine, it will be okay, like you said, there are too many people here, anyway, I wouldn't let any of his blood spoil these boots."

Catherine smiled at him.

"That's better, now let's enjoy ourselves."

They went to the bar counter and got two soft drinks. Catherine took him out onto the terrace, as it was the first time Richard had been here, he was amazed at the sight that greeted him as they walked out of the Hall and onto the big terrace. He went over to the small wall and looked around. He could see most of the city, even the tenements where he and his mother used to live.

"It's a beautiful sight, isn't it, Richard? It is even better when the sun goes down and the city turns its lights on," Catherine whispered into his ear.

"If we can see all of this from here, how can we not see this from down there?"

"Oh, you can, it's just hard to see, anyway I never brought you out here for this, follow me."

They walked along the terrace, and then down a few steps. The steps took them to a smaller terrace that went around the hall. As they walked around it, they came to a huge oak tree, with a bench all the way around it. Catherine sat on it and patted the place next to her for Richard to sit down. Catherine looked into his eyes.

"Richard, I know you might think this is silly but please do it for me. I want you to tell me that you love me and it will last forever and ever."

"You know I do," Richard said.

"Yes, I know but I want you to say it here, under this tree, and it would be nice if you put your arm around my shoulder."

Richard looked into her eyes.

"Catherine, I love you and always will, forever." He kissed her softly on the lips.

"And I will love you forever, Richard." Then she kissed him.

The leaves on the tree started to rustle. Catherine smiled.

"Thank you, tree, for listening," she whispered to it. She saw Richard smiling at her.

"Catherine, you have just said 'thank you' to a tree."

"It heard us swearing our love for each other," she said as if it was an ordinary thing to do.

"Catherine, it is a tree."

"You heard it rustle its leaves, didn't you?" Catherine asked him.

"I heard the wind blow the leaves," he replied.

"No, the wind did not. Richard, this is the 'Hope Tree'. I have always come here and told it all of my problems ever since I could walk up the Hill. I came here on the Sunday when you said you would meet me in the park. When you never showed up, I came back here and asked it to find you, and it did."

"Catherine, it is a tree."

"Richard, it's all right if you do not believe in its power. I will believe it for the both of us. At least it now knows that we love each other, that's all that counts. Now give me one more kiss than we'll get back to the party."

As soon as they went back to the big terrace, Alvin and Beverly came up to them with two other people.

"Richard, this is Martin and Eva Whyte. Rebecca's parents," Alvin said.

"And Robert's," Catherine said. Beverly saw the change in her daughter and she didn't like it, she made a mental note, to get the truth out of Catherine; she had never seen her acting so nastily.

Richard took Mr Whyte's hand and nodded to Mrs Whyte.

"Pleased to meet you, Mrs Whyte," Richard said.

"And I you," Mrs Whyte replied.

"Catherine, we saw your show and we thought it was wonderful," Mr Whyte said.

"Thank you but there are other people in the show so it is not just mine, oh look Richard, there's Andrew, I want you to meet him," Catherine said, not in the least bit bothered if she sounded abrupt to the Whyte's. Catherine pulled Richard away from them and started to walk over to a thin, tall man. Beverly followed them and when they were out of hearing distance to everyone, she said to Catherine.

"Catherine, I want to know what is going on. I have never seen you being so rude to people."

"Mom, I would tell you if I could but I'll promise you I will stop being rude to people all right."

"All right, darling." She kissed Catherine on the cheek then went back to Alvin and the Whyte's.

Catherine and Richard were talking to Andrew, who was a lifelong friend of hers when Robert Whyte passed by them. Richard had never seen Catherine lose her temper but he knew that if he didn't do something now. He was going to see her lose it. She was ready to explode. Andrew shook Richard's hand and left them to see someone else. Richard took hold of Catherine's shoulders and slowly walked her into a corner. He knew Catherine was watching every move Robert was making and she was ready for anything that he might try, she was so tensed up.

If he made a move that looked as if it was a threat towards Richard, she would be ready to really hurt him. She was like a snake just waiting to uncoil and strike. Richard backed Catherine into the corner so that if she had to move, she would have to push him out of the way. The corner was a dark one, and Richard kissed her tenderly as his hand brushed over her breast. He heard her sigh as he felt her mouth open and her tongue searching for his, her arms went around his neck and he felt her start to relax, he brought his lips away from hers.

"Are you all right now?" he whispered into her ear.

"What?" she spoke.

"Catherine, forget about him and let's enjoy ourselves."

"All right, kiss me again then."

Richard moved his mouth closer to Catherine's but stopped just before their lips touched, then he pulled her out of the corner and onto the dance floor where they danced the rest of the night.

"What time is it, Richard?"

"Twenty past one," he spoke.

"Okay, come on, let's go home now." They said goodbye to her parents and then left the hall.

As soon as they were out of the grounds of the hall, Richard exhaled loudly.

"What's wrong?" Catherine said looking at him.

"Catherine, if I ever hurt you in anyway by accident, please remind me of tonight."

"Why?" she asked him, wondering what he was talking about.

"Catherine, you were wanting him to do something, to say something, anything so you could start with him."

Catherine smiled her innocent smile.

"No." Catherine was walking backwards as she was talking to him, she was also glad to be out of the hall.

"Richard, no matter what you do to me, I would never harm you." she started to exaggerate her hips going side to side when she saw Richard looking at her.

"But I know what I'm going to do to you when we get home." She puckered her lips and blew him a kiss. It had been a beautiful night, a warm breeze blew and the sky was full of stars. So when it started to rain heavy, they were caught unawares and they were soaking right through in no time at all. When they turned the next bend in the road it stopped raining again but the amount of rain that had come down in that cloud burst had water running down the road.

"We look like a pair of drowned rats," Catherine said. She put her arms around his neck and kissed him. They stayed like that until they heard a car coming around the bend. Mrs Whyte waved to them and they saw Robert sneering at them in the back. The car skidded and went through the hedgerow. Richard and Catherine ran to the hole in the hedge and saw that the car had slid onto its side.

"Catherine, run back to the hall and phone the Emergency Services." Richard shouted at her. Catherine ran back through the hole in the hedge and up to the Hall.

Richard ran to the car and climbed up onto the side of it. He pulled open the first door he came to. He reached in and grabbed Robert Whyte pulling him out of his seat and up onto the side. Richard lowered him to the ground. He could see that Robert was unsteady on his legs as he leant against the car instead of getting away from it. Richard lay down and looked inside the car. Rebecca wasn't in it.

She must have stayed at the party, he thought. He closed the door, then pulled open the front passenger door. Mrs Whyte was trying to unfasten her seatbelt but she was finding it hard to do. Richard lay down again and took hold of the buckle then pulled it. It flicked open and he grabbed Mrs Whyte, pulling her up out of the car then lowing her down the outside. Robert was still standing there.

"Robert get your mother, then get her away from here, okay?" Richard shouted loudly at him.

Richard could hear the Emergency Vehicles coming up the Hill and he could see their flashing lights although he wasn't looking at them, he was looking at Mr Whyte, who wasn't moving. He lay flat as he could and reached down but he still couldn't grab him. He felt heat at his feet. He looked at them and saw that his feet were in a flame.

"Christ," he said as he pulled his feet out of the flames. He was thinking of his new boots and what Beverly would say to him. He lowered himself into the car careful not to stand on Mr Whyte. He started to loosen the seatbelt and he lifted Mr Whyte up and lay him on the side of the car until he climbed back out. Then he got off the car side and pulled Mr Whyte off. He was turning around ready to run when he saw Catherine running through the hole in the hedge again, followed by a fireman. He shouted at her to stay away. He could see she was shouting back at him but he couldn't hear what she was shouting, he could see the look of terror on her face. His legs felt as if they were still in the flames. He looked down at them and saw that he was on fire. He tried to look back at Catherine to smile at her, so she would know he was all right but something hit his back and he saw the darkness covering him. He thought that the fire must have gone out, then he was on his knees, still holding Mr Whyte. He looked at Catherine; he saw her screaming at him.

Beverly phoned Cora and she and Tom caught the first flight out of New York. They arrived at the hospital four hours later. Catherine was still at Richard's bedside. Alvin and Beverly had been to see how the Whyte's were, Robert and his mother were in shock, Mr Whyte would be okay and all he needed was rest to get over the trauma. Beverly had her arm around Catherine, trying to comfort her when Cora and Tom came through the doors.

"The doctors said that they would have to wait until he wakes up to see what damage the blast did to him," Alvin told them when they sat down.

"It was a very brave thing he did, he—" Alvin stopped talking when Catherine stood up.

"How can you say that, Dad, how can you say that, he almost got killed, and why, why…why, to save that, that." Catherine looked out through the small window and saw Robert Whyte standing against the wall opposite their room. She ran out to him, she started to pound her fists on his chest, not hard, not soft, just pounding as if she was knocking on an old, old door.

"I hate you; I hate you, I, Hate, You," she was shouting at him; tears were streaming down her face.

"I hate you." She cried. They had followed her out of the room. Beverly and Alvin were shocked at her actions. Tom and Cora took her back to sit outside of the room. Catherine was now near to breaking down completely.

"I hate them, hate them," she was saying as she sat down.

"Catherine, what would you have had Richard do, just let them die in the car, because that is what would have happened," Alvin said.

"YES, YES, YES, I would have let them die, yes, yes, yes." Catherine sobbed.

Alvin and Beverly were shocked at the ferociousness in her voice.

"Why?" Alvin asked her.

"Why, why, why, I, I." Catherine realised that she shouldn't be shouting at her parents so she stopped, and just cried again. Alvin and Beverly looked at Tom and Cora.

"What is going on here?" Beverly asked them.

"Tell them, Cora. It's the only why they will understand why Catherine is like this," Tom said.

Cora squeezed Catherine into her and kissed the side of her head.

"Catherine, I'm going to tell them, okay?" Cora whispered to her.

"That thing along there, Robert Whyte with four or five of his friends, met Richard in the park the other week, they punched and kicked him so much, that me and Catherine had to take him to hospital, you can still see some of the foot marks in his skin they made—"

"Why were we not told of this?" Beverly interrupted her.

"Because Richard made me and Catherine promise to say nothing to anyone. But that wasn't all of it, As they were kicking him, they were telling him to get back in the drain where he came from and to never think that he is the same as them." Cora finished and saw Beverly put her hand to her mouth in shock.

They saw a nurse run into Richard's room. Catherine was there before anyone thought of going. When they did get in, they saw Catherine sitting down holding his hand and crying. The nurse said they would have to change a machine because it was not working properly and there was no cause for alarm.

Catherine stayed with him all night, telling him what she wanted in life, how many children she wanted and how they were going to grow old together.

She must have fell asleep sitting in the chair holding his hand because when she felt the doctors hand on her head she looked up and the sun was shining through the windows.

"Do you want me to go out of the room, doctor?" she asked, looking around for him. There was no one there. She looked at Richard and saw him smiling at her.

"Hello, Catherine."

"Oh, Richard," she said, then smacked the button on the wall.

"He's awake," she shouted.

While the doctors examined him, Catherine phoned her mom and dad then she phoned Cora. She told them she would phone them back as soon as she got some news off the doctors. She was standing outside when the doctor came out of Richard's room.

"He seems to be just fine."

Catherine could feel the tears building up, she was so happy. She went into his room as a nurse was busy tucking the sheet around him, he smiled at her, Catherine waited until the nurse, who was blushing left the room.

"Richard, please do not do anything like that again."

"I only smiled at her," he spoke.

"I didn't mean that, I meant put your life at risk," Catherine replied sharply.

"I know what you meant, Catherine; I was trying to make a joke of it." It was then that he saw how much this had affected her emotionally. She broke down on the chair crying her eyes out, sobbing harder and harder.

"Catherine, Catherine, come here, please. I'm sorry, come here."

Catherine slowly got up out of the chair and went over to his bed.

"I will never do anything like that again, now give me a kiss."

Catherine put her lips to his. She could feel her happiness tears falling down her cheeks as she kissed his lips. They talked with each other for over an hour, Catherine telling him that everyone was all right and about her parents knowing what Robert did to him and how they got to know. Richard smiled at his girl with pride all over his face. Catherine phoned Cora and asked her if she would bring some clothes for Richard to wear. Tom shouted from behind Cora that he would get them right now and they would be at the hospital within the hour. Catherine was sitting on his bed and was laughing as Cora and Tom walked into the room.

"I'll bet that's a first for you, babe," Cora said.

"What's a first for me?"

"Richard in bed and there's a sheet between you and him, and you with ALL your clothes on."

They all laughed but stopped when Richard tried to get out of bed and had to grab hold of something as he was still unsteady on his feet. Tom was about to grab him but Catherine was there beside him before he could. Cora saw in Catherine's eyes something she had never seen before. She looked at Tom to see if he had seen it as well. She knew he had when he smiled at her. What Cora and Tom saw was just how much Catherine loved Richard. They saw that her love for him was pure. It was much more than a caring love. It was much more than a friendship love. Cora and Tom saw that the love Catherine had for Richard was an exquisite love, an exclusive love, a one love that covered everything. It was then that Cora realised what Catherine must have went through when Richard was lying there unconscious, she must have been devastated, her heart must have been ready to crumble and fall in a million pieces.

Cora and Tom went out of the room so that Richard could get dressed.

"Catherine, don't take all day please." Cora smiled at her as she closed the door.

Tom drove them to Catherine's house where Sharon and David were waiting on the steps. Sharon rushed around to Richard's side of the car and opened the door for him.

"Are you all right, Richard?" she asked. Richard smiled at her then looked at David.

"You shouldn't have come here; it's not as bad as that." He gave his mother a hug.

Sharon let David and Tom take Richard into the house. She waited for Catherine to get out of the car, then she wrapped her arms around her and whispered.

"Your mother and father have told me everything, Catherine. God, you must have been to hell and back, I'm so glad Richard has you." Sharon kissed Catherine on the cheek.

"And I'm so glad I have got, Richard," Catherine replied.

They all went into the house. Beverly telling David and Tom where to sit Richard, Alvin looking on.

"I'm all right. I can sit down and even walk myself if you two will stop fussing over me." Richard was protesting. Catherine was watching them to make sure that Richard was comfortable. She had not looked at her mother and father.

"I'll go and make the coffees," Catherine said. She went into the kitchen.

Beverly and Cora went to see what was taking her so long as Catherine had been in the kitchen for a while, much longer than it takes to make coffee. They found her sitting at the kitchen table crying. Beverly went to her.

"Catherine, Richard is all right now, please don't cry."

"Mom, I'm not crying over Richard," Catherine looked up at her mother. "Mom, I'm so sorry for shouting at you and Dad at the hospital, I did not mean it, honestly, I'm so sorry."

Beverly put her hands on Catherine's shoulders and lifted her off the seat, then she smiled at her and hugged her.

"Catherine, I'm so proud of you, how you have overcome all of this, what you have been through would drive a preacher to scream, now come on, dry your t's forget all about this." Beverly hugged her harder and Catherine 'ling and nodding her head.

went back into the lounge carrying the coffees, after drinking them and ⸜ɪng between each other Catherine saw Sharon looking at her, Sharon gave a small nod in the direction of the kitchen. Catherine stood up picking the empty cups up as well and walked to the kitchen. Sharon followed her.

"Catherine, how are you feeling?" Sharon asked.

"I'm finem Sharon, why?" Catherine replied.

"You look worn out, are you sure you're all right, is Richard all right, you would tell me if anything was wrong, wouldn't you?"

"Sharon, I'm fine and Richard is going to be all right, now you tell me why all the questions."

"David wants to take me on a cruise but I will not go if there is anything wrong here."

Catherine gave Sharon a small kiss on the cheek and whispered in her ear.

"Sharon, you go, I'll keep Richard safe and happy." When Catherine pulled away from her, she gave Sharon a wink.

"I know you will." Sharon winked back.

After dinner, Richard ask if he could go for a lay down as he was feeling a bit weak still. Catherine was walking with him to the stairs when Sharon caught up to them.

"Richard, I will be away when you come back down, so I will say good-bye now." She kissed him on the cheek and hugged him, then turning to Catherine.

"Catherine, take good care of my boy." She kissed Catherine and winked again. Catherine and Richard went up the stairs with everyone's gaze after them.

Catherine opened the bedroom door and they both went in, then she closed it, she took Richard over to the bed and lay him down slowly, then she went around to the other side and lay beside him, they kissed and promptly fell asleep.

It was dark when they both woke up and when they came down stairs and entered the lounge. Cora and Tom were sitting on the sofa talking to Alvin and Beverly.

"And what pray have you two been up to?" Cora said. They all saw how red Catherine's face went as she looked at her parents.

"We fell asleep," she answered a bit too quickly.

"Yeah, babe, for sure," Cora said.

"Cora if you do not pack it in, I'll swing for you," Catherine said trying to look mad at her friend.

"Sure, babe, if you have any strength left."

Beverly stood up and came over to them.

"Richard, your mother said she would phone you when they got back to California."

"We know you fell asleep; Cora went up to make sure you were all right," Alvin said.

Catherine glared at Cora, who was giggling.

"How are you feeling, Richard?" Alvin asked him. Richard said he was much better, all he needed was a good sleep and it seemed to have done the trick.

"He's got to be aching. He's been in the same bedroom as Catherine." Just as Catherine threw a cushion at her.

Beverly and Alvin went up to bed after saying goodnight to everyone.

"We were just going to bed. Tom has to fly to Mexico tomorrow," Cora said. Catherine and Richard were not sleepy so they decided to stay down stairs.

"Catherine, do you really want us to have a lot of children?" Richard asked.

"Ye, how do you know that?" She sat up.

"You did mention it when we were in the hospital." He had a big smile on his face.

"You, you heard everything?" she stammered.

"No, not everything but I heard you say that." He kissed her softly on the lips.

"Richard, let's practice it now." She purred, loosening the first few buttons of his shirt.

Richard stopped her before she could loosen anymore.

"Nothing I would like better," he said kissing the tip of her nose.

"But, could we go for a slow walk?" he asked.

They put their coats on and went outside, it was one of those nights when the moon has everything lit up, its silver shine is everywhere and it was still warm but with the threat of a cold breeze not far off, as they walked down the drive, Catherine had her arm inside Richard's.

"Catherine, I'm very sorry about—"

"I do not want to hear about it anymore, Richard." She cut him off.

"Let's concentrate on us, about our future, our life together, that is what I want to do Richard."

They walked slowly, not because Richard was uneasy on his feet, it was just one of those lovely smooth feeling nights that come around every now and again and you want to keep it in your memory for as long as possible, so you make it last as long as you can, and also because they were so much in love.

They walked to the end of the driveway, stopped at the entrance and Catherine cuddled into him as they had before, making sure she did not cuddle to tightly, they kissed and smiled at each other, not saying a word, just kissing and smiling, words would have spoiled it. All they wanted was to feel each other's lips and see that each other was happy.

Catherine put her head to his chest.

"Richard, I'm so in love with you."

"An…" Richard was about to say, when Catherine put her hand to his mouth.

"No, listen please, I'm so in love with you that I honestly wouldn't have wanted to live if you had left me in the hospital, I was thinking about it, and, and, I honestly wouldn't know what to do without you in my life."

Richard felt her head press into his chest and her arms tighten around his waist. He kissed the top of her head and said nothing but felt so happy that she felt this way about him. They stood at the entrance holding each other for a while then decided to walk back to the house.

Catherine made them both a cup of coffee and they sat on the sofa. She didn't quite know when they both dropped off to sleep but she woke up and moved Richard to a lay down position and went to the big chair and just watched him as he slept. She must have dozed off again because the next thing she heard was her mother in the kitchen and the smell of breakfast being cooked.

Sharon phoned Richard to say she had gotten back safely and she would phone again as soon as everything was sorted out. Richard wanted to know what 'sorted out' meant but she wouldn't say anything. When he asked Beverly and Catherine, they both said they didn't know but he had seen a glint in Catherine's eye that told him she did know but he didn't press it.

The next few days were spent just walking around the gardens, slowly, and talking. Catherine, Richard and Cora, Tom was in Mexico and wasn't due back for a few more days.

The first performance on Catherine's return was in three days' time, they were all sitting playing a checkers tournament, Alvin of course was winning.

Catherine had drove Richard to his home to pick up some books he needed, she had not wanted to go because she knew he would have his head stuck in them forever but it gave her and Cora a little time on their own to talk women things.

"I think Tom is going to ask me to marry him?" Cora said out of the blue as they walked through the greenhouses.

Catherine stopped walking and turned to her.

"How do you think that?" she asked in a hushed voice.

"Oh, just certain things he does or asks," she replied.

"Such as?" Catherine pushed her on to say more.

"Things like, getting down on his knee and asking me if I would be his wife," Core replied matter of factually.

Catherine had her mouth open; her eyes went wide as she asked, "When?"

"Well, he hasn't gotten down on his knee yet," she replied with a twisted mouth.

"But, well he could have as he was in Mexico when he phoned me and asked."

Catherine was still staring at her.

"And?" Catherine asked her.

"I said, you get your ass up here and you ask me properly."

Catherine almost buckled up with laughter at the serious of the face on Cora.

"Now I do not want you to say anything to anyone and that includes Richard, not until he asks me on one knee, okay?" Cora had her serious head on this time and Catherine knew it.

"You have my word on it," Catherine said putting her arm around Cora and kissing her on the cheek.

****

Richard was well recovered and back at the Uni.

Catherine was still filling the theatre and people were still crying.

Tom had gone down on his knee not just in front of Cora but in front of the whole restaurant that he had took Alvin, Beverley, Catherine and Richard to.

Catherine was sitting reading a few scripts that would get sent to her every now and again and Richard was reading his books, they were both in the study.

The telephone started ringing.

"Hello," Beverley answered it.

"Yes, he is here." She put the phone down and went into the study.

"Richard, it's a Mr Smithson, he wants to talk to you."

Richard went over to the phone and spoke.

"Hello."

"Can we talk, Richard?" the Texan voice said.

"It is very important."

"What, at this time, okay but you will have to come to Mr De Charger's Home."

Richard put the phone down and went back to the group.

"Mr Smithson wants to have a talk with me, so I told him I was here Alvin, I hope you don't mind?"

"We don't mind, do we, Beverly?"

"Not at all, when is he coming?"

"He's on his way now."

Alvin looked at the clock.

"Must be important, to come here at this time."

Catherine felt a knot in her stomach and it got tighter with each tick of the clock.

Cora had been about to go to bed when the phone had rung, now wild horses couldn't drag her away, her curiosity was aroused. Beverly went and made everyone a cup of coffee.

They saw the lights of the car coming down the driveway. Richard went to the door and opened it before Mr Smithson could knock.

Richard showed Mr Smithson into the lounge and introduced him to Beverly and Alvin, when they got to Cora and Catherine, Richard said, "You already know Catherine and Cora."

"Richard, could we talk in private please?"

"No Mr Smithson, I have no secrets from any of these people and I do not want to have any."

They could all see that Mr Smithson was feeling a bit agitated. He looked at all of them and spoke.

"Okay but everyone in this room must never tell anyone outside of it about what I'm going to say."

They all agreed.

"The test you did for me a few weeks ago was to see if you could find that type of virus and hunt it down and kill it dead without any loss of data in the computer."

Richard nodded.

"Well, it seems that you and the English guy were the best and fasted that we tested, and believe me, we tested people from all over the world. The country that we did the tests for want you and the Englishman to go over there and help them rid their computers of the virus that is attacking them."

Mr Smithson was looking straight at Richard and couldn't see Catherine's eyes watering up but he did see Richard's face twist a little.

"I cannot emphasise how important it is to America, Richard. You will be doing more in this six month than twenty years of American, Chinese talks will have done."

"That's putting a lot of pressure on Richard, isn't it, Mr Smithson?" Alvin said.

Mr Smithson looked at Alvin.

"Sir, the importance of this is paramount to America and China's futures." He put his hand into his pocket and pulled out a piece of paper.

"The president told me to give you this, it is his personal phone number, use it, maybe he can tell you just how important this is."

Alvin looked at everyone, one by one, then handed the piece of paper back to Mr Smithson.

"It's okay, I believe you."

"The English guy is on his way there now. It seems he couldn't wait to get out of England fast enough. We promised him that after the job is done, we would set him up in any country that he wished."

Catherine stood up and went to Richard. She took hold of his hand and squeezed it tightly. She didn't like the way he was hesitating.

"I can go with him, can't I?" She spoke.

Mr Smithson looked at her and slowly shook his head.

"I'm sorry, we do not even know where he is going but we think it is in the Tibetan Autonomous Region, in China."

Catherine's grip on Richard's hand got tighter and he could feel her shaking.

"How long will he be gone for, that's if he goes?" She asked, almost dreading the answer.

"It should not take more than six months and you must go immediately."

When Catherine heard 'six months', she put her arm around his waist.

"He is not going, sorry, now please leave. I told Sharon that I would keep him here and look after him." She looked at Richard.

"Richard, tell him you are not going. I promised Sharon, no, he is not going, Richard, tell him you are not going. Richard, please, tell him no, please."

Beverly went to her as did Cora. They both put their arms around her. She slowly moved away from Richard.

Richard wanted to hold her but was afraid to, in case she pushed him away, she knew he would have to go but at this time, she wouldn't allow her mind to think it out properly.

"In China?" Alvin said.

"Is it safe? Will he be in any danger?" Beverly asked.

"I don't care, he, is, not, going, I almost lost Richard when he ended up in hospital." Catherine broke their questions up.

"No, he will not be in any danger whatsoever."

"LISTEN TO ME. HE, IS, NOT, GOING, TELL THEM, RICHARD."

Richard went over to where Cora and Beverly had taken her.

"Catherine. Let's go outside for a minute please."

Catherine broke free from Cora's grip and ran to the door; she opened it and went outside and everyone in the house could hear her crying.

Richard followed her out, he tried to put his arm around her but she moved away saying.

"Not until you tell them you are not going."

"Catherine please, listen to me, you heard what Mr Smithson said, please, I will be doing more for America than all of the talks between the two countries have achieved in twenty years."

"Richard, tell them you are not going. I can't be without you for six months, please Richard, please, say you'll stay with me, please." She was now crying so much her eyes were swelling.

"Catherine, I have to go, you know that."

"NOOOOOOOO, you don't have to go," she screamed at him and ran back into the house, slamming the door shut and running past everyone and up the stairs.

Richard came in and followed her up the stairs, he heard her door slam shut, he tried the handle but it wouldn't budge.

"Catherine, please."

"No Richard, if you go, we will never speak to each other again," she shouted from the other side of the door.

Richard came back down the stairs and looked at Alvin for an answer.

"It's up to you, Richard, but, if it's any help to you, if it was me, I would go, even if it's just to help the Chinese. Catherine will come around to thinking straight soon and will know you had to go."

Richard looked at Beverly and saw her nod her head, he looked at Cora, who immediately turned away from him. Richard looked at Mr Smithson and spoke.

"Okay, let's go." He looked at Beverly.

"Please explain to Catherine and tell my mother."

Beverly nodded and tears started to run down her cheeks.

"Richard, thank you, this is important, the flight is in an…" – he looked at his watch – "an hours' time, C.A.137 flies to Japan first, it has a refuel then on to China, we have been given special permission for you to leave the plane when it is refuelling so that we can hand over clothes that have been pick out for you to wear for the duration of the job."

Richard left the house with Mr Smithson and they got in his car and drove away.

Cora went slowly up the stairs, she tried the door handle but it wouldn't open, she knocked gently on the door.

"Catherine, it's me, please open the door."

Cora entered the room and saw Catherine standing there shaking.

"Please Cora, tell him he can't go."

"Catherine, he has gone."

"NOOOOOOOOOOOOOOO," she screamed and ran down the stairs and to the door. She pulled it open and ran outside. The car was gone.

"O, please Richard come back, I didn't mean it, you know I will always love you, oh please Richard." She came back into the house and stood at the wall, she slides down it to the floor and started to sob.

"Catherine, let's go to the airport. We might just catch him before the plane take's off." Cora suggested.

Catherine jumped up and looked at her parents; they both nodded their heads.

Mr Smithson booked Richard in.

"Richard, you are doing the right thing. I know you must be feeling pretty low. Leaving Catherine back home." He shook Richard's hand and left.

Richard was sitting listening to a man arguing with an airport official.

"Look," the man was saying, "I'm going to Japan to see an old army buddy. I did not know I could get a plane to take me straight there, that's why I bought a ticket for China. I will have to sail back to Japan. But if I could just change it for a flight to Japan, it will save me two maybe three days extra travelling."

Richard went up to the man and the official.

"If it's okay with the airport, I could exchange my flight for his, mine stops at Japan and I'm going on to China," he spoke.

The official pressed a number on his phone and started to talk to someone, he put the phone down.

"It seems to be all right."

Richard exchanged tickets, his new flight was leaving half an hour later, so he went up the stairs to the roof and watched the plane that he was supposed to be on, take off.

Catherine and Cora arrived as the plane lifted into the air, they stood by the car and watched it until they couldn't see it anymore, on the way home Catherine never stopped crying.

"Cora, do you think he has left me? He said he would never leave me, Cora, what happens if I never see him again? I cannot imagine my life without him, oh Cora."

"Catherine, he knows you love him, and you know it as well, no way would he leave you forever. When Tom leaves me, I feel empty for a while, then I just plough into my studies on how creams and shades mix, I even go into the science part of it, just to get rid of the empty feeling."

Richard went back down stairs to the boarding area, he handed over the special papers that Mr Smithson had given him, he was shown through to the plane, he wanted to phone Catherine but thought he had better not. He'd wait until he was in China. He boarded the plane and it took off. He looked out of the window and saw a small car leaving the airport.

****

Chapter Sixteen

It was a long flight and when it finally landed in China, he was glad to get off. He went to the officials and showed them the papers he had been given. He didn't know what was on them as they were all in Chinese but whatever they said it must have been good because they never stopped running around and phoning people, some very official man came up to him and held out his hand. In perfect English, he said, "Sir, it is a great pleasure to have you here at our humble airport but the people who deal with your luggage are having difficulty in finding it." The embarrassment on his face because his airport had lost his luggage was very evident.

"That's okay, I never brought any," Richard told him.

"Ah, that explains a lot." Then the official turned around and started talking in Chinese at the people behind him and all of the serious looking Chinese men started smiling.

"I'm sorry; they thought they had lost your luggage."

"Yes, it happens all over the world," Richard answered.

Richard watched as a small man made his way through the crowd. He didn't know why he noticed him at first, then he realised that people were moving out of his way and he was not pushing through, he was dressed just as he had imagined the Chinese to dress ever since he had seen 'Enter the Dragon'. He even had a long Ponytail and a small round bellhop hat.

The man stopped right in front of him. He bowed.

"Mr Wichard Buckman, I am Hung Sen and I to take you hotel to Mr Mike."

Richard could see that Mr Hung Sen was sweating.

"You here so early, Mr Buckman."

Richard smiled at him; all of the airport officials had gone.

"Come, the sooner we get to Hotel, the sooner we can leave city of sweat and dirt."

Richard followed Mr Hung Sen out of the airport.

When they stepped outside of the air-conditioned airport, Richard's shirt immediately stuck to his body and the sweat started to run down his face, he was glad to get to the Hotel and back into air-conditioned rooms. Mr Hung Sen went to the lift and pressed for the sixth floor, they got out of the lift and Mr Hung Sen knocked on a door.

"Mr Mike, Mr Wichard is here," he spoke.

The door opened and out stepped a tall painfully thin young man, who already had his hand out stretched to shake.

"Hi, Yank," he said with a smile that went right across his face.

"Hello, English." Richard took the hand and they both shook as if they were old friends.

"Ha," Hung Sen said as they all went into the room but before any of them could sit down Mr Hung Sen said.

"Mr Mike is Mr English and Mr Wichard is Mr Yank." He was nodding and laughing.

"Perhaps we go now?" Mr Hung Sen asked.

"At this time?" they both said.

"Ah, you no not what city is like when opens in day time, we go now, please, I dislike city and you like my Old Boiler."

Richard and Mike looked at each other, they were both wondering what he had said.

"Old Boiler?" Mike asked.

"Yes, Old Boiler she good truck."

"Well, I have nothing to pack so I'm ready to leave," Richard said.

"And I ain't unpacked, so yeah, let's go," Mike said while lifting his suitcase up.

The three of them went down in the lift. Mr Hung Sen was smiling.

"Why are you smiling Mr Hung Sen?" Mike asked.

"Mr Mike is Mr English and Mr Wichard is Mr Yank. Mr Hung Sen will be Mr Chinese."

He started laughing loud. It was a very contagious laugh and soon the three of them were laughing.

They were still laughing when they arrived at the parking area below the Hotel and they saw what the Old Boiler was.

"It's an old Army wagon," Richard said.

"Yes, taken from Korea by my father and handed to me, it has many comforts."

Mr Hung Sen opened the back flaps and Mike and Richard stared in disbelief at the three bunks and easy chairs with lots of cupboards.

"It's a bloody home from home," Mike said. Richard just nodded with his mouth wide open.

"You like Mr English, Mr Yank?" Mr Hung Sen's smile was even wider at their reaction.

"Very bloody much Mr Chinese, very bloody much," Mike said jumping up and sitting in a chair.

"You make home, yes?"

"Very bloody much yes Mr Chinese."

Richard jumped up and sat in a chair.

"Mr Chinese, this is superb," he spoke.

"You have Coca Cola in that." Mr Hung Sen said pointing to a cupboard.

"You drink and sleep, I drive, okay?"

Mr Chinese started the engine and they left the city without hearing about the plane crash.

****

Cora was up early as she had to pick Tom up at the airport, he had been back in Mexico but was finished and he was coming back to Cora's house, so she had said she would pick him up as she was at Catherine's. Cora had told Tom everything that had happened and as she waited for him in the arrivals, he came out and they hugged.

"Quick, get to the car and switch the radio on," Tom said urgently.

They walked fast to the car and Cora put the radio on straight away as the announcer was saying about a plane crashing into the hillside at Japan airport.

"Oh God no," Cora cried. She knew no one would be listening or watching the news reports in Catherine's house as they very rarely did, so she drove straight there, her tears making it hard to see. She used her own key to open the door and went to the television, she turned it on and saw the wreckage of the airplane scattered across the hillside.

"I'll go up and wake Alvin," Tom said.

"No, not yet, let's make sure what flight it was, it might not be Richard's."

They sat and watched the reports flashing across the screen. Cora gave out a sharp cry when the flight number was shown as CA 137.

"Right, I have to wake Alvin and Beverly now." He went up the stairs two at a time, he tapped lightly on their bedroom door and when Alvin opened it, he knew something must be wrong as Tom put a finger to his lips and indicated for him to wake Beverly and to come down stairs.

Beverly saw Cora crying; she couldn't see the television but could hear the announcer talking.

Her hand went to her mouth to stop her from crying out when she heard there had been a plane crash, then the flight number. Alvin wrapped his arms around her just before she felt her legs giving way. Alvin put Beverly on the sofa. Cora rushed to get a glass of water; she was shaking so much that a lot of it was spilling over the edge.

"How are we going to tell Catherine?" Beverly asked them all.

"Tell Catherine what?" Catherine said coming down the stairs.

Tom edged his way to the television and turned the sound down and blocked her view.

Catherine looked at him, then down at where the television was, then she looked back up at him and without her saying anything, he moved out of the way, turning the sound back up.

Catherine watched as it showed the wreckage of the plane. She read the words flashing across the bottom of the screen. She turned to her mother and father. It was the first time she had ever seen her mother crying and she could see that her father was holding back his tears as well; she looked at Cora. Cora, her best friend in the whole world was crying. She looked back at Tom, he and her were the only ones who were not crying.

"Why are you looking at me like that, Tom?"

She could see that the question made him feel uneasy; he looked at Cora for a split second then back to Catherine.

"Why are you looking at me like that?" she said again.

He didn't answer her, he just kept looking at her.

She could see the blackness coming towards her. She felt Tom's arms around her. She wanted to tell him to leave her alone but no words came out of her mouth. She felt Tom lift her up. She wanted to tell him to put her down but still nothing would come out of her mouth. She felt the softness of the sofa. Then the blackness covered her and she closed her eyes.

When Catherine opened her eyes again, she was back in her bed.

Thank goodness it was only a dream, she thought as she looked around the room.

Cora was sitting in her chair next to the bed, still crying, her mother was in another chair with bright red eyes as if she had been crying.

Mother never cries, she thought.

"Cora, what's wrong, babes? Why are you crying? I've never known you to cry like this," Catherine asked.

Cora got out of the chair and went over to her. Cora went to the side of the bed then lay down beside her and put her arm around Catherine and snuggled into her, crying more and more.

"Oh Catherine, Catherine, why is all of this happening to you, you don't deserve any of it, all you have done is fall in love," Cora said between sobs.

"Where's Dad?" Catherine said looking at her mother.

"He's flying to California with Tom to see Sharon."

"Why?" Catherine asked.

Beverly started to shake as she fumbled for her tissues.

"To, to, to, tell Sharon about Richard." Beverly started crying again.

"Richard, Richard, is he back, is he back?" Catherine tried to sit up but Cora pressed down on her shoulders so she couldn't get up.

"Catherine," Cora whispered in her ear.

"Richard was on the plane that crashed in Japan."

"No, he wasn't," Catherine replied.

They stayed like that for about two hours. Catherine and Cora laying on the bed and Beverly in the chair. Catherine moved sideways and slipped out from under Cora's arm. She sat on the edge of the bed.

"I'm hungry, let's go and have something to eat," Catherine said.

As Beverly and Cora came down the stairs, they could hear Catherine humming a tune in the kitchen. Catherine saw them standing in the doorway.

"Just go into the lounge, I'll bring them through. I'm not useless you know." Catherine gave them both her usual smile.

"Catherine, you do know what has happened, don't you?" Cora asked.

Catherine was still smiling as she put the coffee in the cups then looked at them.

"I'm not stupid you know, of course I know what's happened." She handed Beverly and Cora their cups.

"Let's go into the lounge to drink them," Catherine said walking past them in the doorway.

When they were all sitting down, Beverly said, "Catherine tells us what you think has happened?"

"Right, I can see that you are not going to give me any peace, are you?"

They both shook their heads.

"All right, Richard was booked to fly to China, the plane that has crashed is the one that he was on, and you all think that he has died, right?" She stopped.

They both nodded.

"Well, I know that he has not died. Now, and I mean this. I do not want to hear another word about this plane crash or your thoughts about Richard being dead. I know he is not and I will not have anyone saying he is, so from this very minute, not, another, word, about it."

Beverly and Cora were nodding their heads, both unsure of what to do or say.

Catherine stood up.

"Now, what would you like to eat?" she asked them.

While Catherine was in the kitchen, Beverly telephoned Alvin and told him what Catherine had just said.

"Okay, darling, we're on our way back home now. Sharon took it very badly but David is doing a good job in looking after her and she has promised to keep in touch with us."

Beverly and Cora were waiting for Alvin and Tom to get back. They had phoned to say they had landed and were waiting for their car to arrive. Cora saw the car coming down the driveway; they both went to the door.

"Please Alvin do not mention the crash, she has totally put it out of her mind and she wants us to as well."

Alvin and Tom said that they wouldn't say a word.

Cora whispered to Tom, "She knows about the plane crashing, and she knows Richard was on it but she refuses to believe that he is dead and she won't have it any other way, Tom I'm getting really worried about her."

Tom kissed Cora.

"I have missed you, darling," he spoke.

"Tom, listen to me please, I'm really frightened for Catherine, I said to her, I think we should phone Jonathon Kranz to tell him we will not be at the theatre tonight. She almost bit my head off. Tom, honest, I'm really, really frightened for her."

"Let's go in and see her," he replied, following Beverly and Alvin into the house.

Catherine had been in the shower and was coming down the stairs when she saw her father and Tom.

As she came down the stairs, she said, "Now I know what you are going to say, you're going to say, Catherine, how are you? Well, Dad, I'm fine and no, I do not believe Richard is dead, so that's it, now let's just get on with our lives, okay? I want no more of it."

She went to her father and kissed him on the cheek as she did with Tom.

Alvin had tried his best to contact Mr Smithson, he had used up a lot of favours off people but not one person knew of him. Mr Smithson had seemingly vanished off the face of the planet.

Sharon phoned to ask how Catherine was. Beverly told her that she refuses to acknowledge his death. In fact, she has banned everyone who comes in contact with her to even mention Richard.

Sharon asks if she should fly there for the reopening of the show but Beverly said it might not be a good idea. Catherine was coping very well with the way she has put things into her life and seeing Sharon might just upset it, and they don't know how she will react. Sharon agreed.

The show reopened to great fanfare, not by the theatre but by the media, who knew nothing of what had happened to Catherine. She went onto the stage and was better than ever. She put her own feelings into her part and had the whole place in tears, critics who had seen the show ten times bawled their eyes out and the reviews of it the following day were all in praise of her.

She even had some of the cast in tears as she brought all of her feelings out. Cora was devastated night after night.

"Catherine, doll. Please ease up on the ending; it's doing nothing for my complexion, all of these tears," Cora would say after every performance. Catherine would laugh and hug her.

"Is it still as good as our first night?" she would ask her.

Cora could only nod, if she tried to talk, she would cry and Catherine would know she would be thinking of Richard, so she just nodded her head.

Two months later and Catherine was still filling the theatre to full capacity. Cora came into the dressing room; she had been to see about one of the costumes that had a slight rip in it and she found Catherine being sick.

"Bit late for stage fright, Catherine," she said hanging the dress up, she froze when she heard Catherine say.

"It's Richard; he's doing this to me."

Cora started to shake, her knees went weak and she dropped the dress to grab a chair.

"I'll make him pay when I get my hands on him again," Catherine continued.

Cora felt a chill go down her back, this was the first time she had mentioned Richard since the plane crash.

"Wha…wha…what do you mean Richard's doing this? Making you sick you mean?" Cora was looking around the room; she had heard so many stories of ghosts in theatres.

Catherine was standing with her hands on her hips, smiling, she knew what Cora was looking for and the thought made her smile even more.

"I've missed two periods now," Catherine stated.

"YESSSSSSSSSSSm," Cora shouted out as loud as she could. She went to Catherine and gave her the biggest hug that she could.

"Why didn't you say something to me, babes, ohhhhhh I'm so happy for you." Cora planted a soft kiss on Catherine's lips.

"There are things that I had to be sure of before telling anyone. But now I'm sure, so you're the first to know, apart from me of course."

Catherine started laughing.

"You should have seen your face when I said Richard was making me sick."

Although Catherine was happy, Cora could still see a touch of sadness in her eyes.

"Catherine, you can't hide much from me, so come on, tell me what is wrong?"

"It's Richard, suppose he believed me when I said I never wanted to see him again, and he keeps away from me, never comes back to me?"

Cora could see that Catherine was getting more and more upset.

"And, and, and he does not know about our baby and how much I really love him. Cora, honestly, I did not mean any of it that I said to him, he must know that, mustn't he?"

Catherine's distress was getting at Cora as well and she could feel her hurt, the stabbing pains Catherine must be getting in her heart.

Cora decided that now would be the best time to get this over with, before all of this anguish could harm Catherine or the baby. Cora held Catherine at arm's length.

"Catherine, Richard is not coming back. He really did die in that plane crash and you know that, you have to see that, Catherine, you're beginning to frighten me with all of this, please don't, you're far too precious to me, my babe."

"He is coming back, Cora."

Cora put her arms on Catherine's shoulders and looked her straight in the eyes.

"Catherine. Richard died in that plane crash, look, you are going to have his baby, you must accept it babes, what are you going to tell him, her, when 'it' asks where is Daddy? What will you say, eh? Catherine please, please accept it, for the baby's sake."

Catherine went and sat down.

"Cora, I know you and everyone who knows me thinks I might be going mad but please listen to me. I can't accept it; I will never accept it. I'm not going mad. Do you think that Sharon struggled most of her life to bring him up, just to be wiped away in a flash? When you look at Sharon, can you not see the happiness he brought into her life and how much both me and Sharon love him? Sharon has David now to love but who have I got? If I believed he was dead, do you honestly think I would be alive? Cora I would have died the very moment he would have. I have to believe that he is alive, because the minute my heart stops believing is when my heart stops beating, when I think it will be safe to admit it, then I will."

Cora knew what Catherine was saying was the truth because she had seen her love for Richard when they were in the hospital, she had seen a love in both of their eyes that was beyond anything she had seen before.

"All right babes, Richard is alive and I'll damn anyone who says different." Cora pulled Catherine up from the chair and wrapped her arms around her shoulders and hugged her.

"Now," Cora said, breaking away from her, "what are you going to call the little papoose, when it makes an appearance?"

Catherine put her finger to her chin and pretended to think about it.

"Babes, I know you far too well for that, you will have its name picked and the school it will be attending, so, come on, out with it."

They both laughed.

"Well, I know it is going to be a girl, so, she is going to be called Sharon. I know Richard will like that."

"How do you know it's going to be a girl?"

"I can feel it here," Catherine said, putting her hand on her heart.

Cora turned away from her and pretended to be busy tiding the make-up desk.

"You know, Catherine, I sometime think of you when I'm in bed at night, well, not sometimes but most of the times, well when Tom is away I should say, and I wonder why all of this is happening to you. I ask myself the same question over and over, why you? You have to be one of the gentlest people in the world and yet you have gone through so much pain and tears, it is not right and I end up crying for you."

"Cora, when Richard comes back, everything will be just fine again, you'll see."

"I hope so, Catherine."

They both got on with what they were doing.

"Cora, have you given any more thought to the movie offer?"

"Well, the show ends next week and I was going to have a talk about it with you but since you have brought it up, I think you should do it."

Catherine smiled and spoke.

"Okay, let's."

By the night of the last show, the theatre people had begged Catherine to stay but she remembered what their attitude to Jonathon had been and how they tried to force him to do what they wanted, so Catherine politely refused all of their demands and pleas to stay.

Crowds of people ringed the theatre. Police had put barriers up to stop the rush of people and making sure no one was hurt by being squashed or trampled, the theatre people had warned the police that with it being the last show, there might be a lot of publics around, they never expected to be so many. Television and radio crews with their mobile transmitters from every part of the country, one crew even came from Japan and they all glimmered to see the leading lady.

When Catherine and Cora came from the special car the theatre had put on for them. They were shocked at the response they got when Catherine waved to everyone. There was a sudden surge forward and she had to be rushed into the theatre by Cora.

"Babe, that was scary," Cora said getting her breathing back to normal.

When the final curtain had fallen and everyone had said their goodbyes, Jonathon came into their dressing room.

"Catherine, Cora, it has been the highlight of my career to work with such beauty. I promise you it will not end here with either of you. Milton Ebbstein has told me that you have decided to work with him, that is good." He was nodding his head in approval. "Cora, you look after Catherine, because there will be people who will try to take advantage of her, and you. And Catherine, take care of Cora, I have a feeling that together, you two can conquer the world and so with that said, I wish you all the best for the future." He went to each of them and kissed them on the forehead, shook their hands and left the room. As he went out, Beverly, Alvin and Tom entered.

They kissed and hugged for a few minutes then Cora said, "Right, I want you all to sit down because Catherine has something to tell you." She looked at Catherine, then at her stomach.

"Don't you, Catherine?"

A smile came to Catherine's mouth.

"Yes, I do, although I wasn't going to say anything until later, but, as usual Cora wants it out now because she will not be able to keep her mouth closed for too long."

Cora looked at her best friend and fell in love with her all over again.

They all saw how nervous Catherine was becoming. They saw her twitching her fingers and wiping pretend sweat off them. They she looked at her mother and father.

"Right, well, erm, erm, okay, here goes. As you know I have never believed for one minute that Richard has gone, well, well, well, God, I don't know how to say this." She looked at Cora and she nodded her head, then she looked at her mother with a plea in her eyes.

"You see, Richard will never leave me, even if he doesn't come back to me. God this is hard, Mother, how did you tell Dad you were pregnant?"

When the shock of her announcement finally came to them, Tom was up out of his seat and hugging her. Beverly was sitting motionless and Alvin just had a huge grin on his face.

"I think we should celebrate and go to a restaurant?" Alvin said.

"We will never find a restaurant with a table at this time of night," Beverly replied.

"I know that Beverly but our daughter is going to make me a grandpa and you a grandma, so we have to at least try, I'll slip the concierge a few dollars," Alvin insisted.

When they arrived at Tiny's Restaurant, it was just as Beverley had said. The concierge was full of apologies but there just was no tables vacant. Everyone else had stayed in the Taxi. Alvin asks to see the owner of the Restaurant. The owner came out and was also apologising to Alvin.

"Mr De Charger, I'm so sorry but we have no tables." He was saying when Catherine came out of the Taxi. The owner saw her, then he looked at Alvin.

"I knew I had seen her before, I just knew it, Alvin, Miss Johnson is your daughter Catherine, am I right?"

"Yes. You are right and if you don't find a table, I will never come back here again," Alvin said his usual response.

The owner knew Alvin was joking as he had said it many times, and when he could not get Alvin a table, he had still came back. The owner walked over to Catherine.

"Miss Johnson, please, would you and your party, including your father," he said, looking down his nose at Alvin but with a friendly glint in his eyes, "please follow me to my private room to await a table?"

Beverly looked at Alvin, who was chuckling, he knew now that his daughter was famous, because Tiny would not allow the President of the United States into his restaurant if it were full.

****

Richard, Mike and Hung Sen travelled for six days and nights to get to their destination. Although it was a rough ride for the two westerners, the inside of the truck made it just that little bit more comfortable as Hung Sen had put two bunk beds at the top, an oven at one side and a small two-seater sofa at the other which when folded up and tied to the side made enough room for the fold down table and three chairs. Hung Sen did everything for his two western friends. It had not taken Hung Sen long to find out how the westerners like things and, although he had never met people from another country, he began to notice that most times they liked to laugh, which made Hung Sen like them better each day. At first, when he had been given the task of getting them and working with them, he had been nervous but as the days and nights came and went, he was beginning to be fond of his two westerners. One night, Mike said he would do the washing up after they had ate their meal and proceeded to do just that, both Richard and Mike noticed that Hung Sen went quiet and stayed quiet the rest of the night, which was pretty remarkable as he usually never stopped talking. They knew something was wrong and asked him what it was but he would not say. They tried and tried to get him to tell them but he just sat at their campfire and said nothing but his hurt look and the fact they had not seen his shining white teeth as he smiled was getting to them and Richard finally decided to say.

"Okay, if you do not tell Mike and me what's wrong, we are not moving from this spot unless it is to go back to the city?"

After five minutes of walking away then turning and walking back to them then away again, Hung Sen finally said, "It's Mr English, he no like my cleaning."

Mike was as surprised as Richard.

"What are you talking about Mr Chinese? I never said I did not like your cleaning."

Then Hung Sen started talking really fast in Chinese and waving his arms about and pointing at this and that. Neither Richard nor Mike had a clue of what he was talking about but his high-pitched squeaky voice told them that he was very agitated. Richard went to him and put his hands onto Hung Sen's shoulders and looked him straight in the eyes.

"Mr Chinese. Please, talk slowly and tell us what you mean okay." Richard was nodding his head.

Richard could feel Hung Sen slowly calm down.

"Now Mr Chinese, in English, tell us what is wrong."

Hung Sen showed them the whites of his eyes just as a puppy dog does when it needs attention.

"Mr English not like my cleaning."

"I never said no such thing, Mr Chinese," Mike shouted but not too loud as he did not want to start Hung Sen off again.

Hung Sen started to point at Mike.

"You said you do cleaning, that mean Hung Sen no clean nice. You no like Hung Sen cleaning."

It now looked as if Hung Sen was about to break down and cry.

"All I meant was, you do too much for us, I was going to do the cleaning just to take some of the load off you, that's all, I never said you couldn't clean." Mike was starting to wave his hands about as Hung Sen had done.

Richard didn't know if Mike was doing it deliberately or not and it was hard for him not to laugh. After a lot more arm waving and shouting, it was agreed that Hung Sen would do everything as he was told to do and the two westerners would just let him do it without any help off them. Hung Sen walked away with his chest sticking out and a look of triumph on his face, and his teeth shining in the bright moonlight.

Lying in their bunks one night, Mike said, "Are you married to that girl of yours yet, Yank?"

Richard waited a while before answering, he wished he was but the way Catherine told him to go made it seem so impossible at this time.

"No, we sort of broke up just before I came here." He felt an ache in his heart; he had tried to keep all thoughts of Catherine out of his mind so that he wouldn't feel sick all of the time.

Mike had not known Richard for too long but he could sense his sadness so he never said any more about her.

The following morning, Hung Sen was in a very happy mood and was singing as he made their breakfasts.

"The deadwood stages is a coming over the hills, oh the deadwood stage is a coming over the hills—"

"Whoa Mr Chinese, please stop, you are hurting my ears," Mike shouted above Hung Sen's voice.

"You no like Dowis Day?" Hung Sen asked.

"How can you sing that perfectly, yet you can't say her name?" Richard asked.

Hung Sen thought for a moment.

"Dowis Day is her name, yes?" he spoke.

"No, Mr Chinese, it is DoRis Day," Mike said.

"Yes Dowis Day, is what I said."

"DoRRRRis, you are saying DoWWWWWis."

"Ahhhh, Doris Day, yes?"

"Yes," Richard and Mike said together.

"Doris Day, Doris Day, Doris Day." He kept repeating until he sat down with them to eat.

Richard and Mike kept looking at the huge mountain in front of them as they put their equipment back onto the wagon and they both wondered if they would have to go around it or not.

"No, we go right through it." Hung Sen had told them as he started the engine up.

"Hospital at other side. We get there today." His smile went all the way across his face.

"Is there a tunnel through its Mr Chinese?" Mike asked him as they got closer.

"Tunnel, no. Road, yes."

"Where is the road?" Richard asked when they were almost at the side of the mountain.

"There, in front of us." Hung Sen motioned.

"Road was built for horses; lucky Chinese horses were big." Just then, Hung Sen did a quick left turn and before Richard or Mike could blink, they had the mountain on both sides of them, it was so tight that they could not put their head out of the window to look up.

After half an hour looking at the shear sides in front of them.

"Erm Mr Chinese, what happens if a car is coming the other way?"

"Car smaller than wagon, it moves backwards."

"And if a big wagon is coming the other way?" Richard asked.

"Bigger than us, we move backwards." Hung Sen started laughing.

After two hours going through the mountain, Mike was getting bored with looking out of the window and seeing mountain.

"Mr Chinese, can we stop and have a cup of your beautiful tea, I'm parched?"

"We stop five minutes."

Hung Sen stopped the wagon but Richard and Mike both knew the doors wouldn't be able to open. Hung Sen pulled a catch on the roof of the cab and pushed a small door up.

"We get out this way," he said as he climbed up and out of the cab.

They were sitting outside at the back of the wagon, it was a little bit cold as no sunlight was shining down, it made a nice change than to be dripping in sweat.

"Who made this?" Richard asked.

"God made the way through the mountains; Mao made the road." Hung Sen gave a little laugh.

Then he stood up and looked at the way they had come.

"There are many of these through the mountains of this glorious land, when I first come here, I was frightened, too much open space but now, I dread when I have to go to city."

"So, you were born in the city?" Richard asked.

"Yes, city far, far away, we were taking out of city and told to work on farm, father went to fight Americans in Korea, came back with wagon."

"Is your mother and father still alive?" Mike asked.

"Yes, you meet them one day, no, day one."

They had never asked Hung Sen his age but he looked about sixty years old and yet his fitness and stamina were that of a much younger man.

"We go now, okay?"

They all climbed back on top of the wagon then lowered themselves into the cab again.

"Mr Chinese, you have one good American wagon here," Mike said.

Hung Sen smiled his huge smile.

"I thank you, Mr English." He started the engine up again.

Another four hours saw Hung Sen turn a quick right and there in front of them was a glass building, to Richard and Mike it seemed to have hundreds of windows. Mike did a quick count of how many windows went up and came to sixteen but there were big brick spaces at some places so he couldn't really say it was sixteen stories high.

"Welcome to the Lotus Flower Hospital, Mr English and Mr Yank," Hung Sen said as he looked at their face and saw the amazement that he had shown when he first saw it. The gates they drove through were of stainless steel and were in the form of two Lotus Flowers bending towards each other and you drove under their stems to enter, the petals of the flowers were painted yellow from the middle then a very light going to dark pink, at the tips they were blood red. They both agreed it was very impressive.

Hung Sen followed the small roadway around to one of the sides of the building, two huge doors were opening and a crowd of people in white came out. They waited at the entrance until Hung Sen stopped the wagon at the doors, Mike and Richard got down out of one door and Hung Sen had got down and walked around to them before they could straighten their legs.

"Mr Yank, Mr English, this istThe Lotus Flower Hospitals welcoming committee." Hung Sen introduced Richard and Mike to everyone personally, everyone was smiling, it took almost an hour for the introductions and as each one was introduced, they went back inside.

Two people were left.

"And Mr Yank, Mr English, this is Papa Chinese and Mamma Chinese, my mother and father."

****

Chapter Seventeen

Catherine told Milton Ebbstein that she was pregnant and if he wished to think again about signing her, she would understand. Milton Ebbstein said to her that she didn't know enough about the movie industry and it made no difference to him if she was pregnant or not; he would just switch the shooting around to cover up her pregnancy. Catherine did all of the body shots before she showed her pregnancy and close ups were left to last. The media were getting little bits of information about the movie and it was being hyped even before the last scenes had been shot, already they were saying that it would be the biggest box office romantic hit ever. Milton knew that if he kept it, someone would get hold of it and release a pirate version so he rushed it out, in as many countries as he could, and on the first weekend, it had taken more money than any other movie in the history of Hollywood and Catherine Johnston was a mega star.

Cora was being sent offers for Catherine to appear in places she never knew existed. All she wanted to do was to get Catherine home to have her baby. Alvin and Beverly were showing up at the studios all most every day as her time got closer and closer. When it finally finished, they took her home. Catherine was fast becoming a 'doughnut woman' as she would often put it although she still had another two weeks to go before, she was ready to give birth. When the day came and still nothing, not one pain, she was going crazy sitting in the house, although her parents had done everything, they could to occupy her mind, Cora had given her scripts to read as well.

"Cora, I need to get out and get some fresh air."

Cora nodded and so did Beverly.

"Yes dear, go and do something, you are the best judge to say when you will give birth not some doctor, you go but please be very careful."

Alvin looked at Cora and Beverly in horror.

"You can't let our daughter go out in this condition."

"Oh Alvin, please be quiet, we women know what's best."

Alvin knew when to keep quiet and the tone of his wife told him that this is one of those times.

"Catherine, the local newspaper wanted to do an interview with you the other week, should I phone them and tell them to send a young reporter to Tiny's and to pay for our meal?"

Catherine looked at Cora and she saw the wicked smile come to her face.

"We have not had any fun for such a long time, yes, let's."

Cora saw the puzzled look on both Alvin and Beverly's faces so she told them what they did while on location once to a local reporter.

Beverly almost collapsed with laughter.

"That is not very nice," Alvin said.

"Oh, we do not go through with it and they do get a good story," Catherine told him.

Catherine and Cora arrived at the restaurant a half hour before they said they would. They had told tiny what they were going to do. He went along with it.

They knew that the newspaper would pull out all of the stops to get the interview and would tell the young reporter to do everything they wanted.

They were already sitting at a table when a young girl came up to them.

"Hello Miss Johnston, I'm Helen Todd from the interviewer." Cora invited the reporter to sit down. They could both see that she was so nervous her hands were out of sight.

And when she took her little notebook out of her shoulder bag her hands were really shaken.

"This is the most exciting thing that has happened in my life," she spoke. Catherine and Cora looked at each other and shook their heads, they both knew they couldn't do it to her.

Catherine had used all of the serviettes on the table and Cora had to ask for more as people kept coming up to them asking for her autograph, when they saw that she was busy, the restaurant people politely asked them to stop before they reached her.

"Okay, ask Catherine anything you wish," Cora said when she finally saw that they wouldn't be disturbed again.

The young girl was fumbling for her questions.

"I'm sorry, I'm so nervous." She was shaken. Cora took hold of her hand.

"Look, how do you expect to make it in reporting if you can't ask a local girl some questions?"

The reporter looked at her and smiled.

"I want to ask you about your pregnancy?"

"Girl, just fire away. Catherine will not bite you, if she doesn't want to answer she won't."

They saw her take a deep breath.

"Who is the father of your child?"

"He is the man I'm going to marry as soon as his work abroad is finished," Catherine said easing herself into another position.

"Is he in the movie business then?"

"He does spend a lot of time at the small screen," Catherine replied watching Cora take a sip of their wine to stop her giggling.

"Is he a television star?"

Cora was watching Catherine easing herself in different positions and thought that maybe the question had better change to another subject.

Catherine eased back in her seat.

"I'll tell you what," Catherine said to the reporter. "I'll give you the biggest scoop of your career." Then she looked at Cora. "That's the third stab of pain in five minutes, Cora, I think you should phone for a car, you can come as well," she said to the young reporter.

Cora kicked her chair away as she stood up and shouted for Tiny to get a car.

The car got them to the hospital fast. Cora had phoned ahead and by the time they got there, the staff were waiting. They took her straight to a private room. Cora holding Catherine's hand every step of the way.

"This is it, babe, now don't let us down, you go in there and give it all you have got."

Cora refused to go into the delivery room when the nurse said that she could.

"No thanks, girl, I only want to see inside one of those when I have to."

"You are not going to let your friend have her baby by herself, are you?" the nurse asked.

"Listen, girl, she got into this state without me, she can get out of it without me."

Catherine knew all along that Cora wouldn't go in the room.

"If you two could please stop talking, I think I need a bit of assistance here."

Cora turned to the reporter.

"Come on, we'll get a cup of coffee." Cora squeezed Catherine's hand tight.

"I'll see you when you are skinny again, babe," Cora said as she walked down the corridor with the reporter.

"You go and get the coffees; I have a few calls to make."

The reporter came back with the coffees as Cora put the phone away.

"Was that the father?" she asked.

"No, it was Catherine's mother and father." Cora looked at the reporter seriously.

"Right, now listen," Cora said to her.

"This is your chance to shine, babe, do you have a camera with you?"

The reporter nodded her head.

"Yes, just a small one. I was going to see if Catherine would pose for a couple of pictures and see if I could sell them." She put her hand into her bag and pulled out a small camera.

"Babe, the pictures you're going to take will set you up for life but only if you promise to not say a word of Catherine's real name to anyone."

The reporter nodded her head in agreement.

They were walking back down the corridor when Cora saw a group of medical people pushing a machine into the same room Catherine had went into, she handed the cup of coffee to the reporter and ran to the room and grabbed a nurse as she was about to go in.

"What's wrong?" Cora asked.

"When was the last time she had a scan?"

"Catherine has never had one, what is wrong?"

"She's breached, if we can't turn it, we'll have to give her a caesarean section." The nurse went into the room.

Cora looked up at the ceiling and closed her eyes.

"What more can you do to her, lord?" she whispered as tears fell down her cheeks.

For twenty minutes, Cora paced the corridor with the reporter.

"It's all right, we have turned it, she will be fine, you can go in now, all we have to do is wait until it wants to come out into the world."

Cora had just crossed the threshold of the doorway and was smiling at Catherine when all of a sudden, Catherine gave out such a scream that Cora's hair felt as if it was curling.

"Oh God, what am I going to put myself into now," she said as she went faster to Catherine.

Cora saw Catherine's legs up in the air and a nurse telling her to push.

Cora took Catherine's hand and squeezed it.

"I'm here, babe, now come on, if you do not get this over quickly, I will never speak to you again, now push, please push so I can get out of here."

Catherine looked at her friend, she tried to smile, then she screamed.

"RICHARDDDDDDDDDDDD."

Cora squeezed her eyes shut, then she heard a very faint cry of a baby, she opened her eyes wide.

Cora looked at the baby in the nurses' arms while she was cleaning it.

"You were right again, Catherine, it's a Sharon." Cora pulled Catherine back up the bed and wiped a towel around Catherine's face.

"God girl, you look at mess." They both started to laugh. The nurse handed Catherine her baby.

Cora went outside and told the reporter to come in.

"Okay, take your pictures, but, only after you have taken one of the three of us together for our personal book."

The reporter nodded. Cora stood next to Catherine who was holding her baby.

"The Three Musketeers," Cora said as the reporter took her pictures.

Alvin and Beverly entered the room and Cora introduced them to the reporter.

Cora took the reported to one side.

"Now you know Catherine's real name, you keep it to yourself all right?"

"For these pictures, I wouldn't tell my own mother who she is. I owe you and Catherine so much, I will always be in your debt. Thank you."

The reporter went away with a skip in her step. Cora looked back around when she saw the reporter go out of the door and saw Beverly fussing over Catherine and Alvin holding the baby, the relief on both of their faces was evident.

Cora was correct; every newspaper had Catherine and baby Sharon on their front page, because Milton Ebbstein had also released a studio news sheet saying that Catherine would also be staring in a romantic comedy later this year. The movie was still at the top of the box office and it seemed Americans loved to have a cry, as one critic had said.

Winter had come and gone and spring was definitely in the air as it was much warmer than it had been. Cora called at Catherine's as she always did on Sunday's, Beverly told her that Catherine had just went for a walk up to the hall with baby Sharon. Cora went up to find them, when she did, Catherine was sitting at the hope tree talking to baby Sharon. Catherine had her back to Cora and never knew she was there.

"This is where your dad said he would love me forever and I said I would love him. I just know he will love you, Sharon, because you are so beautiful, just like your dad. I wish he would come home. I miss him so much." She looked up at the hope tree.

"Please, bring him back to me."

The leaves of the tree rustled as a slight breeze blew through them.

Catherine smiled at the tree. Cora tiptoed back around the hall so that Catherine wouldn't know that she was listening, she had to dry her eyes before walking back around and shouting to Catherine.

"Hi, babes, Beverly told me you were here."

Catherine looked at baby Sharon and spoke.

"Oh, here is that horrible girl who spoils you terribly."

"You're right about that." Cora picked baby Sharon up and swung around with her.

"And I will do it for the rest of this girl's life, wont I, my little darling?"

Baby Sharon was giggling.

"God, I love this girl," Cora said as she hugged the baby to her.

"I know you do, Cora; people are beginning to ask if she is mine or yours."

Cora sat down beside Catherine and she gave Sharon back to Catherine.

"Milton has been on to me about when you feel like doing the next movie," Cora said.

"Well, I'm getting a bit bored." Catherine gave her the look that said, "Anything is good."

Cora gave Sharon a tickle under the chin and Sharon giggled.

"God, Catherine, she is beautiful."

"Couldn't you just love her to bits," Catherine said.

"Oh, I do, as I love her mother to bits."

"And she is going to want for nothing," Cora said as she tickled her again.

"If there is something you want and your nasty mother will not give you it, you come to your best friend Cora, okay little Sharon?"

"Cora, you are going to spoil her."

"I know, babe, and I'm going to love every minute of it."

"Cora, you know I still think he is coming back. I know it has been over a year and it was only supposed to be for six months…but…what we have is more than just love, Cora. I can't seem to find a name for it but it felt that we were meant to be with each other, that even if he was born on the other side of the world, we would have met, we have a thing, I don't know what it is but it is joined to both of us…"

"Yes, babes, and Sharon is the result of what it was joining you," Cora said taking Sharon off Catherine and lifting her up in the air.

"And she is worth every damn penny I'm going to spend on her. We were the two musketeers, now we are the three *amigos*."

"Cora, do you still think I'm a little bit mad for still thinking Richard is coming back?"

Cora looked at Catherine and saw the tears starting to fall.

"I've told you, if you believe he is coming back, then so do I."

"Cora, you are the best friend anyone could wish for but as a liar, you are rubbish, I've known all along that you just say that to give me the support I need and I love you for it."

Catherine gave Cora a hug. Cora whispered in Catherine's ear, "Like you said, babe, it's been over a year now. You should start going out and meeting people. You might even find a man that you want to be with."

Catherine moved away from her.

"Cora, I have made my mind up to not even look for a man. I'm happy with having Richard in my head and baby Sharon on my knee. And please do not say anything like that again."

"Well, if you have made your mind up, that's good enough for me. I just had to say it, Catherine, that is all."

"We'll go and see Milton on Tuesday after I go with my mother and father to the airport. They're off to Singapore to look at a contract he is after, then on their way back they are stopping off at David and Sharon's new house."

******

Mike was mulling over a newspaper, not that he could read it but if something caught his eye, he would ask Hung Sen to translate.

"Here Yank, give me a look at that picture of your girl again," he asked Richard.

Richard took the picture of Catherine out of his wallet and handed it to him.

"Yip, that's her. Mr Chinese, translate this please." He handed the picture back to Richard and the newspaper to Hung Sen. They had been at the hospital for over a year now and they were finally beating the virus. They had found a way to get rid of its months ago but there were so many computers in the hospital and also machinery that used computer systems that had been infected. When they were asked to stay here and help to get rid of it, they did, although at the time they hadn't thought it would take this long.

"It says that Catherine Johnson give birth to a baby girl and she and the baby are doing fine and that Catherine Johnson is top film star in America and that movie is top movie in America."

Richard stood up and walked to Hung Sen, he took the newspaper off him and looked at the picture of Catherine and a baby, his heart stopped.

"So, she meant what she said," he whispered, although Hung Sen and Mike, both heard him.

Richard handed Hung Sen the newspaper back and walked outside of the room and out into the full glare of the sun and heat.

Mike and Hung Sen followed him; they had never seen Yank with such a serious face.

"Well, I suppose she had to get on with her life. I couldn't expect her to put her life on hold while I came here, could I? But I never thought she meant what she said. I thought she said it in the heat of the moment."

The three of them walked around the hospital, not saying anything, although Mike and Hung Sen wanted to comfort their friend, they didn't know how to, so they just walked a few paces behind him. Hung Sen said, "Mr Yank, we take rest of day away from hospital yes, we go to Hung Sen's Garden, you like Hung Sen's Garden, come, I show you."

At the back of the hospital were quite a few buildings, all of them in the typical style of the Chinese, with their curved roofs and red tiles, some had golden paint mixed with the deep red and painted in the forms of Dragon's, Phoenix and of course the Lotus Flower. They followed Mr Chinese into one building; it had become second nature to the two westerners to take off their shoes as they entered a building and as they took off their shoes Mr Chinese gave them each a pair of slippers to put on.

"You follow, okay?" he spoke.

They went through the building, which was nothing but a small enclosed tunnel. At the end of it, it opened out onto a veranda with a beautiful garden surrounded by water with small bridges going across the water, and on the island in the middle were some fully bloomed lilac and apple blossom trees, a lot of the branches had paper lanterns hanging from them.

Mike and Richard had been staying at the hospital even though Hung Sen and his mother and father had asked them to stay at their home, both Mike and Richard had declined their offer as they would be coming and going at all times and they didn't want to disturb others. Mike and Richard had been to the house every Sunday for their main meal, Hung Sen's parents had insisted that every Sunday they would have a main meal with them and Mike and Richard had done so, this was the first time that they had been in this part of their building.

Mike was standing with his mouth open.

Richard just stared at it all.

"Mr Chinese, this is magical," Mike said. Richard was nodding his head in agreement.

The grin on Hung Sen's face went all the way across it.

"If this does not help Mr Yank to rid of his sadness, then Mr Chinese has something else that will," Hung Sen said as he went back into the house and came out with three small cups and a plate of food.

"Come," he said as he walked across a bridge, he walked to a spot that was in the shade of an apple blossom tree and crossed his legs they sat down on the ground.

"Come." He motioned to Mike and Richard. They went across the bridge and sat down.

Hung Sen's mother and father came out carrying various things and sat them out in front of them.

Mike's mouth started to water when he saw hamburgers.

"Hamburgers?" he said and immediately picked one up.

When they had full stomachs, Richard laid back on the grass and closed his eyes. All he could see was Catherine shouting at him to go away. He opened his eyes again and sat up.

"I'm sorry about showing you that newspaper with your girl in it, Richard," Mike said to him.

"I would have seen it, damn, it really hurts but I know she'll be happy, because her friend Cora will not let anything happen to her," Richard said smiling as he thought of the three of them together and Cora told him that if he hurt Catherine in anyway, she would hunt him down and kill him.

"Are you going to look for her when you get back?" Mike asked.

"Nope, it would only open up the hurt."

Mike nodded.

"Are you going back to England when this is done?" Richard asked Mike.

"No, I don't think England will ever see me again."

"Why not, I heard England is a beautiful country."

"It is but it stinks of people who can do what they like, even kill people they don't know. They killed my mother and father and paid their people millions of pounds."

Mike could see Richard looking in a quizzical way.

"I'm talking about the Tory party, they ransacked the North East of England, threw hundreds of thousands of people out of work, my father was one, he died looking for work and six months later my mother died of a broken heart, and the Tories? Well, they patted each other on the back and drank their wine. They ain't going to get the chance to kill me, I'm going to America after this, they said I could go anywhere in the world, so, America is going to get the Geordie."

"Geordie?" Both Richard and Hung Sen said.

"That's what people are called where I come from."

"I'm going to visit my mother and then find a nice school that might be looking for a computer teacher. Then I'm just going to while away my time teaching."

"You like teacher, Mr Yank?" Hung Sen asked.

"Mr Chinese, when you see the faces of young children who have just been shown something new, it is the most unbelievable feelings you will ever get in your life, I love watching their faces."

Hung Sen was nodding his head franticly and the smile was from ear to ear.

"Well, we're almost finished here. I'd say about another four weeks should see this well and truly Kaput," Mike said.

Richard nodded in agreement.

"I still think you should have a talk with your girl, Richard. She is a stunna. Maybe you and her could talk things out, sort of, settle things between you, who knows, she might still love you?"

"Nothing to settle, we were in love, she told me if I came here, we were finished, she's had a baby. There is nothing to settle. I don't have any rights to enter her world. I know she will never enter mine again but I'm happy that I have known her."

"Well, whatever happens, we always keep in touch, okay?" Mike said. Richard stuck his hand out for Mike to shake it.

"You bet we will."

"And Hung Sen," Hung Sen said.

"And Hung Sen," Richard and Mike said at the same time.

Hung Sen and his family made the rest of their stay in China as nice as they could, and the last four weeks went by without any more viruses showing.

****

Chapter Eighteen

Catherine had kissed her mother and father goodbye and she, Cora and Sharon had watched the airplane take off; they were walking back to the car.

"Cora, I think I want a haircut. I'm getting sick of all this hanging down."

Cora threw the car keys to Catherine.

"Okay, you drive. I'll go in the back with Sharon."

"We'll go to Christine's; she'll know what will be best for me," Catherine said, handing Sharon to Cora.

"You go into Christine's. I and this little one is going for a look around Rosewood's."

"Okay, we'll meet back at the car."

Catherine had never felt the same about her hair since Richard had left, although she had wanted it to be the same as when he fell in love with her, she admitted to herself that it was time for something to be done about it.

As she walked back to the car after spending almost an hour in Christine's she managed to make it all the way to the car before Cora recognised her.

"Wow babes, you, you, you sure Christine has taken enough off."

Catherine smiled.

"I needed to change it."

"Well, that you have," Cora replied while looking at Catherine's new 'pixie' hairstyle.

"It's the first time I have seen your ears and neck at the same time."

"Do you like it?" Catherine asked.

"Yes, I like it and it makes you even more attractive."

Tom came to Catherine's house because he was given a few days leave.

Milton Ebbstein had sent Catherine the script of a romantic comedy that he thought she might be interested in looking at. Catherine loved it so Cora phoned him.

"Okay, Catherine will do it, Milton; send us the details."

Baby Sharon was the centre of the three of their lives. Tom would take her out and walk among the gardens for hours on end, more than once Catherine and Cora had to go looking for them.

They were all sitting around the breakfast table when Cora opened a letter, it was from a local small time television studio asking if Catherine would like to do an interview. Catherine saw the glint in Cora's eye the same time as Tom did.

"What are you thinking, Cora?"

"Well, they know they have no chance of getting you to appear at their studio, sooooo, why don't we surprise them?"

"When?" Catherine's face lit up.

"They do a live show and it is very up to date and funny, their anchorman is so witty, obviously there will be a six-to-ten-minute delay, in case of problems but it is live four afternoons out of seven, I think we should call around and surprise them this afternoon."

"Will you be taking Sharon with you?" Tom asked.

"Yes."

"Okay, I'll go and report and see what I'm doing for the rest of the week, if you had wanted me to, I would have stayed here with her."

Cora gave Tom a serious look.

"I hope you are not getting smitten. I was there when Catherine produces this bundle of joy and it looked as if it hurt a little, so get all of those ideas out of your head babes, it ain't happening till I say it's happening, okay?"

Catherine and Tom laughed at the look on Cora's face, then she laughed as well.

"Laugh but no, means no, mister."

Cora drove her and Catherine and Sharon to the television studios but the guard on the gate wouldn't let them in.

"Listen, have a look in the back of the car and tell me you don't know the lady sitting there."

The man looked at the back seat and saw Catherine holding Sharon, then he stood up straight.

"Nope, don't know either of them," he spoke.

"What, you don't know who Catherine Johnson is?" Cora shouted at him in disbelief.

"Well yes I know who Catherine Johnson is."

"Then take another look but remember, woman sometimes get their hair cut," Cora said while making scissor cutting motions with her fingers.

Cora knew the guard had recognised Catherine by the way he almost hit his head as he stood back up and recognition had come to him, he promptly opened the barrier.

"Now go and tell your boss that two special guests are at the parking bays waiting."

The guard shot off as if he had just been paid and the bar across the street was selling drinks for a dime.

The owner of the television station came out to them walking quickly.

"Hello, Miss Johnson, I'm Steven Jones. I'm so sorry, we just didn't think we had any chance of getting you to come here," he said holding out his hand to shake Catherine's.

"It's okay," Catherine replied.

Cora took Sharon off Catherine because as usual when people saw Catherine, they would ask for her to sign this or that, and in a television studio it was no different as word got around that Catherine Johnson was actually walking down the corridors of the studio, people would come out of their rooms to look at her.

"So, Steven, I'm sure you will be selling the rights of the interview to other stations so we didn't think asking for $100,000 for the interview would be a problem," Cora said.

Catherine was just out of eye contact with the owner and he couldn't see her hiding her smile, not that he would have much chance looking at her as she had to turn her head away.

The owner swallowed hard.

"Oh, I didn't know the charge would be so high."

Cora stopped walking and looked at Steven Jones.

"Mr Jones, just now, Catherine is the biggest star in America; did you think you would get her for nothing?"

"Well, no but I, I…"

Catherine started laughing.

"It is all right, Mr Jones." Catherine had to say something because he looked as if a heart attack was on its way.

"Cora is only having a little fun; she likes to see people panic."

Cora looked at Catherine in amazed shock, to think Catherine would say such a thing about her best friend. Then they both started laughing again.

"Mr Jones, who is going to interview Catherine?" Cora asked.

"Alan is, he's, he's on stage now, he keeps this place alive with his afternoon show, without him it would all just collapse."

"Ah yes, Mr Alan Spiaght, he had a go at me when I first went on stage." Catherine reminded Mr Jones.

"It's a good job I do not hold grudges." Catherine winked at Cora but made sure Mr Jones saw it as well.

Cora looked at Mr Jones.

"Do you have a nurse here?"

"Yes."

"Good, get her please."

They watched Alan Spiaght going through his routine. He had the usual desk as all interviewers have but instead of it being near the back or in a corner. It was out in front. There were no chairs or sofas. It was his trademark to have his guests walk on stage carrying their own chair. Catherine and Cora were at the very back and no one could see them watching. Mr Jones came back to them with a woman.

"This is our nurse."

Cora handed Sharon to the nurse.

"Anything happens to her, and you die. Kapeesh."

"Don't move from here unless we say so," Catherine added.

Cora said to Mr Jones, "Two chairs please and no signals to Mr Spiaght."

Alan Spiaght was just finishing a topical joke about a politician but was surprised at the clapping and shouting that the audience gave it.

"It was funny but not that funny," he said while looking around to see if anything had happened.

When he saw the two most beautiful women he had ever seen or would see he stood up and gulped, then he remembered the jokes he had said about Catherine Johnson, his face went from shock at seeing her to pure embarrassment as she and her agent put their chairs down next to him.

"Yes Mr Spiaght, we are within punching distance, so be kind or else," Catherine said.

The audience roared with laughter.

"Ladies and gentleman, may I introduce Catherine Johnson and her agent side kick Cora Johnson."

The clapping lasted a long time and when it stopped, he said.

"You took me by surprise. I will never say another joke about you, ever, this has totally got me flustered."

"Flustered or terrified?" Cora said. The audience clapped again.

"Catherine, will you please tell your agent to stop intimidating me?"

"No, and Cora is not just my agent, she is and has and always will be my closest friend."

Alan Spiaght finally got over the shock and his interviewing skills came back to him, he asked Catherine about her stage show, the movie and what she would be doing next. The audience listened intensely; you could hear if someone was walking past outside, it was so quiet.

"Now if you do not mind, these people will have a few questions to ask Catherine," Cora said.

"Catherine, it's reported that you don't go anywhere without Sharon, is she here?"

"Yes, she is with the stations nurse, just behind us."

"Could we see her?" someone else asked.

Catherine looked at Cora. Cora nodded.

"But not yet, she is asleep. When she wakes up, I'll have the nurse bring her on." Catherine replied.

"Are you going to marry Sharon's father?" someone asked.

Cora froze, she knew a question about Richard would come and she had tried to prepare herself for it but when it came, she was taken aback.

Catherine made a motion as if whispering to Alan Spiaght and stood up. She looked at Cora then handed her the microphone and walked off. Alan Spiaght went straight after her.

"Catherine," he said as they went out of the view of the audience, "is something wrong?"

"Yes, get Cora here for me please. It is all right I will come back on but I need Cora here."

The audience were sitting wondering what was wrong. They couldn't see the tears that had filled Catherine's eyes. All they could make out was that Catherine said something to Alan and got up and left.

Alan came back on and whispered to Cora who got up and left the stage.

"Catherine will be back with us in one moment, she was thirsty and her throat dried up with all of this talking," he spoke. The audience clapped.

Cora reached Catherine.

"Babe, we will go home if you want to?"

"No." Catherine's lips were quivering and she was shivering as if she was cold. "Cora, this is going to be the time you have waited for. I'm going to talk about Richard."

"Catherine, please, you don't have to."

"I do have to and it's time I did. Now come on, let's get back on the stage."

The audience roared with applause as the two of them came back on. They sat down and then it went quiet again.

"I'm sorry about that but someone asked if I was going to marry Sharon's father."

Catherine took a deep breath. Some of the audience took one as well.

"The truth is. No. I can never marry Sharon's father."

Alan Spiaght would have quipped 'is it because he is already married' but knew it was a lot more serious than that by Catherine's tears falling down her cheek.

Cora took out her handkerchief and gave it to Catherine.

"He died the week Sharon was conceived."

Not one sound came from the audience.

Alan Spiaght said, "Catherine, would you like to talk about something else, it is obvious that it is up setting you."

"No. Cora, my mother and father and even Cora's man Tom and the woman who baby Sharon was named after, they have all been so very patient with me and now I think it is time I talked about Richard. When he died, I asked them to never say he was dead and for a year, they have not mentioned his name, Richard. That's the name of Sharon's father." Catherine wiped her eyes again and Cora took the handkerchief off her and wiped her own eyes, as did most of the audience.

"I met Richard when I was at school. He saved me from being very badly hurt, then he vanished for about five years. We met again accidentally and although I had fell in love with him the first time. When we met the second time and I looked into his eyes, I knew they saw me as beautiful and would always see me as beautiful. I…I…saw in his eyes that he was my home, my safe place, a place where I would always be loved and I fell in love with him all over again, and every time I saw him, I fell more and more in love with him. When we woke up in each other's arms, my heart fluttered and my love began all over again, can you imagine, your first love, how it makes you feel? Richard made me feel like that every day. When I was on stage and I had to die, I would think of Richard and how I would feel if I couldn't see him anymore, that's how it was so easy for me to play that part."

Catherine stopped talking to drink some water and she looked at the audience who was spellbound, some were crying and somewhere in a far-off dream world.

Cora was astonished to hear Catherine talk of Richard like this, not even she knew Richard did so much to her.

"And now he is gone from me but he left me with Sharon. I will never marry. It just would not be fair on the man. How can anyone get even halfway to the feelings I get from, even now, thinking about Richard."

The interview lasted three hours and at no time did anyone leave their seat, they were as spellbound as any audience had ever been.

Catherine and Cora and Sharon got back home. Tom was on the phone.

"Oh, here she is now, hang on Beverly." He put the phone to his shoulder and shouted to Catherine.

"Catherine, your mom is on the phone."

"Hello, Mother."

"Are you all right, Catherine, do you want me and your father to come home?"

"No, whatever for?"

"We are watching your interview and we thought—"

"Mom, you're in Singapore?"

"Yes, and the TV was on some entertainment channel and your interview is on."

"But I, but I, I have just gotten back from the studio?"

"Are you all right?" Beverly asked again.

"Yes, I'm fine and no, I want you to stay there. I have Cora and Tom staying with me and Sharon."

"All right, darling. I just thought I should call to see if you needed us."

Catherine put the phone down and asked Tom to put the TV on. He did and they sat and watched the interview.

"God they even left in where I walked off," Catherine said.

"Well, if your mom saw it, they never had time to edit anything," Cora said after wiping more tears from her eyes.

It took about six weeks for the interview to leave the newspapers. They were promising huge amounts of money if anyone could give them a clue about who Richard was or where Sharon is.

But no one who did know would say a word.

Catherine had started shooting the romantic comedy. It was being shot in the studios, which meant Catherine was home every night, sometimes they would take Sharon with them and sometimes Cora would stay with her at home.

"Catherine, we have to film in California next week, so I have asked if we can stay with Richard's mom, and she said we could."

"Aw that's good we have not seen them for a while and I think Sharon will love to see how this little girl has grown since the last time." Catherine picked Sharon up and lifted her above her head, Sharon giggled and said mamma. Catherine almost dropped her.

"Did you hear that, Cora? She said mamma." Catherine hugged her daughter.

David's father had died. David sold the ranch as it brought back to many memories and he couldn't stay there, everything reminded him of his father. His research had ended at San Bernardino, so they moved to his favourite place. San Luis Obispo, he had a house built specially for Sharon.

Alvin and Beverly came to California as well while Catherine was there, they all stayed with Sharon and David. Alvin was being presented with an award to industry for his work in opening up the Japanese markets. Tom was also there because the President would be attending as he was giving some of the awards to people.

They were all seated at the same table. Tom had fixed it so that he was in the audience, so he got a seat at their table. There were about four hundred people in the hall but as most of them were sitting down it made Tom's surveillance much easier.

Cora was whispering in Tom's ear but Tom was watching a man walking towards them. He knew most people that knew Cora or Catherine but not Alvin or Beverly. Although he looked at ease, he was ready for anything that might happen.

"Hi, Tom," the man said in an English voice. Tom noticed he had an award in his hand.

"Oh, hello Cora," he said, then looking at Catherine.

"God, you really are gorgeous, what a shame you are such a heartbreaker." Then he walked away.

Catherine watched him walking away then she looked at Cora.

"Who was he?"

"I don't know, do you, Tom?" Cora said.

"I don't know any Englishmen," Tom replied.

"What did he mean, 'you are such a heartbreaker'?" Sharon asked.

"I don't know," Tom said.

"But I'm going to find out, stay here please? Cora, you come with me."

Everyone watched Tom and Cora go over to the Englishman's table.

He was the only person to be at the table although it was set for two.

Tom and Cora sat at each side of him.

"What did you mean, 'you're such a heartbreaker,' and how do you know our names?" Cora asked.

The stranger was looking at Catherine's table while playing with the name card of the vacant seat.

"No wonder he loved her so much after she dumped him, he would never say a bad thing about her. She must be the most beautiful female on this earth. It's such a shame her heart is made of stone."

"Look, what are you going on about, you'd better tell us or I will kick your reprooooo."

"Reproduction system so hard my eyeballs will hit the ground before I do." The stranger finished for her. Even Tom was amazed.

"I was on the phone when you threatened the man from CIA."

Cora was thinking hard, then she remembered.

"You are that English guy who Richard was talking to when he was doing that test."

He nodded his head. Tom moved closer to him.

"But that doesn't explain how you knew who we were," he whispered menacingly.

"I saw a picture of the four of you every day for about a year and a half."

"Where?" Tom whispered.

"When I was in China with the Yank," the Englishman said.

Cora was visibly shocked.

"You were in China with Richard?" Tom asked, he watched Cora and waited for her to compose herself again.

"Cora, stay here with him, okay?" Tom said, leaving the table.

Tom went back over to the table where Catherine and everyone was watching him.

"I think you had all better prepare yourselves for some stunning news," Tom said, then pointing at the stranger he said.

"That man over there has been working in China with Richard for a year and a half."

"Oh my God," Sharon said. David took hold of her and steadied her.

Alvin took hold of Beverly when he saw her tears.

Tom took Catherine by her shoulders.

"Catherine, you come with me." He led her over to the stranger's table.

"Now tell Catherine what you have just said and can you prove it," Tom said, sitting Catherine down.

"He was supposed to be here tonight." He flicked the name card onto the table and they all saw the name Richard Buckman.

"But why are you all like this? He means nothing to you now. You dumped him when he needed you the most."

"She didn't dump him, you stupid English fool." Cora snapped.

By this time Alvin, Beverly, David and Sharon had come over and sat down on spare seats.

Alvin looked at the name card.

"Is he in California now?" he asked.

"Well, he was supposed to be here, so yes, he is in California. What do you mean she never dumped him, we both saw the picture of you and the baby?"

"Yes, his baby," they all said. Tom stood up and went to another security man, then he came back.

"Okay, we can all go to a side room to talk."

"Where is he?" Sharon asked when they had all moved into another room.

The stranger looked as if he had realised something.

"So, the picture we saw in the newspaper must have been an old one, or an old newspaper, yes, that would fit in, most of the news we got was about six months old but the shock of seeing you with a baby knocked Richard for six, he was gutted. He was sure you had not meant to say it but the picture proved to him you had meant it. I told him when this is finished to go and see you but he said no, you look as if you are happy and he shouldn't spoil it for you by opening up old feelings. So, when we finished in China, he said he was going to see his mother in California and in his letter, he sent me he said he couldn't find where his mother had moved to, so he was going to take a teaching position that had been offered to him."

"You got a letter off him, what was the address on it." Alvin asked.

"But why would you want him, you have to be happy now," the stranger said to Catherine.

Cora said, "I don't know if I should punch you or kiss you numbnut, tell us where he is living."

"He told me to come here and if he could make it, he would come as well but first he had to get some books finished off for his students."

"Where does he live?"

"Well, erm, erm, I don't actually know where he lives."

"You what?" they all said.

"The letters only have the school address on them."

There was a note in Richard Buckman's in box at the reception, He took it out and opened it, it was from the principal.

"Please come to my room as soon as you can."

Richard went to his class and set his students a task on their computers. He was so proud of them, they had worked hard since he arrived here, sure, there were a few slow ones but even they were getting the hang of computers, he had wanted to teach young children but this was the first school to answer his enquiry about a position, so he took it.

Richard entered the principal's office.

"Please sit down, Richard."

Richard sat down.

"You have been here for three months now. How do you like it?"

"This is my first teaching post and I really enjoy it, sir."

The principal smiled.

"Good. I'm taking you off probation now and offering you the post, permanent."

"Thank you, sir," Richard said.

"I had a rather strange telephone call last night, or should I say early this morning, I won't divulge it yet, I have called a meeting in the hall this afternoon. That is all for now, Richard."

Richard stood up and left the room. The principal gave out a large exhale as if he had said all of that in one breathe as was gasping for air. How could he not give the position to such an impressive man as Mr Buckman, even though he thought the teachers were getting younger every day.

The principal called the meeting at twelve-thirty and it was only for classes that Mr Buckman took but it was also for every staff member.

The principal stood at the lectern and looked at all of the students, then turned to the staff, making sure Mr Buckman was there, he was.

"As everyone here knows, Mr Buckman, first I will say that he is no longer on probation." He stopped talking so that the students could clap, and they did.

"Second, I received a very strange telephone call this morning, very early this morning, from the White house." He paused to let it sink in.

"The President of the United States, though I must add it was not the President on the telephone, was at an awards ceremony last night in this City, and he was not a happy president, why I hear you ask. Well, he came all the way from Washington to present this award to a man who only had to walk a few blocks, yet that man did not show up, why did he not show up, I'll tell you why. He had to prepare some papers for this school."

By now, even the teachers were looking at everyone, including the students. There was a faint cry of a baby and someone saying.

"Hush, little babes."

Richard's ears pricked up at the sound of the voice, it sounded familiar.

"The person on the telephone has asked me to give the award to the person involved, saying that the award was being presented for outstanding achievement and the President of the United States was disappointed that he never got to meet this man personally, and so, to present this award is America's favourite, no, sorry I think I should first tell you who is to receive this award. Please step up to this lectern, Mr Buckman."

Richard knew that it was for him and he promised that if he ever set eyes on that Englishman again, he would kill him, he knew that this would be all of his doing, even the phone call from the 'White House', he would have faked it all. But for now, he would go along with it.

Richard walked over to the principal and shook the offered hand.

"Thank you for that rather embarrassing introduction, sir," Richard said.

"Embarrassing? Not at all." Then the principal turned to the students again.

"And to present this award to Mr Buckman is America's favourite little girl. Miss Sharon Buckman accompanied by her mother Miss Catherine Johnson."

Richard heard the names but they were not registering in his head.

Then he saw this little girl, very unsteady walking and he followed the arm that was holding her and stopped at the shoulder, he was unable to look further in case it was all a joke.

"I'll take the babe, Catherine; you go and do what you've got to do," Cora said.

Catherine ran to Richard and threw her arms around him.

"Oh, Richard, I have missed you so much."

The End

Milton Keynes UK
Ingram Content Group UK Ltd.
UKHW022033181123
432826UK00005B/66